The Rose Has Its Own Thorns

HUY NGUYEN

Archway Publishing books may be ordered through booksellers or by contacting:

Archway Publishing
1663 Liberty Drive
Bloomington, IN 47403
www.archwaypublishing.com
844-669-3957

ISBN: 978-1-6657-3538-4 (sc)
ISBN: 978-1-6657-3539-1 (e)

Library of Congress Control Number: 2022923315

Print information available on the last page.

Archway Publishing rev. date: 12/14/2022

Dedicated to my mom, my grandparents, my friends, You are my world.

PART 1

CHAPTER 1

Phuong

Phuong comes home after her shift at the hospital. She is so exhausted and wants to sleep immediately, but she can't. Recently, she got a sleep disorder. She can not sleep even if she is super tired. Today is her son's birthday. So she must try her best not to show the tiredness on her face. Her son does not like it.

She enters the kitchen, opens the fridge, and takes out a bottle of orange juice. She closes the fridge, not too strong, but it makes one of the photos attached to the fridge door fall. Phuong sighs. She hates to bend down because it makes her hips a little pain. She frowns and picks the photo up. She tends to put it back, but after looking at the picture, she holds it in her hand and sits down to watch it again. She takes a sip of orange juice, lays back, and all the memories from that photo come back like waves from tides. It was the photo of herself, her son Michael and her husband, Adam, two years ago. No, not a husband. Ex-husband. It was taken in Disneyland, and no one could believe that after that trip one week, they got divorced.

Phuong is an immigrant from Vietnam who fled away on the sea with her mother, Mrs. Nhu, after her father was killed in the communist concentration camp. Phuong's mother had planned to cross the border for a long time, but it had consistently failed. Finally, in 1989, when Phuong was 15 years old, they successfully disguised themselves as Chinese people and returned to their country. In the refugee camp in Malaysia for one year, they finally came to the U.S. and have lived in California until now.

Like many refugees who first came to freedom land like the U.S., the barrier between the cultures and languages was so vast and so challenging. Phuong had so many troubles when she spoke English, made friends with other people, and of course, had racism too. Remember when she first came to the swap meet to work for a Vietnamese family who sold cosmetics there? A white American lady came from nowhere, pointed into her face, and said. "You do not belong here. Get back to the boat where you came from". And she used so many racial slurs against Phuong. She did not understand some of what the lady said, but the Vietnamese owner saw the situation, and she defended Phuong. "Hey you," she said. "get the fuck out of my store. I am the owner here, ok? You have no right to talk to my employee like that. She risked her life with her mother like every Vietnamese wanted to find freedom after our country fell into the hands of communists. You should respect us and feel sympathy for us instead of hating us. Get out before I call security!"

The American lady left after what the Vietnamese owner said. Then she turned to Phuong, who was crying. The lady put her hands on Phuong's shoulders, looked straight into her eyes, and said. "Look at me!". Phuong looked up. "There is nothing to be afraid of. This is a free country, and you have all the right to speak what's in your mind. If someone says things racist about you based on your skin color, stand up for yourself. Be strong."

Phuong was an outcast in high school. She always had lunch alone when she first came in. Then, even though there were more Vietnamese kids in school, Phuong could not befriend them. When she got into college, it was the time she met Adam.

Adam was born in the U.S. to a Vietnamese family. His father was working for the U.S. government in Vietnam, and after Vietcong came to Saigon, he and his wife were on the helicopter on the roof of the U.S. Embassy. At that time, Adam was in her belly. They settled in Seattle, and Adam was born there. Then they moved to California when Adam was five years old to get him closer to the Vietnamese community and people there, even though Adam's parents loved to live in Seattle more. So when Adam was fully grown up and had a career, his parents moved back to Seattle. Adam was a very energetic boy when he was a kid. He loved playing sports, especially baseball. He was the type of guy that every girl in school must love and wanted to lose their virginity under him. Even though Adam was the idol of every girl, a good friend, and a perfect child that every family wanted to have, he was not like what he seemed to be. Adam was a jerk and a bad kid.

When Adam was in 11th grade, he dated a girl named Casey. Casey was a cheerleader and a typical white American girl with blonde hair. Casey and Adam met in American history class. Casey was good at social subjects, and history was her favorite. She wanted to be a history professor when she grew up. Adam sat next to her, and she had helped him a lot, and they hooked up. Casey thought that Adam loved her but then realized Adam was only using her for goods. Adam made her do his final English essay and history project, even reading books for him. One day, Casey caught Adam kissing another girl outside the school, and she cried a lot. But Adam did not care about it because Casey was out of order to him. The rumor about Adam and Casey was spreading out over the school. Thought that everyone must understand Casey and hate Adam, but they believed that Casey was lying and Adam was being blamed.

Casey had left school.

Mark was a good friend of Adam. They had known each other since kindergarten. Mark's cousin, J.B., was a weed dealer. He supplied all the weed to the kids and people in the neighborhood where Adam and Mark lived. One day, Mark invited Adam to his house to play some video games. After that, Adam, for the first time, was high up in the sky. From that moment, Adam started to fall into the road of perdition.

On Thanksgiving 1993, Adam was in his senior year of high school, and the whole family gathered for dinner. His uncle, who was a police officer, told Adam's father about the problem in the neighborhood where there were so many teenagers who started to fall into drugs and weeds. He reminded Adam to be more careful. Adam nodded. Adam never liked his uncle because he arrested many of Adam's suppliers and could not find anyone who could sell for him. But it did not mean he stopped smoking weed and debauched playing until he went to college, where he needed to change. And that person was Phuong.

Phuong decided to study the medical field, surgeon, more specifically because she loved to help people around her. She remembered that when she visited the hospital once to visit her sick friend who had leukemia, Phuong was so emotional seeing the pain and the suffering that her friend had to bear every day, and her family cried a lot. Her friend passed away at 16, leaving her dreams, family, and passions behind her. At that time, becoming a doctor was only her goal.

Adam, on the other hand, did not know what the future would lie ahead of him. He did not know what to do. His parents expected a lot in him; at least, they had guided him to be a lawyer, but they had to give up because they pushed him too hard, so he left his house for months which scared the shit out of Adam's parents. They finally let him do what he had to do when he came back. The real reason was that he had no money left in his pocket.

On the first day in the English 101 class, Adam sat in front of Phuong. Phuong was still shy. When the professor told every student to start to get to know each other, Adam turned back and said hello to Phuong. Phuong just kept her head low and said hello before. Adam felt a little annoyed.

"Put your head up!" He growled. "I am talking to you."

Phuong put her head up. Immediately, Adam was struck by the beauty on Phuong's face. Adam was frozen.

"My name is Phuong Nguyen," Phuong said.

It took Adam a moment for his soul to return to his body. "Uhm…My name is Adam Le. This is my first year in college."

"Me too."

"Woah, ok," Adam said. "Nice to meet you, anyway."

From that day, Phuong and Adam became friends. They helped each other in their studies. Phuong helped Adam in English and science. Well, mainly Phuong enabled him, and Adam, to be honest, did not help her much in the study. But Adam had encouraged her to become more confident by taking her out to dinner, hanging out with his friends, and practicing her talking in public. And just like that, they fell in love. When Adam graduated, he became a marketing director of a fashion company and was also one of the co-founders. It was so successful. Phuong continued to study the medical until she became a surgeon. Then, they got married, and they had a son. Michael.

And they got divorced after ten years together. Michael was nine years old at the time they got divorced.

On a hot summer night, Phuong had to cover a shift for her co-worker because she had to take care of her mother. That night was their wedding anniversary, and Phuong was supposed to be home to celebrate it. Adam understood the circumstance, and they promised to celebrate the anniversary the next day. After the surgery of a patient, Phuong took a rest. She fell asleep. It was so strange when she had a bizarre dream. A nightmare, perhaps. She saw Adam was in bed with someone else. The mistress with red hair, naked, was under him, giving him a blowjob. Then, they changed their position. Adam was inside her, and he fucked her hard. She groaned and begged for more. Phuong was standing in the corner of the room, and both did not notice Phuong's appearance there. The more Phuong screamed the more they did it joyfully. Rachel, her co-worker, shook Phuong, and she woke up. Phuong breathed hard, and she was sweating.

"Geez," Rachel said. "Are you ok?"

Phuong looked around the room. It was only her and Rachel, and she realized it was just a dream. Phuong massaged her forehead.

"Bad dream, I guessed," Phuong said tiredly. "Uh, can you get me an aspirin?"

"Yeah, of course."

Rachel walked out and returned with two pills and a glass of water in her hands. Phuong took it and drank it.

"Thank you so much."

"Maybe you should go home. It had been a long night." Rachel said.

Phuong sighed. "I would want to, but I have a ton of work I need to do. Writing reports, checking on my patients, and having a meeting. Gosh!"

Rachel placed her left hand on Phuong's shoulder. "You are a human. Not a wonder woman who can save the world. Listen, I will help you to write reports and submit them to the director. You do the other two, ok?"

"But..." Phuong tried to say.

"No, but," Rachel stopped her. "Go home, take a shower, and sleep."

"Are you sure you can write reports?"

"Don't fucking underestimate me!"

Rachel smiled and left the room. Phuong felt pleased when she had an assistant like Rachel. Always energetic and helpful. Even though Phuong tried to keep her calm, she kept thinking about Adam and the girl. What if it happens?

Phuong drove home after she finished everything. On the way home, she passed by Starbucks to buy a cup of hot mocha, which she loved the most. While waiting for her mocha, she noticed a person waiting for the drink. Phuong walked to that person.

"Hey, Ha," She said. "How are you?"

Ha, Phuong's high school friend, looked at Phuong and was surprised to see her. It had been a long time since Phuong and Ha had not met each other since the Thanksgiving dinner at Phuong's house three years ago.

Phuong's mother, Mrs. Nhu, worked in a Vietnamese restaurant when they moved to another place, she met Mrs. Trang, her co-worker, and she helped Mrs. Nhu a lot at work and in daily life. So they had become friends. Phuong and Ha met at school when Phuong enrolled. At first, Phuong did not like Ha so much because she was a shy girl and anti-social; she hated being interrupted and wanted to be alone. And just like Adam, Ha was more energetic and more extroverted. She hated to stay in one place and do nothing. She permanently joined every club (they went to the same high school together), and she was a cheerleader and a president of Key Club back then. Ha always wanted Phuong to be more sociable and get along with friends. She usually came to Phuong's house to get her out of the house and play with her.

"Oh my God, long time no see you!" Phuong exclaimed and hugged Ha. "How are you?"

"I am doing fine," Ha said. "How about you?"

"Well, I am doing well, and the family is still good."

"That's great!"

There was a call. "Hot mocha for Phuong!"

"Oh, it's mine," Phuong said, and she picked up her drink. "Get a table. I wanted to talk to you a lot."

Another call. "Caramel Frappe for Ha!"

Ha picked up her drink and smiled at Phuong. "I would love to, but I have to go right now. I have a case that needs to review. Divorce again."

"Ah, that's huge! Hope that we don't get into that." Phuong joked. They both laughed. Phuong could smell the perfume from Ha. It was so rich, exquisite, expensive, and overpowering. Phuong had already fallen in love with this smell. "Your perfume is so special. I love it so much."

Ha smiled. "Oh really? Thank you. It is Coco Mademoiselle from Chanel. My husband bought it for me."

"You are so lucky," Phuong said. "I will tell my husband to buy this for me. I love the sense of this perfume. Right, how is Thomas? I have not seen him in a while."

"He is doing fine," Ha said. "He is so busy since he has become a chef."

"Send my love to him, ok?" Phuong said. "Maybe next time we can hang out and have dinner. I miss being with you and gossiping about things like before."

"Me too. Good old days. I will call you. See you next time!"

They hugged each other and left Starbucks.

Phuong got home. The house was so quiet. Usually, at this time, Adam must be in the kitchen making pancakes right now. She could smell it from the front door. Adam was the best at making pancakes. But today, she did not smell anything. Maybe Adam was still sleeping. Phuong went upstairs. She walked to her son's room. Michael was not in his room. She freaked out. She ran around the house to look for Michael. But she did not find him anywhere. She picked up her phone and called Adam. The ringtone of Adam's phone was in the house. She ran downstairs, and Adam was standing in the living room with the bouquet of red roses in his hands. He was in a black suit, his hair combed.

"Happy anniversary, babe!" Adam walked closer to Phuong. "I missed you last night!"

Phuong was stunned in front of the surprise that Adam gave her. She was speechless. "This one is for you." Adam handed her the bouquet. "All the roses in here represent my love for you. I love you more than anything and want us to be like this forever."

After a moment of freezing, Phuong could finally open her mouth. "Oh my God, I...I don't know what to say at this moment."

Adam put his finger on the lips of Phuong. "You don't need to say anything. Just follow my lead." Adam took out a black box and gave it to Phuong. Phuong opened the box. It was a diamond heart pendant necklace. That made Phuong completely muted.

"Adam, I...I," Phuong startled. Adam put the necklace on her neck.

"Beautiful babe." Adam smiled. "You deserve it." Adam kissed Phuong, and immediately, Adam lifted Phuong and brought her to the bedroom.

"What are you doing?" Phuong asked.

"Let our anniversary begins," Adam announced proudly.

"What about Mikey?"

"He is with your mother right now. Only two of us. The bed was so cold last night."

Phuong giggled, and a moment later, they were all naked. For 25 minutes, Phuong felt extremely happy, excited, and up to the sky. It made her forget all the tiredness inside her. Adam was always wild with her, like an animal in bed; no one could do better than him. They both breathed heavily because of sex.

"I love you so much!" Phuong said while looking at the chandelier on the ceiling. A crystal chandelier that one of her friends bought as a housewarming gift.

"I love you too, babe." Adam smoked the cigarette. He left the bed.

"Where are you going?" Phuong asked.

Adam covered himself with his blue navy bathrobe. "I felt thirsty. Do you want anything to drink?"

"A whiskey, please!"

"At your service, madam!"

Phuong laughed. Adam walked out of the room and got into the kitchen. Adam put some ice in both glasses, opened the whiskey bottle, and poured it out. He put both glasses in a small wooden tray and returned them to the bedroom. Phuong was lying on the bed and kept watching the necklace.

"You must be fell in love with it!" Adam said. He handed her the glass of whiskey.

"Yes, I am obsessed with it, babe. Thank you!" Phuong kissed Adam. "I will go to the bathroom to fix myself, and we will have a second round!"

"I can't wait!"

Phuong got out of bed, naked, and went to the bathroom. She completely forgot the weird dream that she had last night. She put her whiskey glass in the laboratory. Sitting in the toilet, she kept thinking about what to give her husband. He had given her so many things on their anniversary. But she could not let the sex out of her head. She was obsessed with it. She cleaned herself up and flushed the water. She came to the laboratory to wash her face. The diamond necklace was so bright and so pure. It made her feel like Rose in Titanic. Phuong put some lotion on her skin to make it more moisturized and perfume on her body. It reminded her of the perfume that Ha put on her. She must have that Chanel perfume. Phuong put the perfume back. She accidentally shoved the whiskey glass, which dropped into the laundry basket.

"Shit!" Phuong swore.

The whiskey had poured over Adam's blue shirt. Phuong took out the glass and the shirt. She sighed sadly. But she immediately thought this must be a sign. A gift idea for Adam. She did not know what anniversary gift would be perfect for Adam. And voila, she'd found it. She would buy him a shirt or a suit from Ralph Lauren, his favorite fashion brand.

She was overjoyed and held the shirt in her arms. The smile on her face started to fade away. Phuong noticed something strange. The sense of her husband's shirt. In all of Adam's life, he had never used perfume before. He hated perfume. Only if Phuong made him use, he would use. Maybe Adam used perfume without her consent, but she did not have this perfume in her collection. So strange that this sense was so familiar.

Adam called her. "Babe, the bed is starting to get cold!" Phuong looked at the door where outside, her husband was ready for the second round.

"I'm there right now!" Phuong had no time, and she put the shirt back in the basket. She put on her bathrobe hanging on the door.

As Phuong got out of the bedroom, Adam was already in position.

"Are you ready for the second round?" Adam smiled. "Warning, it will bewilder than round one."

Phuong looked at him without any emotions. She was standing there without saying anything. Adam felt strange. "Babe, what happened?"

"Uhm." Phuong scratched her head and chuckled shyly. "You know what. Uhm. Suddenly I felt a little headache. It must be last night when I did the surgery for a patient. I am sorry."

Adam jumped out of bed. Naked. He came to Phuong and smoothed her. "Oh no, you don't have to say sorry. I understand. Are you ok?"

"Yeah, I need to take a nap. It will be fine."

"Ok, ok. You take a nap, and I will go downstairs. Later, we will go to a fancy restaurant and have dinner there. I will make a reservation."

Phuong gave a fake smile. "Ok, babe."

"Get rest," Adam said, and he left the room. Phuong gasped and burst into tears.

It could not be true. Adam would never cheat on her. The rose bouquet, the necklace, and the sex. If he did all those on the anniversary, it showed that he loved her. There was no way Adam would have done that if he had stopped loving Phuong. Maybe Adam bought a new perfume, or one of his friends bought it for him. There was nothing for Phuong to keep thinking about it. Phuong told herself to take a nap; after that, she would keep it out of her head forever.

The dream came back again. But this time, Adam and the mistress laughed at Phuong when she screamed at them. She could not do anything because there was a glass war between her and Adam with his mistress.

After dinner, Adam and Phuong went home. Phuong was trying their best to be happy with Adam at dinner. The dream and the suspicion kept her waking all night. She walked to the kitchen to get some drinks. She opened the fridge to get some ice. When she closed the door, she noticed the photo on the fridge. It was a photo of Phuong and a girl. Phuong looked at the photo and opened her mouth because the mistress, who appeared in her dream, was in the photo. The red hair, a nice body, and a beautiful smile. Now remembering the perfume on his shirt previously, it was Coco Mademoiselle from Chanel. That person was Ha.

But why was Ha? And why could they fall in love?

For the next few days, Phuong asked a man to set up a small camera in their bedroom. The camera was hiding behind the statue of liberty near the TV. Believe it or not, it was true. Ha, and Adam had an affair. Phuong caught them in the middle of the sex. Adam and Ha did not have anything to explain their affairs. They finally divorced. Their relationship ended, but they still tried to raise Michael without making him feel alone. After the divorce, Phuong moved in with her mother.

Phuong cried a lot, but she calmed herself that she had to be strong to move on. Adam was not worth it; from now on, she would be on her own and never believe in love again.

Phuong wipes the tears from her cheeks and her eyes. She stands up and puts the photo back in the fridge. But this time, she places the photo behind another photo where it can only show the faces of Michael and her. Adam completely vanishes from the photo.

There is a sound of a Ring. It is Mrs. Nhu who comes home from the supermarket. Seeing her mother, Phuong walks out to help her walk inside the kitchen. Mrs. Nhu has been living with disc herniation for over ten years. It is the result of carrying heavy stuff in the past when she was raising Phuong. She would do anything to make money to help her daughter. Even if it was the most difficult work. Mrs. Nhu sits down tiredly.

"Mom, where were you?" Phuong pours a glass of water for Mrs. Nhu and takes two pills from the medicine case. She hands them to her mom.

Mrs. Nhu takes two pills and finishes the cup of water. "I went to the supermarket to buy some food."

"Supermarket?" Phuong is curious. "Who took you there, and where is all the stuff?"

A man with glasses, brown hair, and blue eyes enters the kitchen. He has a buff body, and Phuong could see his muscles through his white shirt. He is carrying two full bags. "Where do you want me to put all of these?" His voice is soft.

Mrs. Nhu turns back. "Oh, you can put it near the washing sink for me, dear. Thank you!" Then, she turns to Phuong. "You must remember Hoa, son of Mrs. Robert, right? This morning I wanted to go to the supermarket, but my back was so painful. So I called Hoa to take me. Luckily he was free."

Phuong looks at Hoa. "Of course, I do remember him. How are you?"

"I am doing well. How about you?"

"Doing ok. I hope your mom is still fine. How is her health? Getting any better?" Phuong pours him a glass of water.

"You know she is still trying to recover. Of course, it will take time, but thank God she survived the stroke."

She hands Hoa the glass of water. "You are right. I can see it was such a blessing when she survived. Now keep praying that she will recover soon. Not 100% recovered, but if she can walk and talk, it will be wonderful."

Hoa smiles. His smile is like the sunshine of early dawn. "Yes, I believe in it too."

"Thank you, Hoa, for taking me to the supermarket today," Mrs. Nhu says. "I hope I did not cause you any inconvenience."

"Oh, don't say that. It is my pleasure. You used to help my family a lot. This is nothing to me. I don't mind. Anytime you want me to take you anywhere, call me. If I am available, I will drive you."

Strangely, Phuong sees Hoa's Vietnamese was so good. Not perfect, but with a kid who was born and raised in the U.S. and can speak Vietnamese fluently like him, it is so rare. Even Adam can not speak Vietnamese as well as Hoa.

"That is so sweet of you, dear. I very much appreciate that," Mrs. Nhu smiles cheerfully. "Do you want to stay to have lunch with me?"

Hoa looks at his Apple Watch. "I'd love to, but I have something to do now at work. Maybe next time I will stay for lunch. Thank you, Mrs. Nhu."

"Oh, that's sad." There is a little disappointment on Mrs. Nhu's face. "Next time you must stay to have lunch with me, ok? Don't refuse it!"

Hoa chuckles. "Of course I will. See you later, Mrs. Nhu."

"Goodbye, dear. Send my love to your mom, ok?"

"I will."

"Let me walk you out!" Phuong offers.

"You don't need to do it." Hoa hesitates.

"I don't mind."

Phuong walks Hoa to the door. He says goodbye to her and leaves. Phuong keeps watching him until he drives away. She tends to go back in the house then Adam's car parks in front of the house. Phuong crosses her arms and looks at Adam. Adam takes Michael to Phuong. Michael immediately runs to her, and she held him happily.

"Happy birthday, my baby!" Phuong says.

"Thanks, mom!" Michael says, and he runs inside the house.

Adam comes to her and hands her Michael's backpack. "Why do you bring him here?" Phuong asks.

"I have an important job I need to do right now," Adam says.

"Fuck some girls?" She says with an ironic voice and despair too.

"Haha. Very funny."

Adams gives the middle finger into her face. They have become enemies since the divorce. All they do when being together are attacking each other with their mean words. "Well, actually, yes, threesome, baby! At least I have somebody else to love more than you. Alone for the rest of your life." Adam says with an ironic voice.

Phuong frowns, and she gets angry. She wants to slap Adam so much into his fucking face, but she would not do it. She is not the type of person who loves violence. Just calm down. He does not deserve to be slapped. He deserves to be tortured and chopped off his penis. You fucking bastard. She thinks.

"I will see you at dinner. We will go to Norms."

"Why Norms?"

"Because Michael loves to eat there. Don't you know that? What kind of mother are you?"

Adam attacks her one more time. That bastard does not know how to stop, huh? When they were married, he was never like this. He changed after the divorce. More asshole, she believes. Meanwhile, Phuong was desperate. She cried and cried and cried, and it was hard for her to move on. Even there was a time she thought divorce was her biggest mistake ever because she was still loving him. So much, actually. Maybe this marriage would not have ended if she had forgiven him, made him change, or spent more time with him. But no, that has been his nature. It has stayed in him for a long time. Then, when the time came, it broke. She realized she was so weak and cowardly when she was like that. The tears were not worth it for him. Adam would never understand her feeling. He just wanted to play with it, and when he finished, he would turn away and never return. So why must Phuong cry because of him? There are so many things for her to cry about in this life. Wasting her tears for that fucking bastard is a big mistake. Phuong would rather choose to be strong than be sad every day.

Phuong smiles coldly. "I am the kind of mother who loves her son so much and will do anything to protect him and prevent him from the way his father has chosen. I don't want him to be like you. Yes, maybe I don't know if he likes Norms, but besides that, I know what he likes and what he wants. How about you? How often since our divorce have you spent time with him or thrown him here and left? I must be the person who asks what kind of father you are. Now excuse me, I have things I need to do too. Get the fuck out of my house!" Then Phuong turns back and shuts the door.

It leaves Adam speechless after what Phuong just said. He chuckles, then turns angry. He kicks the pathway lights on the grass. One, two, three, four, and five. He kicks five of them and leaves. But still cursing. Phuong stands behind the curtain in the living room, leaving a little space to peek out of the garden to see what Adam has just done. Phuong laughs after witnessing him destroyed her property. Phuong shakes her head. "What a fucking child!"

CHAPTER 2

Ha

The black Toyota Camry is parked in front of the big house with a red roof at the end of the street. This house was just being remodeled, so it looks new and gorgeous. Inside the car, Ha is crying out loud. Outside it is raining cats and dogs. She does not want to come inside the house. She stares at the home where she has lived for the past five years, and in this place six years ago, she was given a warning that she would never forget.

Six years ago, Ha was 26 years old with a shiny face and a white silk dress from Givenchy, which was her favorite brand. She was a Vietnamese girl, but since she grew up in the U.S., she had changed herself to adapt to life here. To be a real American girl. But it could not change one thing. Ha was a Vietnamese. The unique thing about her was her hair. It was red. It was like blood mixed with red wine. Because of this hair, so many men in school and at work had crushes on her. At this moment, she was a lovely girl about to meet her fiancé's parents.

She checked herself by the car mirror and put on lipstick repeatedly. She texted her fiancé to tell him that she had come. A moment later, a man with a black sweatshirt and jeans came out. He was a little fat, but overall, he was cute in some way. His name is Thomas Le.

Ha got out of the car. Thomas kissed her left cheek. He took a look at Ha and nodded. "You look amazing, babe!"

Ha smiled shyly. "Thank you so much. I hope that your parents love me."

Thomas held her hand. "Don't you need to worry! They will love you. Besides, I have told my parents about you."

At dinner, in the dining room, they were having pho bo, which was Thomas's mother's best dish ever. Thomas became a cook because of the influence of his mother. Ha sat next to Thomas, and his parents sat in front of them. Mr. Tan Le, Thomas's dad, poured everyone a glass of wine. He loved wine so much that he even had a collection full of every kind of wine he bought each time he went to Europe. Ha took a sip of wine and gave the compliment. "This wine is so good and so soft. I like it."

Mr. Tan smiled. "Well, it must be good because I chose it," He drank some more. "I have a collection of wine. Maybe I can show you later on."

"That will be great," Ha felt excited. "I'd love to."

In her mind, she had crossed out one thing of many things that she should do when she met Thomas' parents in her list, which she had created a few days before. She wrote down every task she would do to impress her future parents-in-law. Ha did a little research on the internet. Some research has shown that Vietnamese family is complicated when their son brings some girls to introduce to their parents. Ha grew up in the U.S.; so. with her, she did not know much about Vietnamese traditions or what a Vietnamese family would expect from their future daughter-in-law. She asked her mother about this topic, and Mrs. Trang just smiled. "You are too worried about this, darling. Remember, this is America, not Vietnam. There is no way their family will make it difficult for you. Everything will be fine. Besides, you are a strong independent girl, and there is nothing for you to be afraid of. If their family makes it difficult for you after you become their daughter-in-law, I believe you can fight back. They should feel lucky when they have a daughter-in-law like you."

Those words of Mrs. Trang made Ha feel less stressed and scared. Indeed, Ha was strong and independent.

During her childhood, like Phuong, she was outcasted and bullied by other popular girls. She used to be a nerd at school. She did not care much about her looks. Old clothes from Goodwill, not doing makeup, wearing a large pair of glasses, and hair were horrible. So dry and damaged. That made everyone in school try to stay away from her as if she were a disease.

After school, because Mrs. Trang worked in the restaurant, she usually picked Ha up after five p.m. when school ended at two forty p.m; Ha spent most of her time in the library. She did all of her homework and found books to read. After the library closed, she waited outside the school.

One day after school, the library closed because the teachers had a conference, Ha waited for her mother outside, and she spent the time reviewing for the exam tomorrow. Suddenly, there was a group of girls which everyone in school called Five Fab Gals because all of those girls were pretty and popular. All of them were cheerleaders. The group leader was Francesca Wilkerson, a spoiled brat living by her daddy's money, she saw Ha was all alone, and the whole group stood in front of ha. The silhouette covered Ha. She looked up at them. Frighten.

Francesca popped the bubble gum in her mouth. "What's up? Nerd!"

Ha did not answer. She returned to her homework. Francesca grabbed Ha's workbook and threw it away, then slapped her. "Are you deaf?" Francesca got angry. "I am asking you."

Ha kept silent. She picked her workbook up and put it back in her backpack. She tended to leave, but the Five Fab Gal did not leave her alone. They surrounded Ha. Now, she was trapped in the circle. Francesca touched Ha's face. She felt annoyed when Francesca did it.

"What do you want from me?" Ha spoke up. Frustrated.

"I just want to play with you a little bit," Francesca said sarcastically.

"I don't want to."

"Just come." Francesca smiled, and that smile haunted Ha because of its horror.

Ha followed the group. They came to the back of the school, which led to a small alley. This place was where the neighborhood around the school put their trash. It was so stinky but a perfect place for the students in school to smoke weed or deal with other problems here. Ha was freaking out. Francesca crossed her arms while others were in a position to do something nasty. Their faces were like monsters with no blood, ready to eat prey.

"I hate you, Ha," Francesca said angrily and despairingly. "Since the day you were in this school, I have been disgusted by what you did. You are so fucking fake. A good student of every teacher. A nice person from every friend," She imitated the puking sound. "You made us feel like losers in this school, stole our spotlights, and never showed any respect to us. It.

Is. Enough! A fake girl like you should be taught some manner," Francesca called her group. "Girls," She flicked her fingers. "Let's do it!"

In the small alley that afternoon, the Five Fab Gals had beat the hell of Ha. They tore her shirt, threw everything in her backpack out, slapped her, pulled her hair really hard, and kicked her stomach brutally. Ha kept screaming and crying, but no one could listen to her because this alley was separate from the neighborhood, and people didn't pay attention unless they wanted to throw their trash. In this case, Ha was like trash now.

After the Five Fab Gals group finished their sweet vengeance, each of them spitted at Ha, and they left her alone. Ha cried, got all her stuff, and walked back to the school. She was so miserable. Her mother was already there. Seeing her daughter from the car, Mrs. Trang was horrified and immediately got out of the vehicle.

She held her daughter. "Oh my God, what's wrong with you?" Ha did not say anything but hugged her mother tight and cried out loud. Mrs. Trang did not know who did this to her daughter, but in her mind, she already knew why.

"That's ok, babe," She smoothed slowly. "Don't cry. Look at me."

Ha looked into her mother's eyes.

"It's over, ok?" Mrs. Trang continued. "Pains only last for a while, and then, it'll go away. Let's go home, and I will make you your favorite dish, ok?"

And together, they went home.

After dinner with pho bo, Ha took a shower. She wanted to wash away all the pain and shame she had been through that afternoon. But she couldn't. It kept appearing back in her mind. A scar from physical and mental abuse would never go away unless Ha knew how to make it gone.

Seeing her daughter like that, Mrs. Trang was so painful. She could not believe that her daughter was being treated like that. She wanted to cry, but she told herself not to do it. The last time she ever called was the time she gave birth to Ha when they were in Vietnam. Mrs. Trang must think of a way to help her daughter. She went to the backyard to smoke. Suddenly, something caught her attention immediately while she was smoking. She smiled.

Ha locked herself in the room after the shower and still crying on her bed. She was angry because she was humiliated and ruined her dignity.

How could she ever go to school? How could she ever look at her friends and teacher? And how could she ever recover from the pain those bitches had caused her? As she kept thinking, she cried even more.

Mrs. Trang knocked on the door while holding the particular thing she found in the backyard. "Sweetie," She called Ha. "I know that you are upset. But crying cannot help you anything. I know it is not your fault that they treated you like that. They will never understand what they have caused you. That is their nature. Could you open the door for me? I have something that will make you feel better."

Ha wiped her tear and shouted out. "Go away, mom. Leave me alone."

"Sweetie, if you keep being like this, they will laugh at you even more. Then, it is your fault for being so easy on them. I know what you need to do. Let me in."

Now, Ha was a little convinced by her mother. She knew that her mother was more substantial than her. She knew that her mother had taken all her courage to get on that tiny boat to the fleet on the high sea to be here now. She knew that her mother was not afraid to start a new life and take risks to do the best things for her daughter. And mother knew best. So the only person that Ha could trust was her mother. Ha got out of her bed and opened the door.

Mrs. Trang walked inside, put the thing on the desk, and sat down. Ha sat on the bed in front of her mother.

"How are you feeling right now?" Mrs. Trang asked.

"Painful," Ha sniffed. "Both from inside and outside."

Mrs. Trang nodded slightly. "I can understand that. But don't worry because I have something to cheer you up and can help you change yourself." She took the thing from the desk and handed it to Ha.

Ha looked at that thing and did not get it. "A vase with roses? How can it help me?" Ha asked curiously.

Mrs. Trang smiled and leaned back in the chair. " I have a secret to tell you. I am hiding a secret from you and have no intention of telling you because I am ashamed of it."

"What is this?" Ha asked.

Mrs. Trang sighed and began. "I was not a good person before. I was a prostitute. I satisfied every man each night, and they paid me high for my service. Every single penny that I made, I never kept it all for myself.

I sent them to my parents in the countryside so that they could cover their lives. I said I went to Saigon to work as a teacher. But I lied. Life was too harsh, and it pushed me to this way. Every time I wrote letters to my parents, I told them I was fine and had a good life in Saigon and hoped I could someday come back to live with them. Then they told me they were proud when they had a daughter like me. A daughter who is a prostitute? What is proud about that? I thought I could keep this secret. But my parents silently came to Saigon and found out what I was doing. They were so shocked and so embarrassed about me. They told me not to return to my hometown, and I was no longer their child. From that moment, they disowned me. Even when my dad passed away, my mom told me not to come back. She wanted to let him rest in peace. Then my mom followed him for four months after that. I met the end of my life, you know. I had no one left."

Mrs. Trang wiped the tear quickly from her eyes. "When the unfortunate events keep coming, it's coming for good. I was alone on the street one night, and suddenly, a man walked through me and offered me so much money to satisfy him one night. I smelt the alcohol from him. I denied it because I did not have a mood. But he did not leave me alone. He grabbed my arms from behind and covered my mouth with another hand. Then, he dragged me into an empty alley. He shoved me to the ground, pushed me down, and tore off my shirt, bra, and pants. My hands were pinned down. I tried to scream, but he covered my mouth with a cloth. Just like that, he dropped off his pants and raped me. I was crying, you know. I passed out. The next morning, I was alone in that empty alley. Naked. There was no sight of that man, and strangely no one saw me. Three months later, I found out that I was pregnant. I did not know what to do at that time. I could not raise a child when I had nothing in my hand. I decided to do an abortion. But I could not. Something inside me did not want me to do it. So I kept the baby, and it was you. When I gave birth to you, I was all alone. Holding you in my arms, I could not keep my emotion. You were sleeping peacefully in my arms, and that made me happy. You were the motivation for me to move on with my life and keep living and keep going."

Mrs. Trang wiped the tears from her eyes again, as well as Ha. "Listen, I have been through many bad things in my life. I cried, I crumbled, and

I decided not to give up. And you, young lady, have just met the first challenge of your life, and you have already given up? No. There are so many more terrible things and challenges waiting ahead of you. You must be strong, firm, bold, and smart to overcome those challenges. Do you understand me?"

Ha nodded, but Mrs. Trang was not happy about that. She yelled. "DO YOU UNDERSTAND ME?"

"YES, I UNDERSTAND," Ha screamed back.

Mrs. Trang felt satisfied. "That's my girl!"

She looked at the vase of red roses Ha was holding. "I always admire the beauty of roses. My favorite flower. But it has thorns on it. I realize that the roses are beautiful and elegant, but it is also strong, dangerous, and unpredictable. People will be hurt when they touch the rose without paying attention to its thorns. Beauty has attracted everyone by its beauty, and that beauty will kill back. You are like roses. Beautiful but dangerous. You have not shown the danger inside you, but it is now the time for you to show your thorns. Take them down with it and be strong. Show them that you are not the kind of person who can easily be overpowered like that. Be like roses."

Ha was never wrong when her mother was a strong independent woman. What her mother just said was so right. Ha was just at the beginning of her life challenges. There was a road full of obstacles; if she did not hold the strength, how could she overcome those? And be like roses. Beautiful but dangerous. It was the time she had to change herself. Those bitches who had humiliated her would pay a price because they had touched the thorns on it.

Those girls from that group were jealous of her, what she did, what she achieved, and what they didn't have or couldn't do. Let them envy, then. They did not know they had burned the marches for a great fire.

Ha decided to dye her hair red; she started to put on makeup, learn how to talk back, and remove her old personality. She joined more clubs, was more sociable to get more people on her side, and was easier to manipulate them to do jobs for her, spreading out the gossip about that group. Ha also got more attention from teachers when Ha told them so many bad things about each bitch in that group. And soon, she finally made the whole group destroyed, and everyone turned their backs on them. Even one girl in the group moved away because of the tension at school. Then, Ha became a cheerleader, which kicked Francesca out of the team by exposing the real personality of her and her group. Knowing what Ha was doing at school and her nature had changed, Phuong, a shy girl at school, hated her so much.

Confidence and strength could not help her when she had to impress Thomas' parents. The father was not the person she should be afraid of. The mother, Mrs. Linh, was the one who made the final decision on whether Thomas could marry her or not.

In some research that Ha had done, there were thousands of information talking about the tension between a mother-in-law and a daughter-in-law. For many years, this topic was discussed in books or movies. Usually, the relationship between them could be better. Mother-in-law puts so much pressure on daughter-in-law. The mother-in-law would be everywhere in the house, interfering with everything, annoying for no reason because once her son gets married to a woman, the woman would live with her husband's family. That is the rule. She would watch that daughter-in-law doing everything from cleaning the house to cooking, from how they talk to how they breathe, and she would be careful when they made love with their husbands. If they go against what their mother-in-law was expecting (well, nothing that a daughter-in-law did would please a mother-in-law once she hated her from the beginning), they will be despaired and outcasted by the whole family, where the mother-in-law spread out the rumors about her daughter-in-law. There would be only bad things around that poor daughter-in-law.

Many Vietnamese brides can not take their mother-in-law's life or the pressures they are being put on, so they kill themselves. Their deaths do not mean anything to those mothers-in-law because they claim that they do nothing wrong, want their daughter-in-law to be better and understand more, and choose to die. No one tells them to die. Because of the ignorance of every mother-in-law, they encourage their sons to remarry or stay alone. There are thousands of reasons that a mother-in-law hates her daughter-in-law. First, it can be social status. The husband's family is wealthy, and a poor girl with difficulties getting married to him. Immediately, that mother-in-law will despair that girl's family and claim that she married her son for money. Second, it can be that the bride can not give birth to a son.

Most Vietnamese families or Asian families, in general, have a tradition that the first son in the family must have a son to succeed the family. This tradition has been around for a long time. If the girl had no son, the mother-in-law would hate that girl. Third, it can be jealousy inside the mother. She loves her son so much that she would not let any girl love him or marry him because they would take her son away from her forever. She wants her son to stay with her forever. She would find all the way to stop that marriage, or once they get married, she would destroy that marriage. Or maybe learn from the most explicit example from Norman Bates.

Ha could not stop being horrified. Facing Thomas' mother, Mrs. Linh, Ha's heart was like jumping out of her chest. She ate, but her legs were shaking. Lately, Thomas told Ha that his mother was friendly, sweet, and dedicated. She would love her from the first meeting. Mrs. Linh looked at Ha and asked gently. "How is the soup? Do you like it? I hope it is not too salty for you. My husband and Thomas liked to eat salty."

Ha swallowed the soup in her mouth. "Oh, no. It is delicious."

"That's great." Mrs. Linh said. "So, how do you guys know each other?"

Thomas and Ha gave each other a sweet look. "I met him in a coffee shop where I usually hung out with my friends. One of my friends was a friend of Thomas, and he brought Thomas with him to join us. I did not pay any attention to him at first. But then, when I went to the bathroom. It was so strange that the bathroom was not in that coffee shop. We had to ask for a key and walked outside to go to that bathroom. Thomas also wanted to go, and we went together. After I finished, Thomas was waiting for me outside. I asked him why he stood there and said he wanted to wait for me. I was so surprised and impressed by his action. Then I asked for his phone number. We texted, hung out, and he cooked for me, and we fell in love."

Thomas kissed Ha's left cheek. "And I love her so much."

"I see," Mrs. Linh said. "It sounds so nice."

"Thank you," Ha said.

"So, Thomas told me you are a lawyer, right?" Mrs. Linh continued immediately

"Yes, I am currently working for a law firm," Ha said.

"Ah, you must get paid a lot, right?"

"Mom!" Thomas exclaimed.

Ha turned to Thomas. "That's ok," Then she turned back to Mrs. Linh. "Enough for me to live with my mom."

"Your mom must be very proud when she has a daughter like you. I am glad." Mrs. Linh took a sip of wine.

Ha smiled shyly. "Thank you for saying that. My mom is everything to me in this life. She sacrificed a lot for me and never stopped loving me. I love her too."

Mr. Tan wiped his mouth with napkins after finishing his pho bo bowl. "Nice talking. Yes, I always agree that our children should be grateful for everything their parents have done for them. Even though we live in the U.S., the tradition of "*drinking water, remembering its source*" should live forever and pass from generation to generation. I expect that a lot from the next generation."

"I will remember that, Mr. Tan."

Mr. Tan nodded happily. With him, Ha would be a good daughter-in-law. He could be proud to tell every one of his friends that he had a daughter-in-law who was beautiful, lovely and a lawyer. Turning to Mrs. Linh, the real woman of tonight, she poured herself another glass of wine. She took a sip and looked at Ha again. But this time, she got more serious. She was not satisfied with what Ha had just said.

Mrs. Linh responded immediately. "Are you sure that your mom is everything to you?"

The whole room was silent. They stopped what they were doing after the question from Mrs. Linh. Mr. Tan threw a surprised look at his wife. "Darling, what are you talking about? Of course, her mother is everything to her. What kind of question is that?"

Mrs. Linh turned to her husband. "Babe, I don't feel what Ha just said was right. I have my witness and my reason. Now let me ask her."

Thomas looked at Ha, who was now freaking out at Mrs. Linh. She knew that Mrs. Linh did not like her in the first place. But Ha still tried to keep her calm. "Yes, my mom is everything to me, and no one can replace her in me."

"Really?" Mrs. Linh chuckled and gave a stern look at Ha. "So why do you love my son and be here to have dinner with my family? Why don't you stay at home with your mom tonight?"

Ha did not know how to respond to that appropriately. She just responded to her instinct. "I heard Thomas say that you made pho bo good, and I want to try it. Just like Thomas said, it is super delicious. I have not tried this bowl of pho bo before in my life. I want to learn more about how you cook this, or maybe I can protect this recipe under the law so that no one else can steal yours. What do you think about that?"

Nobody said anything. Ha was a brilliant girl. She thought before she spoke. She must consider whether it could hurt anyone or not. Mrs. Linh had underestimated this girl. She laughed. The laugh startled everyone in the room and cut off the scary silence. "Good answer. I am glad that you have a special impression of my pho. When you are my daughter-in-law, I will show you how to cook in my recipe." Then, Mrs. Linh raised her glass of wine. "To Ha and Thomas. To their happiness. Cheer." She gave a toast.

Everyone cheered. Mrs. Linh's eyes kept staying on Ha, and Ha still kept looking at Mrs. Linh. She could sense the danger from Mrs. Linh. Something was not good about to happen.

After helping Mrs. Linh wash the dishes, Ha followed Mr. Tan to the living room to see his collection of wine, as he said before. They had a conversation together, and they had already bonded. Mrs. Linh called Ha from the kitchen. "Ha, dear, can you come here and help me to prepare the fruits?"

Ha gently said. "Yes, of course. I will be there right now." She excused Mrs. Tan and Thomas to go inside the kitchen. She could feel the danger was coming, or Mrs. Linh wanted to understand her more so she could keep in touch with Ha.

When Ha entered the kitchen, a dish with apples, strawberries, and kiwi was prepared carefully and decorated beautifully on the table. Mrs. Linh smiled and told Ha to sit down next to her. Ha pulled the chair and sat down.

"What do you want me to help?" Ha knew that she had prepared everything. It was just an excuse for her to talk to Ha.

"I want to talk to you a little bit. You know, to understand you more." Mrs. Linh said.

"Ok, what do you want to know from me?"

"I think that you did not understand my question lately."

"What question, Mrs. Linh?"

"If your mom is everything to you, why are you here tonight?" Mrs. Linh asked coldly. "I knew your answer was false, but I did not want to break the dinner. I hate to do that."

At this moment, the terrifying in Ha began. "What I just answered was true and thoughtful. I love my mom, but I also love Thomas. I hope you and Mr. Tan can accept me and this marriage."

Mrs. Linh chuckled. "Marriage? You have already thought of marriage? That's funny!"

Ha looked curiously. "I don't understand. You don't want me to marry Thomas?"

"It is not about that," Mrs. Linh said. "You are too confident. Maybe Thomas brought you home to introduce us today, but we are not sure that you and he are still together tomorrow. Or if you are married, what makes you think it will be a successful marriage?"

Ha could not say anything. Mrs. Linh continued. "You put your mom on first in everything. Even above Thomas, his father, and me. How terrible you are. Once you get married, you will follow your husband, and your husband will be everything, as well as his family. If you keep thinking about your mom daily, what place inside will you be for us? It is not because I got jealous of your mom, but I feel my son will not be happy when he is with you. You have no respect for him or us. How can my son live with a woman while her mind only keeps thinking about her mother? How can we stay in one house when her heart and belief are only for her mother? You just answered my curiosity. You are a smart girl but don't try to be smarter than me. My husband might like you, but I don't. I despair a girl like you who pretends to be better, to be the center of everything, and manipulate others while you are nothing to this society. I can accept the marriage between you and Thomas because I want my son to be happy, and I don't want to hurt him. But it doesn't mean that I can love you. I will watch out for a woman like you. If you ever break my son's heart, be prepared to pay the consequences. Do you understand?" Mrs. Linh threw her a cold smile. "By the way, your red hair annoyed me the whole evening. It looks like the flag of communists."

In front of Ha right now was the appearance of a monster in the body of a human. Looking at the eyes of Mrs. Linh, Ha could see that Mrs. Linh was just like other mothers-in-law in that she had done the research, but this lady was worse than anyone else. She realized that Mrs. Linh would destroy her if she broke Thomas's heart or ever hurt him or disobeyed her. Whatever Ha did, Mrs. Linh would know, and once she found out, Ha would meet the end of her life.

Knowing that, after five years of marrying Thomas without doing anything that made her mother-in-law uncomfortable or annoying, Ha had made a terrible mistake when she had an affair with Adam, the husband of Phuong. After being exposed to their relationship with Adam by Phuong, Ha felt guilty so bad that she did not know what to do. She just wished that Mrs. Trang was here with her at this time.

Mrs. Trang passed away because of colon cancer two years ago. Ha always asked her mother for help, but she was on her own. But if she was still alive, what Mrs. Trang would think about Ha, the daughter she had raised. Mrs. Trang would have been so disappointed.

Ha could not make up her mind.

CHAPTER 3

Phuong

Every Monday, Phuong takes Mrs. Nhu to the chiropractor to help her with the pain in her back. She has to live with it for so many years. With Phuong's well-known connections, she has contacted every best hospital or city doctor who can help her mother with the pain. But because her back goes too far, there is no way to make it disappear. They could only somehow reduce the pain for her. Usually, Phuong will stay with her mother until the therapy is done. But today, she has to leave to pick up Michael after school and buy him some school supplies. Adam must be the person, who did it, but he said he was busy with some work at his company. And Phuong knows it was just a fucking lie. There was no business, only wanting to find an excuse for him to do something else.

Phuong knows Adam is irresponsible, and she thanks him for that because she can spend more time with Michael, and Michael will love her even more. Her purpose is that Michael must hate his father, and soon she will tell him about who his father is. *A scumbag, a bastard, a cheater*, and *a motherfucker*. Oh yeah, she will tell him everything, every bad thing about Adam, how he treated Phuong and abandoned Michael when he was living with him, and she will make up more stories that a best-selling author can not think of about writing in their accounts. Phuong is so excited about that time to come. She wishes Michael would grow up faster and what Adam's face would look like when Michael knows the truth and will despair his father so much.

Phuong laughs like a villain on the way to Adam's school.

Every parent is waiting for their children in front of the school. Seeing Phuong coming, a few ladies are calling her and waving. Phuong has to put on her pretending happy face as usual to greet them. Inside them, she hates those women and does not bother remembering their names. They always gossip and then spread fake news.

"Hey, Phuong," the purple-haired woman says. "Long time no see you. Where have you been lately?"

Phuong smiles. "Well, I was a little busy in the hospital. But everything is fine in my life. Thank you."

A white woman with brown hair frowns at Phuong, whom Phuong believes this lady does not like. "At least you should come and pick him up sometimes or go with your husband. It would be great," Then, she changes her tone to exciting. "Talking about your husband. He had been so great recently. What a wonderful dad!"

"I agreed," Another blond mom adds. "I wish he was my husband. Danny is such an asshole. He did not even care about his children after the divorce."

Phuong looks at the woman. Her name is Jenna. She knows about Jenna's family. A little bit. Danny is a dentist at Phuong's hospital. They met a few times in the hospital cafeteria but did not talk. Jenna calls her husband "an asshole" because he is just like Adam. He slept with his assistant and was caught. The whole school knew about it after Jenna shared her story on Facebook and immediately received other people's comments, shares, reactions, and attention. Everyone felt sympathy for Jenna. That was quite a big deal at that time. After what happened to Jenna, every parent at school waits for another family scandal to stick their noses in and spill some tea.

Understanding that kind of toxic thought, Phuong stopped sharing her family problems on social media. Nobody knows that Phuong and Adam got divorced. Phuong told Adam to keep this secret because she was afraid that those mothers at school would gossip and judge her or Adam. Once they know about the story, they will change it in their own ways. That is so strange. Phuong never liked those women nor wanted to hear anything they said. She pretends to be friendly with them so they will not tell their kids to stay away from Michael.

After listening to what the brown hair woman has said nice things about her husband, Phuong is surprised, which activated her desire to gossip a little bit. Inside her, she hates her ex-husband so much, and suddenly he is praised. It makes her a bit annoying.

"Really? Why?" Phuong asks.

The black short hair woman standing next to the brown hair woman cuts in. "Well, recently, we had a fundraiser for our children's concert at school. Michael was so gentle when he baked cookies to sell and helped the concert as an executive producer. The parents of the school were appreciative of what he had done. By the way, he is now the president of the Parent-Teacher Association at school."

"Woah," Phuong is getting shocked right now. "President of the PTA. How nice it is!"

The red-haired woman in the group shows her curiosity. "You don't know about this?"

Phuong laughs. "No, I don't. He has not told me anything."

The purple hair woman, who is a single mom, says. "That's weird. He has been elected for six months. Haizzz, this guy. I think he doesn't want you to be worried about him because he knows you are very busy and he is too. I wish I have a husband like Adam."

"Yeah, right." Gosh, Phuong disgusts these women so much.

There is no doubt that Adam has built a perfect image in every parent's eyes, and he fools around a lot. That makes Phuong nothing in their eyes. She is an irresponsible mother who never cares about her husband and an ignorant wife who knows nothing about her son.

He is so intelligent. Always one step ahead. *Nice move.*

The school bell rings, and all the children run out to find their parents. All parents are so happy to see their children. Seeing Michael, Phuong calls his name and waves. Michael sees Phuong, and he runs fast to her. She catches him in her arms.

Phuong kisses his forehead. "Hey, sweetie, how is the first day of school?"

"It is good," Michael says delightfully. "I made some new friends at school today."

"That's great. Is the teacher nice to you?"

"I think so." He grins.

"What do you mean you think so?"

"I don't know. She looks so mean."

Phuong smiles and smooths Michael's head. "Aw, don't say that. She is a kind, sweet teacher who cares for her students. Don't judge a book by its cover."

"You think so?"

"Yes, I am sure with you." Phuong holds his hands. "Ok, let's go shopping for your school supplies, ok?"

"Yes, mom," Michael says.

On the way to the mall, Phuong looks at Michael. He is playing with the iPad. Phuong does not know that Michael has an iPad.

"Since when did you have this iPad?" She asks.

Michael keeps his eyes on the iPad and answers. "Daddy bought it for me two weeks ago as a gift for the first day of school."

"Really? And you brought to school?"

"Yes, mom."

Adam bought Michael an iPad without consoling Phuong. *He destroys the childhood of his son*, Phuong thinks. She always wants Michael to grow up full of memories with friends at school; Phuong wants Michael to grow up knowing how to go outside to play all the fun outdoor games. Phuong wants Michael to be fun and happy. Not putting his eyes into that fucking tablet.

Phuong looks at Michael through the mirror again.

"You know what," Phuong clears her throat and changes her voice to firmer. "I will talk to your dad about you playing iPad. It is not healthy at all."

Michael now gets his eyes out of the iPad and looks up. "No, mom," He protests. "I like to play with this."

"I know, sweetie. But at your age, you should go outside and play with your friends or toys. I bought you many toys." Phuong gets into the parking lot of the mall.

"Playing with toys is suck," Michael says while his eyes are on the tablet. "iPad is much better."

Phuong parks the car and turns off the engine. "Ok, let's get you some school supplies and clothes." Phuong turns back to Michael. "Give me your iPad."

Michael resists. "No!»

"Mikey, give me your iPad. I won't say again."

"NO!" Michael screams.

"Hey, don't yell at me, young man!" Phuong raises her voice. "All right," Phuong quickly grabs the iPad from Michael's hands. "If you don't give, I'll take."

Michael prepares to cry, but Phuong knows Michael is just pretending. Phuong pointed at him. "Stop. Don't get started here, young man! I will give you back later. I swear to God, if you start, I will break this iPad immediately, and no more iPad for you. Do you understand?"

Michael nods in fear.

Phuong puts the iPad inside her tote. "Good. Now, come with me to the mall."

They spend half an hour buying school supplies for Michael at Target inside the mall. She can see that her son is missing many things from the list Adam sent her yesterday. How can Michael go to school today with a few old school supplies? And why the hell did Adam not buy him anything before? After that, they go to the clothes shop for Michael. Phuong often chooses clothes for Michael from GAP, which is fashionable and affordable.

Phuong goes through every T-Shirt, jeans, and jacket. She tries on Michael, who is so bored and tired. He keeps looking at his mother's tote, where his iPad is being locked up.

Michael groans tiredly. "Are we done yet?"

Phuong is holding two shirts. One is red, and one is black. "Which one do you like the most?"

Michael groans more. Phuong smiles. "All right," She takes the black shirt and puts the red shirt back. She grabs the rest of the clothes. "Let's check out, and we will get some ice cream, ok?"

Michael nods. "Ok, mom."

After purchasing everything, Michael and Phuong get out of the store. Suddenly, Phuong meets Hoa in front of the store. The man with brown hair, a buff body, and a smile of sunshine.

"Hey," Hoa says. "Nice to see you again. What are you doing here?"

Phuong smiles. "I go shopping with my son. You know, school supplies and some clothes. How about you?"

"Well, same as you," Hoa says. "Not school supplies. I bought clothes."

"That's nice."

Hoa looks at the little boy holding his mother's hand and has no idea who he is. "So this must be your son."

"Oh," Phuong forgets she is holding Michael's hand or the appearance of Michael here. "Sorry, this is my son, Michael," She looks at Michael. "Michael, say hello to Mr. Hoa. He is…Uhm…"

"I am your mother's friend," Hoa says to Michael. He bends down as low as Michael. He smiles. "How do you do, little boy?"

Michael shyly responds. "I am doing fine."

"Good, good. Have you had a good time in school today?"

Michael nods. Phuong chuckles. "He is a little shy."

Hoa waves his hands. "Nah, don't worry. The kids are always like that. So where are you going right now?"

"We are going to get some ice cream. Michael loves ice cream."

"Oh, that's nice!" Hoa says delightfully. "You know what, I know an ice cream place in this mall is so good with so many wonderful flavors. Also, they serve coffee too. Five stars on Yelp."

Phuong smiles. "That's great! Can you show me?"

Hoa shakes his head. "It is not for you, unfortunately," He turns his look to Michael. "It is for this little boy. Is that right?"

"Yes." Michael gets excited.

"All right, let's go to the ice cream shop," Hoa says.

Phuong pretends to sulk. "Oh, now I am being outcasted. I think that Mr. Hoa doesn't want me to join you. So I guess I have to go home now."

Hoa asks Michael. "Do you want your mom to join us?"

"I do," Michael says. "Because my mom told me not to go with strangers."

Hoa and Phuong laugh out loud after what Michael says. Then, they walk to the ice cream shop that Hoa just introduced. Michael orders a chocolate chip ice cream, which is his favorite flavor. Phuong orders a vanilla milkshake. Hoa orders a caramel frappe. They sit at the table.

"What do you say to Mr. Hoa?" Phuong asks Michael.

"Thank you, Sir," Michael says and continues his ice cream.

"You're welcome," Hoa says.

Near the ice cream shop, there is a playground with so many kids playing. It immediately gets attention of Michael.

"Mom," Michael says. "Can I go over there and play?"

Phuong looks out to the playground. That is what she wants from Michael—hanging out with friends and playing with ordinary things, not technology. "Of course, dear," Phuong says. "But be careful, ok?"

"Yes, mom." Then quickly, he runs to the playground to play with those kids.

At the table, Hoa leans back and enjoys his frappe. Phuong looks at Hoa. She has a strange feeling at this moment, as if someone has to wake up that feeling inside her on her behalf. Hoa is so handsome and so attractive. It has been a while since Phuong is not so close with men like that. It is like a fire starting to burn inside her. But Phuong does not consider it a fire of love because she has shut down that fire since the day she signed the divorce paper.

Hoa turns his look from Michael, playing with those kids over there, to Phuong. He gets startled because Phuong is staring at him. He chuckles. "What? Why are you looking at me like that?"

Phuong smiles. "Nothing. It's just..." Phuong tries to come up with something to say. "You have a good body." Dammit, there are so many things to say, and she chooses to say about his body. What can be more stupid than that? Phuong feels like other middle-aged and beyond women who have a major crush on young guys. Like they say. Young pilots fly old ladies—cougar style.

Hoa takes a look at his body. "Thank you for saying that."

"I hope that you don't mind if I just said things that were... inappropriate." Phuong can see the weirdness in this situation. She blushes. She returned to her vanilla shake and sucked it, trying to look away to avoid Hoa.

"I don't mind," Hoa chuckles. "So many people used to say that about me. I feel normal. Besides, I like people who have compliments on my body."

"You must go to the gym a lot."

"Three times a week. And I have a healthy balanced diet for my own."

"That is great. You must tell me about it sometimes."

"I will."

Then, for a moment, they both fall into an uncomfortable silence and watch Michael playing. Hoa speaks up to break the awkward silence. "Did Michael know about it?"

Phuong gives Hoa a puzzled look. "What do you mean?"

Hoa meets her eyes. "About your divorce."

"Oh," Phuong smiles shyly.

She wants to avoid this question from people, especially from all the mommies at Michael's school. But in front of Hoa, she feels comfort and trust, which she can open up to share her divorce story, and there is nothing to be embarrassed about. It was over, and there was nothing between her and Adam now. Adam is the reason why they got divorced. She is not the reason leading to the divorce. *That motherfucker caused it.*

But Hoa does not ask why Phuong Adam got divorced. He asks about the aftermath and whether Michael knows about it or not. Phuong feels heavy in her heart. She feels guilty and irresponsible because she let Michael live in this situation where he no longer has a happy family and must live today with his mother or tomorrow with his father. Michael is innocent and deserves to have a happy family, but Phuong and Adam can not give him one. Sometimes, Phuong feels regret about her decision when she gets divorced. "He hasn't known about it yet. We're both trying to make him feel happy and not lonely."

"Does he ever ask why you and Adam are no longer living together?"

"We told him that because I took a new job at a new hospital. So I moved to my mom's house near the workplace."

"And he believed it?"

Phuong nods. "He is still a child."

"I can see that," Hoa stirs the straw in his frappe for nothing. His cup is only left with whipped cream. "A play where you and your ex-husband are trying to play along even though you are not happy to play your character. Bravo to your performance."

Phuong is bewildered at what Hoa said. *A play,* he says. What play? For just a moment, Phuong loses all of the best things she has thought about Hoa. He feels that Phuong is just pretending to be happy with Michael; behind Michael's back, she wants him to look bad at his father. That has been true all along. But Phuong does not like people who expose her in front of her like this. What if Michael hears about this? What will he think about his mother?

"You know what," Phuong gives Hoa a cold smile. "You are nothing. You are just a stranger, an outsider. What do you know about us? All you see is a surface but did you go deep inside it? So don't sit there and try to outsmart me, young man. You know nothing about marriage. You're still young and need to learn a lot."

Hoa laughs out loud. He leans forward. "Oh yeah, I am an outsider, and I am just a little boy to you, aren't I? But let me tell you this. I used to be in Michael's position, right now. Do you get that? And I can see it in Michael. I am sick of people pretending they are happy in front of their children and trying to fool them."

Phuong gets frozen. She cannot believe what Hoa said. He is a product of a failed marriage. She immediately changes her feeling toward him. From anger to something. A mixed feeling. "I...I don't....know about this," Phuong says, but she is still shaking.

Hoa sighs, but he still keeps optimistic. "That's fine. I am so sorry when I said that to you. I was so rude."

"No, no. I don't mind at all. Don't worry about that." Phuong smiles. She thinks about what to do to get out of this awkward situation. Suddenly, she remembers that she has to pick up her mother, who is in physical therapy. She looks at her watch. It is almost 5 p.m., and her mother must be done. She stands up. "Oh my God, I have to pick up my mom. I almost forgot." She grabs all her stuff, including her shopping bag and tote bag.

Hoa stands up with her. "Oh, ok, Uhm... Maybe I can see you next time?"

Phuong looks at him. She is not so sure that she wants to see Hoa again after today.

"Let's see about that. Thank you for the ice cream and the drink. Goodbye." Then she quickly leaves without letting Hoa say goodbye to her or Michael. Phuong picks up Michael at the playground, who does not want to leave. He frowns. But Phuong knows what to do with him. She gives him the iPad, and he stops resisting immediately and follows her. Phuong goes to the physical therapy clinic and picks up her mother, who has done the therapy thirty minutes ago.

After dropping off Michael at Adam's house, Phuong returns to her mother's house. Mrs. Nhu is cooking pho for tomorrow. Adam would be here to eat. Mrs. Nhu invited him a week ago. Phuong walks to the kitchen. Mrs. Nhu sees her daughter and gives her a spoonful of soup.

"Try this one," Mrs. Nhu says. Phuong takes a sip. "Is it good?"

Phuong smiles. "Always, mom. Never doubt your cooking."

Mrs. Nhu nods. She returns to the soup pot. She reduces the heat and lets it simmer. When she turns to Phuong, she can see the disturbance and the suspicion on her face.

Mrs. Nhu pulls the chair and sits down. She pours herself a glass of water and drinks it. "What is the matter?"

Phuong turns to her mom. "Mom,"

She wants to ask her mom about Hoa. She wants to know about him, who he is, and what his life is wrong. But she stops because it sounds like she wants to investigate Hoa.

Hoa has his own life and might want to keep the secret for himself. If he wanted to share about himself, he would have told her everything to Phuong this afternoon. Phuong feels she has no right to get into someone's life like that.

"Have you taken medicine yet?" Phuong asks

"I've already taken those pills," Mrs. Nhu says. "Do you want to check?"

"No, mom"

"Seriously," Mrs. Nhu returns to the disturbance on her daughter's face lately. "What happens to you? You look strange."

Phuong laughs. "Nothing, mom. It's just that I am tired. Maybe I spent time with Michael today and had so much fun."

"So much fun, and you completely forgot me." Mrs. Nhu talks with a sarcastic voice.

"I'm sorry."

"I'm just kidding. If you feel tired, go to sleep. Get relaxed."

"Ok, mom," Phuong says. "I will go to sleep. It will help if you go to sleep early. Don't stay up late."

"I know. I know. But I must finish the K-Drama before I sleep." Mrs. Nhu says.

She loves watching K-Drama so much because every movie she watches has all the leading men who are all handsome and charming. She is obsessed with those Korean films. But not only because of attractive leading men but also loves Korean movies because of the content and the value. After watching the movie "Parasite" for the first time in the theater, she immediately fell in love with that movie and has watched it five times in a row. How crazy it is! First, she watched it with Phuong. Second, she watched it again after watching some YouTube analysis videos. Third and Fourth, she watched it because she wanted to watch it again and again. And fifth, she watched it for entertainment.

Phuong sighs. "You can watch it tomorrow. Not at a late hour like that. It is not healthy for you."

"All right," Mrs. Nhu agrees. But it cannot stop her from doing it, and Phuong knows about that. "I will try. Now, get rest."

"OK," Phuong kisses her mother's left cheek. "Good night, mom."

"Good night, sweetie."

Phuong goes to her room and lies on the bed tiredly. She is staring at the ceiling. She can not let the thought of exploring Hoa's life out of her mind. When he said he used to be like Michael, Phuong is curious about it. Hoa did not say anything further and left a cliffhanger on Phuong's mind. Only Phuong can assume that Hoa did not have a happy family and was left alone. His reaction in the afternoon showed that he was serious about the whole divorce thing and the life of a child after that. Phuong wants to know about Hoa so that she can treat Michael right and what to do with her son.

But how?

Suddenly, her phone rings. She looks at the phone. It was an unknown caller. She picked up.

"Hello?"

On the other side, with a sweet voice, someone answers. "Hey, it's Hoa, Hoa. What are you doing?"

Phuong is surprised. She remembers that she has yet to give Hoa any contact information. She asks how he got her phone number.

"Well, your mom gave it to me," He says. "I hope you don't mind."

"Not at all." Phuong chuckles. She gets out of bed and comes to the window. "Why are you calling me at this time?"

Before Hoa could answer anything, Phuong somehow predicted

what Hoa would say. He clears his throat. "Uhm, I feel a little awkward about what happened this afternoon. I hope that I did not make you feel uncomfortable. I am the kind of person who would like to speak my mind and talk about what I observe. It would make people feel annoyed, but it is true. I am sorry if I offended you and your ex-husband or Michael."

Why would he want to bring this up? Phuong does not mind what Hoa says because everything is accurate. It is a big fucking play. But what Phuong wants to know is Hoa's life story. A big fucking cliffhanger. Phuong truly hates that. An unhappy family? She would have asked Mrs. Nhu about him, but she does not want to invade other people's privacy. Now talking to Hoa impulses her more. Should she ask him?

"Hello, are you still there?" There is a long silence. Hoa must find out whether Phuong is still listening because of a connection.

"Yes," Phuong returns the call. "I am listening. Well, there is nothing. I don't mind that. You are right. Everyone can speak their minds, and I don't get angry if someone talks about me. I got used to it. So don't worry about that, ok?"

"I understand. So, uhm," Hoa clears his throat. "Are you free next week?"

"For what?" Phuong gets surprised.

"I would like to take you out for dinner. I know a good restaurant in the city," Hoa says. "I want to make peace with you, and I think you would like to know about my story."

Oh, hell yeah, Phuong thinks. Finally, he opens up about this topic. Phuong feels so released after Hoa says that. Now she is like *ok, you bring this up, you want to talk about it*, and she doesn't force him to talk about it. All she knows is that Hoa intends to make peace with her. A wish comes true.

"Well, of course," Phuong says delightfully. "I will check my working schedule next week and call you back. Ok?"

"Sure. No problem," Hoa says. "Have a great night."

"You too. Bye."

They both hang up. Phuong right now can get a good sleep because everything is about to open. Every single layer.

CHAPTER 4

Ha

It was 6 in the morning of the fall. This was when the sun was still under the horizon and getting ready for the morning. The street lights were still on. Street sweepers cleaned up all the leaves and dirt on the road to ensure it did not block the drain and make the street cleaner. Even though it was still early, some cars were driving on the street whose owners were hustling to go to work early, their workplaces were far away, or they were moving to nowhere. Some food stores had opened for breakfast. People loved to have a cup of coffee to start the morning. Anyone walking past some Vietnamese banh mi stores could smell the fresh baguette in the morning or croissants. The fall came and brought the cold breeze in the morning mingling with the thin fog that had made things around so chill strangely.

Ha, a well-known lawyer in the Vietnamese community, also wakes up early to enjoy the vibe of early morning in the fall while her family is still sleeping, except her mother-in-law. She is exercising in the park with her friends, or at least that is what Ha believes because, according to what Mr. Tan, her father-in-law, says, Mrs. Linh never does any exercise in her life. Not even one. And now, suddenly, she exercises so early in the morning like that. Someone may have possessed Mrs. Linh.

Ha does not enjoy the morning vibe even though she wants to. She is too busy. Yes, the time at the firm with a pile of cases can not give her any spare time for herself. She would love to have one day to enjoy the day. She was going shopping, driving around, having drinks, or simply walking along the beach. She needs to escape.

The firm would open at 9 a.m. But Ha has gone out 3 hours before. *Who would want to have a lawyer in the early morning like that?*

Arriving at the place, Ha checked herself on her phone. She was wearing a black T-Shirt with the line "Keep Calm and Fuck", which she would never wear in her house, a pair of leggings, and Sketcher running shoes. Whomever Ha was about to meet. It was not about the law stuff. Ha knocked on the door. A man with a blue shirt and black jeans opened the door for her. It was Adam, Phuong's sweet husband. He was glad to see Ha again. Maybe happier than seeing his wife.

"Hey," Adam said with a smile. "Come in. You arrive on time."

"Why not?" Ha said. "It's an important business, right?"

Ha walked inside the house. She turned back to Adam, who had just closed the door. She kissed him immediately on his lips romantically. Then, she was released.

"I miss you so much," Ha said as if she had not seen him in a long time. They just had sex two weeks ago.

"I miss you too, babe," Adam held her belly. "Do you want to warm up before we get into action?"

"I always love your tequila."

Then, hands in hand, they went to the kitchen.

Ha sat on the cabinet near Adam, where he was preparing tequila. Ha looked at Adam with a sweet look. "Where is Michael?"

"He was with his grandma," Adam handed Ha her tequila. "Salute."

"Salute," Ha finished her drink. After the tequila shot ran down her throat and the alcohol transferred immediately to her brain, Ha came up with an idea.

"Babe, why don't we try to do it here?" Ha suggested.

"What?"Adam looked at her surprisingly. "Here?"

"Yeah. We always do it in your bedroom, living room, closet, garage, and even Michael's room. We have never done it in the kitchen. I watched some sex scenes in movies, and they were all great. What do you think?"

The whole business they were about to do was having sex. This affair worked because of all the "actions" on the bed that Adam and Ha sponsored. They had been putting on many hot shows throughout their dirty love affair. And soon, morning sex had become their routine.

Adam took a quick peek at the floor. A little dirty and maybe smelly because the robot vacuum cleaner would not clean the house until 2 p.m.

Adam grinned. "I...I don't know if it is a good idea or not. I mean, the floor is pretty dirty."

Ha laughed. She placed her glass down and came near Adam. She put her hand on Adam's cheek and fondled it. "Babe, we are naked when we fucked. Why the hell are you worried about the dirty floor."

Adam was still considering this. He did not know whether it was a great idea or not. But he tried to remind himself that wherever Ha picked a place to have sex, they would have the best sex and orgasm.

The first time they had sex was in Adam's car in the garage because they did not want to leave any traces in the house. The second time Adam changed the sheet in his bedroom so that when Phuong came home, she would not smell suspicious. The third time was in the living room, where they did not need to do anything to cover their sex because Adam needed to throw away the old couch and replace a new one on that day. The fourth time was in the closet, right after they went shopping in the mall. And the fifth time was in Michael's room. The fifth time was not intentional. It was an accident. Ha came to Adam's house and found him in Michael's room to clean up his toys. She had this idea inside her head because at her hospital, in obstetrics, her colleagues told her that they sometimes caught many couples having sex in some empty delivery room, and nine months, ten days later, the doctors delivered their child in that same room. Ha found it very interesting, and she wanted to practice. Adam had Michael, and he had his room. So why not? Just like that, they fucked on Michael's bed.

"All right, if you want to do it right here in the kitchen, let's fuck!" Adam declared.

He immediately took off his jeans, ran his hands inside Ha's dress, and took out her underwear. Then he grabbed her vagina hard. Ha groaned.

She kissed him badly from his neck to his mouth.

"You are better each time we fuck." Ha exclaimed.

"I learn from the best," Adam took his hands off her vagina. "It is just a starter. Now get into my favorite part."

Adam lifted Ha. He put his dick inside her. One, Ha groaned in joy, and her hands were around his neck. Two, Adam pushed in harder, harder until Ha reached her orgasm. Three, both moved around the kitchen. They did not care about the stuff in the kitchen. Some of them dropped and broke.

"Yeah, Yeah, Yeah," Ha screamed out loud. "Fuck me, fuck me, fuck me to the moon."

"You like that?" Adam asked.

"Don't ask. Just do it." Ha groaned harder.

After they finished, the couple would lie on the bed and smoke, just like in every movie. Instead, they were lying on the floor of the kitchen. They both stared at the ceiling. They were like losing their souls.

"It is.... so sexy," Ha said.

"You think so?"

"Yes, absolutely," Suddenly, Ha just remembered that she had an appointment with one of her clients today to sort out the divorce for them. She turned to Adam. "What time is it?"

Adam looked at his watch. "It's 8 a.m. Why?"

Ha sat up. "Shit, I have an appointment today at 9 a.m. I gotta go."

She stood up and picked up her bra, clothes, and underwear. She put them on. Adam put on his blue shirt but still needed to get his jeans. He put his arms around Ha, who was trying to fix her hair. He kissed her neck.

"You have to go right now?" Adam was sad.

Ha turned back, put her hands around Adam's neck, and kissed him. "I guessed so. I had great sex. Next time, you will pick a place. Maybe somewhere else."

"Well," Adam said. "I will think about that." He slapped Ha's asses when she was about to go into the bathroom to change her casual clothes for work.

"Ouch!" She exclaimed. Then, she kissed him again. "Take time, babe, to think. But don't take it so long."

After Ha finished everything, Adam walked Ha to the door and watched her drive away. Then he immediately ran back to the kitchen and cleaned up the mess they had just made. Then, he went to the bathroom and took a shower. He returned to the bedroom, went to the closet room, and chose the black suit. After wearing the suit, he combed his hair carefully and walked downstairs. He opened the closet near the kitchen, where he hid the rose bouquet and the necklace. He looked at the bouquet in his hands. Suddenly, Adam realized that it was not right all along. He knew today was his wedding anniversary with Phuong, and he still had sex with Ha this morning. These things, which he was holding, were lies and betrayal. He had betrayed Phuong, the love Phuong had given him, and crossed himself when he had already fallen in love with Ha.

Inside Adam, the image of Ha was the only thing right now. But he must continue the whole lies with Phuong. He wondered when it would be over.

While driving on the street, Ha noticed a Starbucks on the right. She took a look at the clock in the car. It was 8h30. Still early, she thought. The clients could wait and would not mind if Ha wanted to be fully refreshed after her morning sex. Ha walked inside the store. She was so pissed because this store did not have a drive-thru.

Ha ordered for herself a venti caramel frappe with extra caramel drizzle. She loved sweets. Then, she stood at the corner to wait for her drink. Even though it was 8h30, it was still early, but the Starbucks table had been full of people. Students came to study, and others discussed business. Even some homeless people were here to do nothing. Ha used to love staying at Starbucks to enjoy the music, read a book, and smell the roasted coffee bean. But that moment ended abruptly after she got married. She did not even have time to sit here to enjoy. She went home immediately after work to cook dinner for the family, she had to go to the supermarket to buy food for the whole week, and at night, she had to work on her cases. A hustle life made Ha want to get away. But when she thought of the idea that she would have sex with Adam, the tiredness disappeared. Adam would fuck all of the burdens, the depression, and the anger inside Ha out and recharge her.

But the question was, "Why didn't Ha and Thomas have sex?". Not so difficult to answer that. It was all because Thomas could not provide the real need like Adam. There was nothing wrong with his health or his penis. It was just that Thomas was such a coward in the sex game. If talking about sex, Ha was the only girl he had ever had sex with. How ironic it was! He did not even know how to do it properly. Ha had to show him how by buying books or watching porno movies. But there was no use. Ha felt so depressed. But it was not the only problem. Thomas was working in a famous restaurant downtown as a head chef. He worked from lunch to late at night. So when he came home, he was already tired, and Mrs. Linh told Ha not to disturb him and let him rest. Just like that, the distance of love between Thomas and Ha started too far apart. Whenever Ha wanted to pull the distance closer, Thomas pushed her away. With force from her mother-in-law, who told her to leave her son alone because he needed to have his own time, Ha gave up, and there was nothing she could do.

Luckily, at the end of the dark road, a light of hope always shone for Ha.

It was Adam.

At the corner, Ha was checking her email. Suddenly, from somewhere, somebody was calling her name. A woman with long hair in the scrub for the doctor came to Ha. In a moment, her heart was beating fast for no reason. In front of her right now was her best friend, Phuong. Ha had not seen Phuong the Thanksgiving a few years ago.

They are best friends but don't see each other much after high school. They each went to different colleges and pursued different dreams. Unlike Ha, Phuong has a happy family with Adam. Ha is a little bit jealous when there is one time Phuong and Adam invite Ha and Thomas to dinner. They had shown love in front of Ha. She looked at her husband and wished Thomas could be one of Adam's.

Whom could she blame? Fate had settled for her. Somehow, that fate had jokes on her; right now, Ha was having an affair with Adam. She understood she had betrayed her best friend, whom she always considered Phuong as her sister. She felt guilty. Sometimes she wanted to stop this affair and return Adam to Phuong. But it was too late. Nothing could be retrieved right now. Ha, and Adam had finally fallen in love.

Ha had to pretend to be glad to see Phuong. Deep inside, she did not even want to look at Phuong's eyes; at that moment, those sharp eyes wanted to denounce Ha's guilt. It made Ha feel heavy in her heart.

After meeting Phuong at Starbucks, Ha could not hide her shock. When she was in her car, she gasped and breathed heavily. *Shit, shit, shit.* Ha just had sex with Phuong's husband, and the karma had already come. So fast.

She grew up with her mom, who always taught her about the Vietnamese culture so that Ha would not forget her origin, and as a

Buddhist, Ha believes in karma so much. Good people will get good things, and bad people will get bad things. In this case, Ha just did a bad thing, and bad karma would come to her any soon. Seeing Phuong was evident as a bad omen at that moment. Too many bad things in her head right now. She tried to clear everything up and focused on the divorce case she had to deal with later.

It was a rainy Thursday, but the lousy weather outside could not stop the sex of Adam and Ha. Ha called Michael a day before to ask him to cancel the sex today because she was not in the mood due to the bad weather. But somehow, with the enchanting words of Adam, he convinced her to do it. He said that Ha might look sexy when she was wet, and they could do it in the shower. It immediately turned her on, and she changed her mind at the last minute.

Phuong had a shift at the hospital that afternoon and would not be home after dinner. Adam and Ha had more time to fuck.

Adam always loves interior design. When Adam and Phuong bought this house, it was so horrible from the inside and outside. It was like a haunted house. Despite the look, many people wanted this house because of the low price. They could spend a little more money to redecorate the home. Adam and Phuong were somewhere on the list, and the chance to get this house was short. But luck had smiled on Adam and Phuong. They were the chosen ones after offering the realtor a price. Before Adam could do anything with the house, he bought books on interior design to learn how to decorate and organize the house. He ordered all the furniture from Ikea to Bed Bath & Beyond, from Home Depot to Ashley Furniture. To keep the surprise, Adam required Phuong to live with her mother for a few days until he finished everything in the new house. When it came to the bathroom, Adam was amazed by the toilet size in his room. It was the main bathroom. So Adam would take advantage of all the advantages of that bathroom. An oversized bathtub would be the center of this bathroom. It was a square bathtub. Normally, Phuong would spend one hour soaking herself in that bathtub with candles and essential oils. She felt so relaxed but never had a chance to have sex with Adam in this bathtub.

That chance was given to Ha.

They were in the bathtub full of water and bubble from the bath bomb and some bath oil. After having wet sex, they dried themselves (Not with a towel) and then moved to the bedroom for a second round.

But just in five minutes they did, Phuong came into the room and caught Adam and Ha. *So busted.* Ha and Adam got startled and tried to cover themselves with the blanket after seeing Phuong. Their faces were pale and white like blood had been sucked out of their bodies.

Usually, a lady who caught her husband having an affair would get mad and jump into the scene to beat up the girl in bed with her husband. But Phuong was not that kind of person. She was quiet, bit her lower lip, and left the room.

Surprisingly, Adam did not follow Phuong when she left. *Fuck*, he mouthed.

Ha got out of bed quickly and put on her clothes. They looked at each other without saying anything. Ha left.

"I'll call you," Adam shouted when Ha was at the door.

Ha turned back to look at Adam. She did not know what to say to him. Then she went away, and that was the last time she saw Adam.

Ha walked down the stair, passed through the living room, and saw Phuong sitting there and crying. Ha was about to come in, but she did not know what to say. It would be all bullshit if she said something, and Phuong would not want to listen to it.

On the way home, Ha was crying. She held the wheel tight, which made marks of her nails on it. It was so fucked up and so humiliating. In her mind, many thoughts were crossing through right now. A full sequel on what would happen after today. First, she thought of what Phuong might do next. She might share the story of her husband's affair with her best friend on social media, and people would know about Ha, a whore destroying other people's happiness. Second, her husband's family would soon find out about it when Phuong or her mother tells them about the whole affair. Usually, her mother-in-law hated her, and the love affair would be a big chance for Mrs. Linh to get rid of Ha once and for all. Third, Ha would be kicked out of the house, and Thomas would leave her. Soon, the whole firm would know about this scandal, and Ha would lose her job; nobody wanted to hire her. Ironically, a lawyer who is the best at every divorce case and gets all the benefits for clients after divorce, and has been so fierce, so strong, so firm in court, turned out to be a nasty bitch.

"SHUT UP!" Ha shouted out bitterly. The tear rolled down to her cheek and dropped on her lap. She kept crying without knowing she had been home. Looking at the house from the car, she hesitated to come in.

Mrs. Linh was sitting in the living room chair reading Vogue magazine. Seeing her daughter-in-law walk into the house with wet clothes and hair, Mrs. Linh felt annoyed because she had just mopped the floor, and now Ha had made the bed get dirty.

Mrs. Linh put the magazine on her lap and sighed. "Next time, use the umbrella when you walk in the rain," Mrs. Linh demanded. "You are not Gene Kelly."

Ha took off her boot and left it next to the shoe shelf. She did not want to make other shoes dirty and, of course, did not want Mrs. Linh to yell at her. She had enough trouble for today. "Yes, mom. I will be careful later."

Mrs. Linh never liked every action Ha took in this house. She never cared about her. Even right now, Ha was soaking wet, and she might catch a cold, but Mrs. Linh was like, "Ok, clean floor first and if her daughter-in-law was sick, get some medicine." Ha quietly walked in.

Mrs. Linh returned to the magazine and spoke up. "Do you know what day it is?"

Ha turned her look to her mother-in-law. She did not know what day it was, or even she could not remember what the date was today. Her mind did not have time to think about what day it was. Whatever the day Mrs. Linh was talking about, Ha definitely did not give a shit. It was not more important than being caught during sex today.

But when Mrs. Linh asked her about that, it was a big deal, and she would be as mad and so disappointed as usual if Ha did not remember.

Ha scratched her head and answered tiredly. "I...Uhm, I don't know, mom."

"Haizzz," The disappointment of her daughter-in-law showed clearly on Mrs. Linh's face. A very familiar face. She put down the magazine and looked at Ha. "You have been a daughter-in-law of this family for a long time. It was not like the first time you walked into this family. You could not even remember what day it was. Let me remind you. Today is Thomas' grandfather's death anniversary."

Ha did not remember. Usually, Mrs. Linh will prepare everything. Ha is busy with her job. Thomas is active in his restaurant. It is hard for both of them to catch up with important family events.

"I am sorry, mom," Ha said. Her hand was on the forehead. "I completely forgot about this," She lied, of course. "Let me change my clothes, and I will take you to the supermarket to buy food."

Mrs. Linh shook her head. "Never mind. I have done everything. Later the relatives come, you help me. Pay attention, please."

Ha kept her head low. "I am sorry, mom. Next time I will...Uhm... remember." She left the living room. She walked to the stairs and stopped suddenly because of what Mrs. Linh was saying.

"Their daughters-in-law always care about their families. This daughter-in-law is just like a guest. Leave when she wants to leave, return when she wants to return. Never pay any attention to the husband's family. This family is so miserable."

Ha could not move another step. She held the stair handle tightly. Those harsh words of her mother-in-law made the hatred inside her rise up more. Sometimes when she watches crime movies or reads thriller novels, her favorite genre ever, she wants to pick up a pistol and shoot her mother-in-law in her chest or butcher her body into pieces and feed some dogs. Actually, after that affair scandal, Ha would want to do it immediately. Nothing to lose, right? She would go to the kitchen, choose the sharpest knife, come to the living room, and slit Mrs. Linh's throat. She did not care if she went to prison or was executed. Her worst nightmare would be over. Ha knew that deep inside her, she had the gut to do it, but something just popped up and stopped her from doing that horrible thing. Today was enough for Ha.

Ha walked into her room. Thomas was sitting on the bed and working from his MacBook on his lap desk. Thomas looked up. His expression did not show any sympathy when seeing his wife soaking wet. If a husband truly loved his wife, they would have gotten up their feet, found a blanket for their wife to dry themselves, helped change their clothes, checked on their health, and ensured that everything was fine. Oh my, Ha desperately needed that gesture for her husband. But the wish was just a wish that would never come true. It was like how Ha wished Thomas could be better at sex.

"Geez," He hissed. "You look fucking terrible. Where have you been?"

Ha went to the bathroom and spoke out. "I was at work."

"You're all soaked up. Were you working in the rain?"

Ha returned to the bedroom with a flower dress. "I forgot to bring the umbrella."

Thomas did not say anything. He just kept focusing on his recipes for the restaurant.

"Do you know today is your grandfather's death anniversary?" Ha asked while she was brushing her hair.

"Yes, I do," Thomas said. "You don't?"

Ha turned to Thomas with wide eyes open. "You remember your grandfather's death anniversary?" Ha scoffed. "I doubted that."

"No, I remember my grandfather's death anniversary. It is always in my head."

"How great," Ha groaned. "I forgot, and mom just taught me a lesson. Why didn't you remind me?"

"Darling," Thomas took off his glasses and closed the laptop. "You should pay more attention to this house's business. Please don't ignore it, and don't blame me for not reminding you. It was your responsibility as a wife and a daughter-in-law. You know they will judge you if you show your irresponsibility, your mom, and my family. They will look at me and tell me that I am married to a terrible wife. I don't want it to happen. Keep my family's reputation, ok? Now, if you have understood what I just said, go downstairs and help my mom to prepare. I will go down soon."

What a nice thing to say to a wife from a husband! Ha looked at her husband with a bored look. *Why did I ever marry you?* She thought. Thomas opened the laptop, put on his glasses, and returned to work. Ha crossed her arms and frowned. She shook her head but did not say anything because she did not want to make a scene. She left the room.

When they were dating, Thomas was super friendly to Ha, with all the nice words he learned from somewhere in romantic novels. Ha immediately fell in love as if she was voodooed. Thomas always cooked for Ha, and they had dinner or lunch in the parks. Sometimes in Ha's backyard in her house. They were both busy with their jobs but always spent time with each other and never let themselves apart.

After getting married, Thomas lost all of that romance. But to Ha, it was just how he tried to win Ha; deep inside, Thomas is not that romantic, and he has taken off his mask. Living under one roof with Mrs. Linh, Thomas is nothing more than a mama boy. Thomas is pissed off each time Ha does not clean the house and leaves it to his mother. He yells at Ha, and they fight for days. All the time. Or when the house had a party, Ha helped Thomas and Mrs. Linh prepare the guests' food. She accidentally burned the meat and messed up some dishes, Thomas was not pleased, and Mrs. Linh told her to get out of the kitchen. Then, Mrs. Linh told Thomas that Ha was a useless wife and a loser. Or the times when Ha had a party with her old friends from college, and she came home late, and she was drunk, and she forgot the house key, instead of helping her to change her clothes or getting her to bed or letting her in, Mrs. Linh did not let Ha come inside the house because she hated to have drunk people inside her house. And Mrs. Linh told Thomas to go to bed and did not need to bother about Ha. Ha was freezing outside and felt so sad. She called, but they all ignored her. She came to her mother's house but did not tell Mrs. Trang anything about what happened because she did not want Mrs. Trang to be worried for her, and she wanted her mother to be pleased that she was still happy.

After so many things happened like that, Ha discusses with Thomas about moving out. Ha has a client who is a realtor, and she can help Ha to find an affordable house for Ha and Thomas. She wants to stay away from this house as soon as possible. She wants to be freed from Mrs. Linh. Thinking that Thomas would agree, Thomas tells this to his mother, and his mother yells at Ha badly. She tells Ha she is a cold blood monster and a heartless woman. Mrs. Linh claims Ha despairs her, hates her, and wants to steal her son. Matter of fact that everything Mrs. Linh says is correct. Ha does not deny it, but the thing is that Thomas doesn't listen to Ha, not just consider it. Thomas never protects her even once.

Ha feels so depressed and can see that she is forever stuck in this house.

When it came to the dinner with relatives from Thomas' family, it turned worse. The relatives of Thomas' family still has their old thought inside their heads because Mr. Tan is the first child. So, it is his family who gives birth to a boy to the family's heritage. Not only, but they also separate people at the table. Men will sit in the front. Women will sit in the back. Mr. Tan has lived in the U.S. for a long time and has changed this concept. He no longer minded this tradition. Whoever is his child of him will be forever his child. Whether the child is a girl or a boy, he would love them with all of his heart. But Mrs. Linh is still keeping that old tradition.

Before Mrs. Linh became a mother-in-law, Mrs. Linh used to be the daughter-in-law of Mr. Tan's family, and her mother-in-law put pressure on Mrs. Linh she must give birth to a boy. It would be one of the most severe sins of filial piety if she couldn't do it. Her father-in-law expected a lot from Mrs. Linh. And she did not fail them. Thomas was born under the name "Khanh." The family was so happy. But that happiness had not lasted for long. Saigon fell in 1975. Many people were trying to get out of Saigon. The chaos grew more extensive than ever. In 1976, when Thomas was two years old, Mr. Tan decided to join the wave of people crossing the border on the sea. But Mr. Tan's family refused because they wanted to die in the homeland even though it had fallen into communism. Vietnam was still Vietnam with them. Before they left, Mr. Tan's mother pulled Mrs. Linh into her room and told Mrs. Linh that whatever happened, she must keep the tradition of this family and when that child grew up, he must have a boy to heritage this family. Mrs. Linh would never forget that.

Mrs. Linh never forgets that. If anyone ever comes to Mr. Tan's, they will never believe that the head of the house is Mr. Tan.

In the family, there is not only Mrs. Linh hates Ha but also Mrs. An, who is Mr. Tan's sister. Not sure why she hates Ha so much, but when she meets Ha in front of Mrs. Linh, she always mentions the giving birth topic even though there are so many topics to discuss. For example, Thanh, Thomas' first cousin, fails many classes in college. Jenny, Thomas's second cousin, does not make much money but still goes shopping using her dad's credit card. Mr. Tung, Jenny's father, and Mr. Tan's youngest brother had trouble dealing with hit-and-run. Each person at that table was covered with dirty truths that no one wanted to talk about and be afraid of being exposed at any time. Thank God Ha was here. They could point all attention to Ha if Mrs. An spoke up.

"So," Mrs. An said after taking a coke. "Do you have any plan on having a child, Ha?"

The whole table talked about something, then reticent after what Mrs. An asked. Mrs. Linh looked at Ha and waited for her answer. Ha was trying to finish her egg roll. She put down her bowl and her chopsticks. She smiled. "Uhm, I don't know about that. We are busy, and of course, we are trying to. I hope we can have it soon."

Mrs. An laughed out loud in the meanest way. "Sweetie, you have said like that for a long time ago. My brother and sister-in-law have been waiting for your child for a long time. Every time I asked you about this, you always answered like that. You don't want to have a child or something?"

That old bitch. Why does she never keep her mouth shut? Ha had difficulty conceiving. She and Thomas had tried many times. Of course, one part was because Thomas was terrible at sex. But nothing happened. Ha was desperate, and no one, even Thomas, was there to encourage or understand her. Only her mom and Mr. Tan were there for her. They understood what Ha had been through. Ha could feel better when her mom and her father-in-law were beside her.

Ha never likes Mrs. An and tries to stay away from her. She knows that Mrs. An was nothing good. She used to set up car accidents to get indemnity from the insurance. She used to work in a wire where other people could qualify for driver's licenses without taking any tests. She used to work in an illegal gambling organization where she could hold any gambling activity underground. Karmas always came to bad people. The police found out what Mrs. An and her partners in crime did. They were all sentenced to prison and later deported back to Vietnam. But somehow, thanks to the defense by Ha at court, Mrs. An only served two years in jail. Ha did not want to defend somebody who committed a crime, especially Mrs. An. She despaired about what Mrs. An had done because her crimes made the image of Vietnamese uglier.

Now, Mrs. An insulted her with all the giving birth thing. Ha held her fist tight and wanted to jump into Mrs. An and beat her up.

But Mrs. Tan slapped the table hard. His face was angry.

"You can keep your mouth shut right now, An," Mr. Tan talked to Mrs. An. "I don't want you to talk like that to my daughter-in-law."

"Brother, I want to know why they have not had kids yet. Why are you angry at me?" Mrs. An asked.

"You don't need to know about that. That is the privacy of Ha and Thomas." Mr. Tan said.

Mrs. Linh looked at her husband with a surprised look. She stood for Mrs. An. "Darling, An was asking a question. She was curious, and she had a right to ask. That was the right question. Don't you see Ha has been living in our family for a long time, but she has not had a child yet? I believe that everyone wants to know about that too." Then she turned to Ha. "Ha, can you answer it for Mrs. An? Show some respect."

Mr. Tan stopped Ha when she tended to answer. "You don't need to answer it," He looked straight at his wife. "You can stop it right now. This is my father's death anniversary, and I want to spend this evening remembering him and talking about his memories. And this is the time for a family reunion. Not Family Feud. If anyone talks anything that insults others at this table, stand up and leave."

No one dared to talk after what Mr. Tan said. They were all afraid of him at that moment. Mrs. Linh was so angry because her husband had shut down her plan to insult her daughter-in-law so that people in the family could discuss that. With Ha, she was so grateful for what Mr. Tan just stood for her. She looked at Mr. Tan, smiled, and mouthed. "Thank you." Mr. Tan just nodded, slightly agreeing.

Later that night, Ha stayed awake. She went to the backyard and sat there to watch the sky. After the rain, there were many stars in the sky. It was so beautiful. At this moment, Ha lighted up a cigarette, smoked, and thought about what had happened today. Being caught in the middle of an affair made Ha feel so bad and guilty. But after the controversial dinner lately, Ha did not feel anything guilty because she knew that she loved Adam and Adam loved her. Their love for each other was real. Ha thought in her mind that if Adam got divorced, she would divorce Thomas too. Ha could not see any love from her husband anymore. He was just a mama boy. How her mother-in-law had treated her so far in this house was enough. She got to leave. Now, contradicted with what she was worried and scared about when she came home earlier, Ha wished everything would be ended soon so that she could be with Adam even if Mrs. Linh found out and insulted her badly.

But what about Mr. Tan? What would he think about this?

CHAPTER 5

Phuong

I t has been a long time since someone invites Phuong for dinner. She feels so excited. Phuong goes shopping the whole morning to find the best outfit for tonight. She wants to be beautiful and youthful. But she is afraid that everyone will think she and Hoa are on a date and that she is a cougar. No, she has to stop thinking about that. Be happy and enjoy dinner with Hoa. Also, she must listen to Hoa's story.

Makeup is always torture for Phuong because she does not know how to do it. Usually, she puts on some powder and some lipstick. Sometimes, she adds mascara or some cheap eyeliners. Rachel has taught her how to apply makeup, but it never worked. Rachel could have been here to do makeup for Phuong, but she is busy with her shift. Phuong tries her best.

Before leaving her room, Phuong looks at herself in the mirror again to ensure she is okay.

"Remember, Phuong," She talks to herself. "It's just a normal dinner. No other purpose beyond that."

She smiles and leaves.

Phuong goes downstairs to the living room, where Michael is doing his homework, and Mrs. Nhu is helping him. Both turn their attention to Phuong as she walks in. With a blue navy dress from Prada, she turns around for Mrs. Nhu and Michael to see.

Michael claps his hands happily. "You look so beautiful, mom."

Phuong comes near him and kisses his head. "Thank you, dear."

"When will you come back?" Mrs. Nhu asks.

"I don't know, mom," Phuong says as she stands up and fixes her hair. "But don't wait for me if I come home late. I have left the medicine for you on the table in the kitchen. You take it before you go to bed and eat something before you take it. Besides, take Michael's iPad when he is ready to sleep."

"I got that." Mrs. Nhu looks at her daughter. Inside her, she feels happy and pleased when her daughter can enjoy her life one more time. The affair and the divorce have pushed Phuong down to the bottom, and she loses herself somewhere where she does not have any more taste in life. Mrs. Nhu has always been hoping Phuong could be better.

"You are beautiful, Phuong," Mrs. Nhu says. "I like it."

Phuong smiles. "Thanks, mom," Then, there is a phone call. Phuong looks at the phone. It is Hoa. She picks up. "Are you here?.... Okie, I am out right now." She hangs up. "I have to go right now. See you!"

"Goodbye, mom," Michael says.

"Bye, sweetie."

"Have fun." Mrs. Nhu says. She always wants Phuong to have fun and do something new to forget all the old things away.

"Bye, Mom."

The blue RAV4 parks in front of her house. Hoa is standing next to it, and in his right hand, he is holding a red rose and smiling. With the same smile, same hair, and in a black suit mixed with the sense of Dior Sauvage and a pair of Jordans? Gen Z! But they all make Hoa more charming and attractive. Hoa is still a young man, and they mostly don't wear suits. Phuong thinks he must wear something active, a street style suitable for his age. But no, Hoa is a true gentleman.

"How do you do?" Hoa asks.

"I am doing fine. You?"

"I am ok," Hoa hands Phuong a red rose. "This one is for you."

Phuong is like, *"What?"*. She can not believe that Hoa can act like that. So lovely. But Phuong hopes that there is nothing between him and her. She responds immediately without giving Hoa a compliment or a thank you. "Don't mistake tonight for a date. Just a friendly dinner."

Hoa smiles. "I understand that."

Then, he opens the car door and invites Phuong to get in. And they go to the restaurant.

Arriving at a fancy restaurant on a small hill outside the city, Hoa shocks Phuong with surprises followed by surprises. How can Hoa afford to be in this restaurant? Du Coeur. This guy is so mysterious, and tonight must be the time for Phuong to dig into each layer of his life.

The restaurant is like a medieval castle under the moonlight. Phuong has known about this restaurant through some of her colleagues and some Gen Z nurses. They praise this restaurant as the most romantic restaurant ever. They have jazz, they have wine, and they have food that is worth every single dime. Indeed, the chief of *Du Coeur* is among the top chefs in America and has won many prizes and awards in culinary competitions. He used to run a restaurant in Paris, then became the instructor for *Le Cordon Bleu* for years, and finally, he became the chef for *Du Coeur* after a friend of his, who is the owner of this restaurant, invited him. Prices for each dish are costly. But they say once the guests ate, they would know why they paid much money.

The car parks in front of the restaurant. Hoa gets out of the car and runs to Phuong's door before a man outside opens it. He opens the door and gently gives Phuong a hand to help her out of the car. The man stands there, bowing his head slightly. "Good evening, sir and madam. May I have your key to park your car?"

"Sure," Hoa hands the man his key. "Thank you so much."

"You're welcome, sir. Enjoy your evening."

As an act of a gentleman, Hoa offers Phuong a hand for her to hold. Phuong chuckles.

"Please," Phuong hesitates. "I won't do that."

"Why not?" Hoa asks.

"I don't want people to misunderstand us. You know, like a couple."

"I can see that," He grabs Phuong's hand and puts it around his arm. "But tonight, I will control the game."

It catches Phuong's complete surprise. She feels a little bit uncomfortable when Hoa does that. She resists but finds it useless. Finally, she gives up and walks inside the restaurant with Hoa. As a couple. The receptionist sees Hoa and Phuong coming in, and she greets them.

"Good evening," She says. "Have you made a reservation?"

Hoa says. "Yes, I have. Hoa Nguyen. H-O-A N-G-U-Y-E-N"

"Oh, here you are," She gets off the counter and invites them to follow her. "Please go this way."

Phuong hears the jazz coming from the band on stage as they pass through the hall to get into the dining hall. They are playing blue jazz live. Phuong always loves blue jazz because it suits her feelings and mood. The receptionist introduces them to a table that views the city at night. Looking down on the hill, with a million lights coming from houses and buildings, the view is even more romantic, especially the moonlight. Hoa pulls the chair for Phuong.

She sits down. And Hoa sits in front of her.

Phuong is amazed by the view of the city, with lights coming from buildings and houses. And above the sky are millions of stars and a bright moon.

"Woah, it is magnificent, isn't it?" Phuong exclaims.

Hoa looks at the view. "Oh yeah."

"Don't you see it is beautiful?" Phuong asks after ignorance of Hoa. "I have lived in this city for a long time, but I've never seen the whole city from this position."

"Yeah, it's great. I know it." Probably, Hoa has been watching this view many times before. So, it is nothing new to him. He does not pretend he loves this view in front of Phuong. He prefers to tell the truth.

Phuong shakes her head disappointedly.

A waiter comes to their table with two menus in his hands.

"Good evening, Sir and Madam," He says with a British accent. Phuong always adores British culture and their pronunciation. It sounds so romantic and so polite. That is why she loves watching Downton Abbey. "My name is Harry, and I will be your server tonight. Here is the menu, and I will give you minutes to choose the best dishes for you. And tonight, we will serve cheesecake for free if you like."

"I'd love to. Thank you," Hoa says. "I want to begin with a bottle of the best chardonnay of this restaurant. And you know what I am talking about."

"Of course, sir. I will bring it out for you." Then the waiter leaves.

Phuong seems curious. "Best chardonnay?"

"Yes," Hoa says. "This restaurant had the best chardonnay ever. They make it by themselves. You should try it."

"All right," Phuong holds up her hands. "You control the night."

A moment later, they finally decide what to eat, and the waiter brings out a bottle of chardonnay and two glasses. He opens the chardonnay and pours it into each glass.

"Thank you so much," Hoa says. "Can you leave the bottle here?"

"Of course, sir," The waiter says and puts down the bottle. "Are you ready to order?"

"Yes," Hoa says, offering Phuong to order first. "You go first."

"Me?" Phuong asks.

"Yes, you."

Phuong looks at the menu. "I would like Duck Breast a l'Orange with a side salad."

The waiter writes everything in his note. "Ok, madam," Then, he turns to Hoa. "And to you, sir?"

"I would like to have New York steak with red wine sauce. Medium rare, of course. And that will be good from now."

"Ok," The waiter says, and he takes the menus. "I will be right back."

They both enjoy the chardonnay, which Hoa says is the best. Phuong loves this one. She has tried many wines before, but this one is perfect.

"Woah, I agree with you that this is the best wine I have ever had," Phuong says.

"I told you," Hoa takes another sip and clears his throat. "Do you know what we look like?"

Phuong is confused. Would he say that they look like a couple? There are so many possibilities that he is thinking like that. And it does look like they were a couple. But Phuong shakes her head and pretends to be naive.

"No, I don't."

"Vincent Vega and Mia Wallace," Hoa says. "I can feel like that?"

What the hell is he talking about? Who are they? Phuong does not know anything about them. She thinks that they must be very famous. Actors maybe? Like Elizabeth Taylor and Richard Burton?

Phuong does not want to be humiliated for her lack of knowledge of everyday life. So she nods and smiles.

"Oh, how cute." That is all Phuong could say.

Hoa looks at her with an understanding that Phuong does not know what the hell he is talking about. Hoa is not an easy person. He does not like when he talks about something, and they have no ideas on those topics. He has to explain it to them and pull them into the story he is talking about. If he knows, people will have to know.

"You don't know them, do you?" Hoa did not let this down.

All right, Hoa had pushed Phuong near to the dead end. He would make her confess. What a strange guy. Never back down.

"Of course, I know them," Phuong laughed. "They are celebrities, right?"

"They are not real."

"What?" Game over. Phuong once again loses in front of Hoa. If Vincent and Mia are not honest, why does Hoa even talk about that?

"They are just characters from a famous movie. Just like us, having dinner but not a couple," Hoa says. "Remind me to open this movie for you to watch."

Thank God that this conversation ends when the waiter returns with a tray of food in his hands. He served and they started to eat.

During the dinner, Phuong and Hoa talk about their interests, pet peeve, and taste in music. They don't say anything about their personal stories of each other. Phuong crosses her fingers, wanting Hoa could spill some tea about his life. It is the whole purpose of her in this dinner tonight. She could have asked him straightly. But she does not want to be impolite when asking about private things like that. It's up to Hoa. If he wants to talk, it would be great. If he does not, well, nothing will be severe. But Phuong still prefers Hoa to speak out.

The food, the wine, and the music make the evening comfortable and not intense. Phuong must agree that it has been a long time since she does not have a fine dinner like this. Of course, she usually hangs out with some nurses or with Rachel. But they only go out for burgers, tacos, or Vietnamese food, not in a fancy restaurant like this. According to her memory, the last time Phuong has been to a restaurant like this is with Adam on their previous wedding anniversary.

"In the last time seeing you, I mentioned that you and Adam were acting a play in front of Michael," Hoa begins to say. "How is that play going?"

Phuong thought he would go directly into his story, but it seems like he has turned his wheel into a corner, which Phuong cannot expect. That is so mart of him.

She smiles and takes a sip of chardonnay. At this time, she is a little drunk. So she does not care about anything. To lure the rabbit out of the hole, the hunter must prepare the trap for the rabbit to fall in.

"Well, you are right. We are acting in front of Michael. It is a perfect play, and we are still playing well. And maybe better than ever." Phuong says without any regret.

"But do you feel comfortable when you do that?" Hoa leans forward.

Phuong laughs. "Why are you asking me like that?"

Hoa leans back and rolls his glass of wine around. "Last time I told you I was in Michael's position. I understand his situation more than anyone else."

Phuong chuckles. "Oh, please! Don't be the superman trying to save a world!"

"I am not trying to save anyone. I want to tell you my story. And I think you want to hear about that, or you should hear."

"I am curious too."

Hoa pours some chardonnay and takes a sip. He leans back and looks outside the city. He wants to begin his story by watching something that can recall the memory. Stars are above the high sky. A beautiful night like this is the same beautiful night that a tragedy struck Hoa when he was a little kid. A tragedy that haunted him throughout his teenage years till he was a grown-up man. He never likes sharing this story with anyone because it is a bad memory he wants to bury deep and never intends to dig up. But when he sees Michael, whom he never gets too close with, Hoa can understand what that kid is going through. The kid is being blindfolded and hidden by his parents. A happy life with both mom and dad? It is just a fantasy. It has no longer been real. Hoa feels sorry for Michael and is frustrated because of how Adam and Phuong act in front of their son. Hoa finds nothing good about it. Just speak up that they are no longer together but still love Michael no matter what. Of course, Michael may react negatively and be angry. That's normal. But once he understands everything, all those anger, and negative thoughts will go away, and he will be happy again.

Things are so easy. But Hoa never understands why Adam and Phuong have to do it. Why don't they have the guts to tell Michael the truth?

Hoa was born in Austin, Texas, into a Vietnamese family. His parents met each other in a Hong Kong refugee camp in 1986 and fell in love. When they came here, they got married and had Hoa. His mother was a house cleaner for a company. She worked from early morning till evening. His father was a construction worker. His working schedule was the same as his wife's. Life was difficult for both of them, with many worries about finance and a lack of materials in the family. They both worked hard to provide for their family; their love could not be like it used to be. They fought all the time. Hoa's father complained about why his wife never cared for the house, cooked, or cared for Hoa. They usually sent him to the next-door neighbor, who was so kind to look after Hoa. Hoa's mother had her reason too. She argued that she was busy with her job and had no free time for herself, so she could have time to take care of the family. Both had reasons to avoid their roles in the house — even the parts of parents. In the end, they got divorced when Hoa was two years old.

From that moment, Hoa was nothing in the family.

After the divorce, Hoa lived with his mother, and when he was five years old, his mother remarried a wealthy man with two children. She loved him because he provided her with everything she needed, which she no longer needed to work. But he did not like Hoa. He always considered Hoa an outcast in the house and told Hoa's mother to let him with his father. Without any hesitation, she agreed. She dropped Hoa in front of the house of his father on the next day with all of his belongings. Although Hoa was crying and begging her not to leave him, his mother did not care a bit and just said bitterly. "I never want you in this life, ok? Stop bothering my life!"

It was the most painful thing that Hoa had ever heard. Watching his mother go away made him heartbroken; it was the last time he saw his mother.

When Hoa's father came home from his shift, it was late. Seeing his son sitting alone in front of his father's house, he felt angry and in pity for him. At first, he took care of Hoa properly and loved him. Sometimes, Hoa listened to them fighting over the phone because of him, of his appearance as their burden. Hoa cursed himself why he was ever born in this house or appeared in this life. Like his wife, Hoa's dad remarried too. She was ten years younger than him. She was annoyed with her voice, character, arrogance, and laziness. Hoa could see his dad had turned into her slave. Seeing himself as an outcast in this house, too, Hoa decided to run away. It was when he was 12 years old.

He had saved some money for himself. Enough to buy bus tickets and some food and drink. It was an afternoon after school. Hoa got on the bus and went to California. He had no regret at all. His parents got scared, and they looked for him everywhere. They called the police, and in the end, they found no information about Hoa. He had disappeared forever.

Arriving in California, Hoa usually slept in some shelters for the homeless. During the daytime, he asked for money from people on the street. People stole money from him and even beat him if he resisted. After six months of living like nothing, Hoa was finally exhausted. He found there was no life or no future in front of him. So he decided to end his life. But at the end of the tunnel, Hoa had found himself a light to hold on to.

When he was sitting on the street, thinking about how to kill himself on that day, a charity foundation was coming to that area, where many homeless people were sheltering. They provided clothes, food, and drinks for them because it was going to be cold soon. An American couple saw Hoa on the street with a chubby face and a sad mood, and they decided to talk to him. Hoa ran away and told them to leave him alone. He returned to his spot at night, and the couple was still there. Hoa had no choice but to ask them what they wanted. The couple gave Hoa some warm food. Hoa ate like a bird because he had been hungry for a day. They asked him kindly what had happened to him and why he became like this. Suddenly, Hoa burst out and cried. He told them everything but asked them not to hurt his parents. Hoa thought they were bad guys. But they were not.

They had been for five years, but they had no kids. They had been through so many orphanages for adoption, but none wanted to be with that couple. Now, as if fate had settled, they found Hoa and wanted him to be their child. Hoa's life had been opened into a new chapter. He had a new family, he could go to school again, and he was reborn.

Phuong has been crying through half of Hoa's story. She can not believe it is a tragedy that no one could imagine. But in the end, it has a happy ending. Phuong feels relief.

"Oh my God," She wipes the tears from her face. "I...I...I don't know what to say right now. It was so shocking and terrible. I am sorry. I believe there are no words that can describe that terrible time."

Hoa smiles. "There is nothing. It is past, and I have moved on. It is only a bad memory."

That's true. Hoa finds no emotions on his face during the story.

"It must have been so difficult for you to overcome."

"It is. Thanks to my new parents, who love me with all of their hearts, I can have a purpose to continue this life." Hoa says. "My story is not relating so much to Michael's situation or yours. But in some ways, the lie you and Adam are trying to hide is even bigger and more severe than ever. Right now, Michael is still a little kid, and he can be easy to forget. But once he got older, in his teenage year, when he found out the truth about his parents, his reaction would be out of control because he felt like his parents betrayed him. I don't want that to happen.

"You know, Michael is a good boy, and he deserves to have the best things in life with the love of you. What Adam did was wrong, and I know you hate him deep inside. You are probably tired of playing this fake character in front of Michael. It is time for you to talk to your son about his father. Try to make him understand but still remind him that whatever happened between his mother and his dad, you still love Michael, and nothing can change that love."

Hoa leans forward and holds Phuong's hands by surprise. "I can see that you have suffered a lot from the pain Adam had caused you. The feeling of being betrayed is so painful. It is like a thousand knives stabbing into our hearts. It is time to let go of the past and stop playing with the character you don't want to play. Live the real life that you want and be happy."

A young man like Hoa is so thoughtful, Phuong thinks. It was beyond what Phuong had felt about him before. After what Hoa says, she nods.

Hoa takes Phuong home after dinner. It is 11 p.m. Parking in front of Phuong's house. They sit in the car for a few minutes. Of course, they don't say anything. What else can they say? Phuong decides to break the silence.

"Thank you for dinner. It is enjoyable and... nice," Phuong says. "Also, thank you for this flower. It is lovely."

"You're welcome," Hoa says. "I am glad that we had fun."

"Me too. So, uhm, have a good night, ok?"

Phuong tends to open the door, but suddenly, Hoa holds on to Phuong's other arm and pulls her back. He kisses her on the lips. It is all so sudden that Phuong does not see that coming. She is frozen completely.

Hoa looks into Phuong's eyes.

"I love you," Hoa says.

Phuong is stunned. Her lips are like being sewed together and cannot know what to do. It happens too quickly. She gets out of the car immediately and goes into the house. Leaving Hoa alone in the car and bewilder.

Phuong shuts the door. Her back is against the door. She puts her hand in her heart and breathes. Her heart is beating fast. She runs straight to the living room and looks through the curtain. She is watching Hoa's car as he starts to leave.

The house is tranquil. Phuong walks to the kitchen and gets some water. No, water is too normal. She returns to the living room, moves to the minibar, and pours herself a glass of whiskey. She knocks it in just a sip.

Phuong sits down on the couch and thinks about what just happened tonight. Ok, he gave her a red rose, which is her favorite flower ever; he took her to one of the fanciest restaurants in the city, where the food is so delicious; he told her about his life, which is what Phuong has wanted the most and it surprises her too. But the weirdest thing was when they kissed in the car. Hoa kissed her, not Phuong. She cannot believe that Hoa has a love for her. Or a crush? Phuong has no idea what the fuck was that about.

She runs her fingers through her hair tiredly and groans. She just met Hoa a few times recently, and he did that. That was so awkward. Wait, the dinner must have been a date to him? He just dated Phuong without her understanding. No, no, it can not be like that. Hoa cannot have a crush on her. One BIG reason Hoa should stop loving her is the big age gap between Hoa and Phuong.

Phuong is going to be 40 years old soon. And Hoa is only 25 years old.

Walking upstairs, passing through Michael's room, she pushes the door to come in. Michael is sleeping with the lamp dinosaur shape on. She sits next to him and kisses him on his forehead. Phuong thinks about what Hoa just said at the dinner. Yes, she is too tired of being someone who tries to be happy with her husband in front of her son. Michael needs to know the truth about his father and this marriage. It is time to say. She has to end this.

But mind and action could never go together as friends. Phuong has not had the gut to tell Michael the truth.

CHAPTER 6

Ha

Like other women, Ha always wants to have a child. She desperately desires to have a child cry or laugh in the house. Since her husband's family has treated her like shit, a child can be her appeasement and her only light in that house. And also that is what her husband's family wants. Ha always envies Phuong, her best friend or ex-best friend. Phuong has everything. A great husband, a good mother, a respected career, a beautiful house, and a lovely son, Michael.

Ha loves his smile whenever she sees Michael in person and through pictures. Michael has a jawline like his mother when she was young, a face like his father, and attractive blue eyes.

It is a perfect child, which Ha often dreams about.

And yet, Ha is a cold-blood killer who murders the happiness and everything that Phuong had built and axes the family of Michael, a sweet child who always calls her "Auntie Ha."

Every time Ha thinks about that, she feels stung in her heart. It is stronger after she is exposed to being in bed with Adam.

So, the ability to have a child with Thomas is so challenging. Her oval does not work, and her uterus is hopeless. Even though the doctors tell her that there will be no chance at all and she probably can think of adopting, Ha never stops believing that a miracle can come one day, even though the stakes are so small.

Ha is a Buddhist. Each month on the first day and the fifteenth day of the moon calendar, she goes to the temple to pray. Ha used to think she might go vegetarian, but the doctors stopped her because they wanted Ha to be healthy and full of nutrition so she could have a baby. But Ha cannot have that luck in hers. She has failed many times. Any recommendation, any good doctors in the city or outside the city, Ha has been there.

Money with her is not a big problem. Her salary at the firm is being divided into two-part. One half is for her husband's family, in which when it comes to a special occasion, she can use that money to buy things under the order of her mother-in-law. The other half is for herself. She could have used it for shopping or something that pleased her; instead, she spends for a better purpose in life. To Ha, it is worth it for her to try.

The pressure of Thomas' family, especially Mrs. Linh, has pushed Ha to reach her limit. She is so tired and wants to stop. But Ha doesn't let herself give up.

As an attorney who deals with divorce cases, Ha usually sees couples who get divorced when their children are so little. Ha often advises them to think carefully before making the final decision. Some listen, and some don't.

Many years ago, Ha witnessed a case that was a tragedy to her. It was not a divorce case she handled. It was a real example of how an unhappy family could push to the brink of destruction.

Back then, she was just in the law firm for two months, and her boss and mentor, Joseph Phan, famous in the indigenous communities for helping their relatives to America, handed Ha her first case. There was a family where the father always gambled, and the debt was above the roof; meanwhile, the mother was a doctor and had helped to pay the debt, but he never changed. The wife could not take it anymore, so she told him that she would get a divorce. The husband heard that and beat her up because he would not have money to continue his toxic hobby without her. Suddenly, she found there was blood. It was not blood from her flesh.

She had a miscarriage then.

The husband had been found guilty of domestic violence and sentenced to 3 years in prison. After the husband was released, despite the restraining order from the court, he convinced his wife to go back with him with some of his miracle words coming from his mouth. And because she was so lovely and so naive, she agreed. Together they had a daughter later on.

He thought he would change, but he still walked the same road. This time, it got to a new level, a tragedy. One beautiful day, he came home and tried to take his daughter away. He said that one family needed a child, and he thought his daughter would be perfect for them. But the real purpose was selling the child to some human traffickers for the money to gamble. His wife opposed and fought back to keep the daughter away from him. She warned him that he would be over her dead body if he wanted to take her daughter away. As she wished, the husband pushed the wife hard, making her head hit the table, and she passed out. When she woke up, she discovered she was in the hospital. Her mother and a police officer were with her. They both looked sad, and they told the wife to calm down. The bad news was that her husband and daughter had a car accident. The husband was still alive and injured badly. But the daughter had died on the way to the hospital.

After listening and watching the case, Ha could not hold her emotion. She cried throughout the trial. The judge had to order her to stop; if she did not, she had to leave the courtroom. Looking into that woman's eyes, Ha understood that she must get justice for her and her daughter. That bastard would be punished for his horrific crime against his family. With her defense and her firm words, Ha had put that bastard in prison forever. Not only that, Ha wanted to help that woman in life. So she shared the story on social media through the firm's page and raised funds on GoFundMe. The story got sympathy from everyone, and the money was raised over $150,000. The woman felt so grateful for what Ha had done for her. But she told Ha that even though the money was a lot, it could not erase her daughter's pain forever. Ha just smiled and said. "Life is a journey full of unexpected things. Don't let the past pull you back. Let it become a base for you to be stronger to begin a new life. You are like a rose. Like my mom told me, the rose had an attractive beauty everyone wanted. But to get the rose, they must be careful with its thorns. Beautiful but dangerous."

From that case, Ha promised herself that when she had a family, she would be more cautious, more careful with the man she loved, and try to keep her family as happy as she could. But Ha has failed that completely. This marriage, sometimes in Ha's mind, is a big mistake because all she sees is that it only comes from her. Only Ha tries to work this marriage out. On the other hand, Thomas is nothing more than a mama boy. He does not even bother to love her or try to understand her feeling.

Ha is all alone. She embraces that pain alone and tries to bury it deep. For the very first time, she did it alone. But since she welcomed Adam into her life, he is the only person to save her from that fucking hell.

Now, she is all by herself again.

Like many previous times, Ha walks out of the clinic with a sad face. She fails again. She could have cried too, but she isn't crying because this happens so often. Every doctor often sees the most painful part: Ha goes here alone without her husband. Ha always tells them that Thomas is busy.

But it is not fucking true.

Ha hides this from Thomas.

Watching every couple leave the hospital with a baby in their hands makes Ha feel more desperate. Sometimes she blames the Buddha that Buddha does not care about Ha. Buddha has punished her. But maybe it is her destiny. She has a successful career in the law firm, and being unable to have a kid is the price she has to pay. Or simply karma for destroying the happiness of a family.

On the way out of the clinic, Ha suddenly meets Phuong, walking opposite her with the files in her hands. Phuong is elegant as usual, even in her lab coat. She has the sense of Chanel Mademoiselle. Thanks to Ha, of course. Looking through her face, she probably has overcome the pain from the affair between her husband and Ha.

Phuong sees Ha, and she ignores her. But Ha follows Phuong to stop her. She grabs Phuong's arm.

"Phuong," Ha says. "Can you talk to me?"

Phuong sighs tiredly. "What do you want, SLUT?"

"Fine, you can call me whatever you want. But I want you to listen to me. Adam has nothing to deal with the affair. I came on him first. Whatever you saw on that day was my fault. Don't blame Adam!"

Phuong looked at Ha and laughed as if she had heard a good joke. "Oh my God, you love him so much, don't you? Why don't you defend more for him more? Adam is a jerk, a motherfucker, and an asshole. Why didn't he stop you from the beginning if you came on him? He fell in love with you in the first place. And so did you. Both of you are so fucking good when you covered this affair so well." Phuong shakes her head and smiles.

"Besides, I don't care about it anymore. We all finished. You can come to him at any time you want."

Ha is bewildered. *Are they all... finished?* So Adam and Phuong have divorced. That is why Phuong looks cherished. Isn't that what Ha always wants?

Ha is speechless. She cannot think of anything to say about their divorce.

"How about Michael?" That is all Ha could ask at that moment.

"Don't worry about that," Phuong comes near Ha and points her finger into Ha's face. "Even if you and Adam can come together, don't think you can become his stepmother. You are not the person who can stay near my son."

Then, Phuong walks away. Ha stands alone in the hallway. She does not feel happy or sad. It all mixes up. It is a warning from Phuong. It means that even if Ha and Adam can be together in the future, there is no way that they can be happy.

Suddenly, someone calls Ha as she is about to leave. A nurse runs to her.

"Mrs. Le," The nurse says. "You forgot this paper."

Ha turns back. "Oh."

Ha gets the paper. It is a paper of recommendation to another doctor. This time she failed again, and the doctor here still wants to help Ha, but it seems so hopeless and so gloomy. They would like to introduce her to other best doctors in the city by writing her a recommendation.

"Oh, thank you so much. I completely forgot." Ha says.

"You're welcome," The nurse smiles at Ha and holds Ha's hands. "Listen, I always believe good things will come to good people. Soon luck will smile, and you will have the child you are desperate to have. I will pray for you."

Ha is bad at controlling her emotion. Every word that the nurse said touched Ha deeply inside. She has watched Ha coming in and leaving this hospital for years. All she can see is the disappointment on Ha's face. The feeling of a woman being told that the chances of having a baby are so low can kill that woman immediately. No doubt that a woman like Ha, who always receives terrible news, never expresses any hopelessness. She never stops believing.

A few tears are coming from her eyes. "Oh my God, you make me cry. It is so sweet of you to say that." Then, they hug each other in tears.

"Good luck to you." The nurse says her final word, and they say goodbye.

Usually, after she visits the hospital, Ha will go straight home and take a nap. Sleeping can help her to forget all the sadness she has been through. Despite her mother in law tells her she is lazy. How the hell can she understand the pain Ha is dealing deal with? Mrs. Linh forces her to give birth to a son for her family.

Eventually, Mrs. Linh still "cares" for her daughter-in-law in her way. As a woman who grew up in a family full of old traditions, she believes that Ha needs to use old methods like inviting a shaman to help Ha to expel the evil spirits inside her soul because Mrs. Linh comes up with a funny thought that an evil spirit has stopped Ha from having a child. But it was all bullshit. The shaman used some weird burning things to cleanse her oral which Ha was allergic to.

Next time, Mrs. Linh forced Ha to drink unusual drinks that almost caused Ha poisoning. Also, she made her special meals containing all the bitter foods Ha could not swallow. Sometimes Ha could not take anymore. She resisted. Mrs. Linh was pissed off and complained about everything in this world, which made Ha feel a headache. Even though Ha understands that her mother-in-law wants to have a grandson as soon as possible and Ha also wants to have a child, Ha keeps her pains inside to obey her mother-in-law.

But it is Wednesday today. It is the day Ha brings the fresh flowers to her mother's grave.

Mrs. Trang passed away a few years ago because of breast cancer. The whole world collided in front of Ha. She lost a shoulder to lean on. She lost a person who could give her advice whenever Ha was in trouble, or she was crying. And she lost a mother, whom Ha believed never had one day for herself. Mrs. Trang spent all her life until she died devoting herself to her daughter and wanting all the best for her.

With Mrs. Trang, no matter how old Ha was or how high Ha could fly, or how badass Ha was out there, Ha was still Mrs. Trang's little daughter. When Mrs. Trang was still alive, she used to say this to Ha. "You must remember this is your home. You can go wherever you want, do whatever you like. You can stay in every best place on us. But whenever you need it or fail in life, or something bad happens, this is where you can return because it always welcomes you to come back. And you still have me".

The house is still there. But right now, when Ha walks in, her mother is not seen. Only the empty house with the altar of her mother. After Mrs. Trang passed away, Ha decided not to sell this house or use it for other purposes. She wants to keep it for herself. It is a house full of memories between Mrs. Trang and Ha. It is the house that Ha bought for her mother. It is the house where Mrs. Trang used to sit next to the window every winter to knit a scarf or a sweater for Ha. It is the house where Ha came in, and she could hear her mom's voice. And it is the house where Ha left behind her mother to get into the marriage world. It is everything.

Ha came by the floral shop to buy a bouquet of white roses, Mrs. Trang's favorite. The owner knows Ha because she is a regular customer of this shop. Every Wednesday, she always prepares Ha freshest roses, wraps them carefully, and sets them on one side; so that when Ha comes, she needs to pay and grabs them away.

Then, she drives to her mother's grave. She carries a plastic bag, which she has prepared at home. She puts down the bouquet into a china vase, which is attached to the ground. Next, she gets a water bottle out and pours it all over the dark grey granite gravestone. There, Mrs. Trang's picture is clear again.

She places three paper cups on the gravestone and pours each cup of artichoke tea, which is Mrs. Trang's favorite. She burns the incense sticks and plugs down on the green grass above the gravestone.

"Hi, mom," She looks at her mother. "As usual, I failed again. It sounds so sad. But I think I got used to it. Perhaps it is a price I had to pay after I'd done it to other people, and you must be disappointed in your daughter. You probably can never believe that I could do such things as that. You used to teach me that never in life should I break somebody else's heart because it would be the last thing you do in this life," Ha chuckles bitterly. "And yet, I don't do what you said. I met Phuong today. Can you believe it? I am too ashamed to speak to her. I tried, but she did not listen. I destroyed my best friend's happiness, and now, they divorced. My heart feels so heavy, mom. It is like someone trying to put a brick pile on it and crushing it. Strangely, even though I feel guilty, I cannot stop loving Adam. He is the person who carried me out of the burden and the misery that I was carrying. He is the person who gave me the love that I lost. Phuong and Adam got a divorce. I asked myself, 'Is this what I've wanted to happen?'. Well, I don't know. I know I have to stop loving him and disconnect with him forever so I can forget him and return to my normal life."

Ha wipes the tear on her cheeks. "I think I...Uhm..."

Ha tends to stand up, and there is a silhouette covering all over her.

"Hey," A voice comes from that person. "I did not know that you would be here."

Ha looks up and squeezes her eyes because of the sunlight. She stands up immediately and looks frightened. She almost falls back.

It is Adam standing in front of her. Ha has not seen Adam for months. She has blocked all the connections between her and Adam. There is no way he could know about her.

Ha gasps. Now facing him suddenly like this has shocked Ha, and she feels uncomfortable. She does not even know why she reacts like that.

"It is so surprising to see you here," Adam says. "It has been a while. How are you?"

Adam is carrying a bouquet of white roses. It has explained a big question in her mind. Every time Ha comes here every Wednesday in the afternoon; she notices there are white roses on her mother's grave. She always wonders whose flowers they are.

Today, she has found out.

"Normally, I come here on Tuesday," Adam says. "But yesterday, I had something to do. So, I...Uhm. I do not know if you are coming here too. What a coincidence!"

Ha ignores everything Adam says and tries to leave immediately, but Adam holds Ha's left arm. Ha turns back.

"Please, I miss you and want to see you," Adam begs her.

She looks at Adam. Adam releases her. Ha sighs. "Adam, we can't do this."

"Why?"

"I don't know," There is a choke inside Ha's voice. "I just think it is wrong."

"That's ok. If it is wrong, let it be."

They both stand still without saying anything. Both take their looks on Mrs. Trang's gravestone. This is all sudden, and Ha hates sudden things.

"So, are we going to keep silence like this?" Adam asks.

There is no answer from Ha.

"Phuong and I divorced," Adam says and in his voice is not that sad or regretful.

There are two kinds of men that Ha knows in this world. One, it is the man who loves and cares for his lover at any chance. They would sacrifice everything to protect, care for, and make their lovers happy. Those men would love their lover from the beginning until death separated them. That type of man is the one that Ha needs. The man loves his lover from the start and changes after that. Those men cannot keep the love with their lovers, and because of some reasons, mainly bad ones, they break in the middle of the road to happiness. Talking about Thomas as the second type of man is correct, but Adam, unfortunately, falls into that category too. He left Phuong and came to Ha. How many chances are there that can guarantee Adam might love Ha the way he loved Phuong before? That is what Ha had thought after Phuong told her they got divorced in the hospital a few hours ago.

Ha looks up after what Adam said. "I've already known about that," Ha says, which surprises Adam.

"How do you know?" Adam asks. "Did someone tell you about it?"

Ha quietly nods.

Adam sighs. "It doesn't matter right now. I am so glad to see you again and coincidentally meet you here. I tried to contact you, but you blocked my phone number, Facebook, Instagram, and even my email. I feel so sad. But what else can I do? It all happened so fast, and we could not do anything more. I miss you, Ha. I never stop thinking about you or loving you. Now everything is over, and nothing can stop us right now."

Ha changes her facial expression immediately. Right now, she feels weird and confused. Does he tell her that nothing could stop them from getting together? What does that even mean? Wait for a second...

"You mean I should get a divorce from Thomas and come to you?" Ha asks.

"What's wrong?" Adam asked. "Isn't that what you ever wanted?"

Ha is angry and shakes her head. "No, Adam, no. This is what you want. I don't want it. That's not funny. You have a good image of yourself and me in the future. It would be best if you become a movie director. We are all over, and I have nothing to deal with you. My life with Thomas is wonderful, and we are happy." Ha sighs. "I understand right now you are sad, and you need someone to be with you. But I am sorry. I am not the one that you need."

Adam can sense the lies inside her voice.

"You are lying to me. I know you are not okay or happy with Thomas, and you love me. Please don't do this to me. I miss you, and I love you, Ha." Adam holds Ha's hands. "My love for Phuong was over. Our fate could only go that far. Now you are the only person I need and love." Adam starts to shed tears. "Don't leave me, Ha."

The tears of Adam fall on Ha's hands. She does not know for sure whether the tear of Adam is actual or not. Adam has left Phuong to come to Ha. It can show two possibilities. First, Adam truly loves Ha and never stops thinking about her. Now, at this moment, Adam has opened his heart to welcome Ha to come in. And this is the love that Ha has wished for. Sometimes when she was with Adam, she asked herself why she had not met Adam before Phuong or Thomas. But after all, it is just a big fucking "if." Being caught in the middle of the affair made Ha think about her relationship with Thomas and whether she should continue with him or not, also her relationship with Adam because she would be called a third person, who stepped inside the life of a happy couple and stole away one of them. Usually, the third person will be blamed for everything, and that person will be judged by people around. So many bloody scenes of jealousy occurred because of the third person. But is it the fault of the third person all the time?

Ha should feel fortunate that Phuong did not beat the shit out of her. Even though there is no bloody scene of jealousy, Ha is still worried that one day her husband's family will find out, and it will be a big drama. The second possibility is that Adam uses Ha to replace the whole inside his heart. Maybe he is just like other jerks. Using Ha in a short amount of time, after Adam finds another woman for his life, he leaves Ha like he left Phuong. If that possibility is genuine, her life will be nothing like a piece of shit. Or maybe it is her karma for her affair.

Everything happening right now in front of Ha is so quickly, and she does not know what to do. Ha takes her hands back.

"I'm sorry," Ha says. "This is not right."

She collects all of her stuff and leaves without saying goodbye. Adam is standing alone at the table, and he wipes the tears from his face. But it does not stop him from crying.

Inside her car, Ha tries to calm herself after everything that happened. She covers her mouth and screams. She needs to be alone and gets all these out of her head. Ha knows deep inside her that she is lying because she still loves Adam and wants to be with him.

But in her mind, it tells her to act differently. It wants her to reject everything against what the heart truly desires.

What happened today? Failure in trying to have a baby. Meeting Phuong and being taught a lesson. And seeing Adam so suddenly like that. Could it be more terrible for Ha for the rest of the day?

Yes, things have not been over with Ha yet. When Ha comes home, the whole family of Thomas is sitting in the living room. All of them look so angry. Thomas gets out of the chair and comes near Ha. He slaps her hard in the face.

"You fucking cunt," Thomas says in an angry voice. "It must be happy for you when he fucked you, hah?"

Finally, they know everything. But how?

CHAPTER 7

Phuong

They once said that love is only beautiful when they have not married, and love would be ruined when they take the vows. The fate between Phuong and Adam only came that far. The day Phuong picked up the pen and signed the divorce paper, her heart was crushed and felt like it was about to explode into a million pieces.

About to…

Until the moment the judge finally gave her final decision that they were longer husband and wife, Phuong realized one thing. Whomever you consider as your life partner, it is not one hundred percent that they can be your forever love.

Life is full of unexpected moments. The person, whom you met yesterday, can die tomorrow. The person, who is your enemy, can be your friend some days. The person you trust, like your friend, can stab behind your back at any time or sleep with your lover. You might be poor today and be rich tomorrow.

That is all depended on fate.

Fate is very luxurious, fancy, or crucial that people would never be able to reach out, see, or change. All bets are off. Fate has arranged for Phuong and Adam to be together. But it is in such an amount of time. When the fate of love is over, whether they want it to stay, it still goes away.

After things were said and done, Adam and Phuong walked out of the courthouse as strangers. They looked at each other. It was no longer the look of love or care. It was the look of hate and fury.

Adam put on his Ray-ban sunglasses. Aviator one. "I think this is it,"

He said. "We are officially nothing for each other. It's funny, however. I thought I could be happy, and you should be pleased that you finally got rid of a husband like me." Adam chuckled. "But look at us. It is so obvious that we feel a different way. I don't feel happy at all. Do you know what I feel? I feel lost. I lost you. I lost directions, and I lost my happiness. But I won't regret this divorce. It is the right thing to do, Phuong. Good for you because you won't be near a husband like me. I will never forget all the days we were together because those were real love."

Adam stopped talking and wiped off the tears. He cleared his throat. "Well, I'd better take off. See you around!" He walked down the stairs. But he remembered something and turned back. "Oh, by the way, remember what we have agreed to do in front of Mikey. Don't let him know!"

With some weird feelings inside her, Phuong could not continue walking. She sat down on the stairway outside the courthouse and burst into a cry. No one, who was walking around the area, even cared about Phuong crying. It seemed like nothing new about a woman who collapsed and called in the stairway of the courthouse. In her mind, so many memories between her and Adam kept running through her mind as if it was a movie showing only for her. But only at this time does the film comes to an end.

Phuong wanted to forget everything or wished everything was just a nightmare that she tried to wake up.

Phuong returned to her mother's house, where she had been staying for a couple of weeks. She walked into the living room and saw so many boxes that named her as well as her luggage. Phuong sighed. She had expected this would happen.

Mrs. Nhu walked inside the living room. From behind, she hugged Phuong tightly.

"I am sorry, dear," Mrs. Nhu said. "I am so sorry."

Phuong turned back. "When did this happen?"

"There was a group of men who brought all of them here earlier and said it was the order of Adam. Those are all of your stuff in that house," Mrs. Nhu put her hands on Phuong's shoulders. "Are you ok? How were things going in the court?"

Phuong quickly wiped the tears from her face. She tried to smile. "Everything is over, mom. What to say right now? I'm freed from the marriage I thought would be happy for the rest of my life." Phuong turned away from her mother, and sat down on the couch near her. She covered her face with both hands. Mrs. Nhu sat down next to her.

Mrs. Nhu continued to calm her daughter. "Darling, people constantly change. They can change into good or bad in an unexpected way that we cannot prepare for. Like you, a shy girl transformed into a strong woman like now. That is a good thing. Listen, I know that inside you right now is full of hatred, feud, and anger but let's think on the positive side when all of the things Adam has caused to your life are a motivation for you to be stronger and gustier. Also, a lesson for you to choose the right man if you are ready to move on.

"Adam is a bad man but don't blame him. Everyone who passes through our lives, even just a moment, could greatly impact our lives. You have a life in front of you. Especially, you have Michael as your strength to hold on to. Don't let this whole Adam thing ruin your life. Life is short, and enjoys it as you want because you don't know what lies ahead of you tomorrow. You get it?"

Phuong nodded slightly. She held her mother's hands. "Thank you, mom. I'll try."

Mrs. Nhu kissed Phuong's forehead. "Good. Now I will go in the kitchen and cook bun bo Hue for you, ok?"

Then Mrs. Nhu left the living room. Phuong looked around the living room full of her boxes. She felt tired when she saw all of those boxes. She wondered why on earth she had so much stuff. Suddenly, she noticed a small box placed near the fireplace with her name written in silver marker (unlike other packs with black marker), and next to her name was a golden star sticker.

Phuong got the box. She used her car key inside her pocket to tear off the masking tape. She opened and looked inside the box. There were an album named "The Journey"; a black box; a photo frame; a DVD; a red box; and a small journal. Phuong knew what was inside the album. It was all the photos of Adam's and Phuong's happiest time, and near the end of the album were all the photos of Michael. Adam named this album "The Journey" because he wanted all those memories through the photos as a journey of their life from how it started to how it was going on through time. But that journey ended like Titanic had sunk in the middle of the Atlantic Ocean, and their happiness could not dock in the peaceful destination.

Phuong set the album aside and opened the black box. It was not locked. There was all the jewelry of Phuong, which Adam bought for her from Tiffany or sometimes Pandora. She always loved jewelry and wanted a complete collection of expensive jewelry when she traveled around with Adam. Phuong continued with the red box. A crystal rose inside the box, which Adam bought as Phuong's birthday gift a few years ago. The photo frame with a photo inside was a wedding photo of Phuong and Adam. Adam was in the Calvin Klein suit, his favorite fashion brand, and Phuong was in the wedding dress her friend designed. With Phuong, it was the happiest day of her life because she thought that was it; she finally found the love of her life and a happy ending for a fairy tale story. The DVD was their wedding video, in which Phuong told the photographer to record every detail of the wedding so that they could watch it together on every wedding anniversary. And the journal was about what Phuong thought about Adam, which she had written since she married.

It was all the good things.

Everything inside this box was full of memories with Adam. When she looked at those, the face of Adam appeared in her mind. She used to love to see those things every day. Now, she wanted to throw everything away immediately. No. She had a better idea.

Phuong opened the album and took out all the photos of her and Adam, only keeping the images of Michael inside. Then, she got the journal, the DVD, the crystal rose, and the wedding photo inside the frame with her. She went to the backyard. There was a BBQ stove in the corner of the backyard. Phuong placed the journal, the DVD, and the wedding photo on the BBQ stove. Before returning to the house, she smashed the crystal rose into pieces. She got into the kitchen where Mrs. Nhu was cooking bun bo Hue. Mrs. Nhu did not know what Phuong was doing when Phuong opened every cupboard.

"What are you finding, dear?" Mrs. Nhu asked.

"Where are your matches and fuel?"

"What for?"

"I am gonna kill the past."

Mrs. Nhu did not understand what Phuong was talking about but just showed her where she kept the matches and fuel. She hoped Phuong would not burn down this house. Phuong got both and went immediately outside the backyard. Mrs. Nhu followed her, but she stood quietly at the door and watched what her daughter was doing.

Phuong tore each page of the journal. Then she put the fuel on everything inside the BBQ grill. She lit up one journal page and threw it inside the grill. The flames started to rise. It burned everything. It burned the wedding photo. The fire caught the face of Adam in every photo first for no reason. Maybe it was God's intention when God wanted Phuong to forget Adam as quickly as possible. Seeing the flames burning, Phuong felt her heart crushing her tightly. She collapsed and cried, then screamed. Mrs. Nhu, seeing her daughter like that, could not hold her emotion. She wanted to go outside to reassure Phuong, but she didn't. She thought Phuong would like to be alone at that moment. Let it be.

Things had turned to dust and ashes.

After dinner, Phuong handed her mother the black box with her jewelry inside. Phuong told Mrs. Nhu to sell all of those and get the money in whatever the price was. Phuong did not want to see that jewelry anymore. Mrs. Nhu agreed. Just like that, Phuong swore that from now on, she had to be stronger, and she would get all the memories of Adam and his image outside her mind and her life.

It had taken a long time for Phuong to get back to the orbit of her life.

But even though she can return to everyday life, the flames of hatred never stop burning inside Phuong. When she can open her heart to forgive Adam and Ha, the image of Adam and Ha having an affair on the bed where Adam and Phuong had spent many years together, and from this bed, Michael was born, keeps spinning in her head. It sounds ridiculous because it is only a bed. Why is it so crucial to Phuong like that? Because with her, every single thing that had given her special memories would stay forever in her mind, and she never forgets until this day. Thus, she is a person who appreciates everything she has and never complains. And yet, thanks to a jerk and a scumbag like Adam, she started to change her views on many things. Especially man.

The morning after the dinner with Hoa, Phuong wakes up with a strange feeling. She touches her lips, which are so soft. Usually, Phuong's lips are so dry that people can see the crack and blood, and she has to use chapstick every time. Phuong is a person who always drinks water every day, even when she is not thirsty. She also reminds her colleagues and her family to stay hydrated. Water is never enough for Phuong. The doctor checks her lips, but no one can explain why her lips are always dry, even if it is not in cold weather.

And yet, today, they are so soft and tender before Phuong puts some chapstick on them. She runs immediately into the bathroom and looks in the mirror. There are no cracks or any sight of dryness on her pair of lips. This one is new. Maybe she is dreaming. Phuong slaps herself hard. Ouch! That is hurt. So it is not a dream. By some miracles, they are healed.

After changing her clothes, she goes downstairs and gets into the kitchen. Michael is eating his breakfast. Bacon, sausage, egg, toasted bread, and a glass of orange juice, as usual. Mrs. Nhu is drinking her coffee, and a bowl of cereal is next to her.

"Do you want me to make you breakfast?" Mrs. Nhu asks.

"No, thanks, mom" She pours a cup of coffee. "I still feel full from last night's dinner." Then, she came near her son and kissed his head. "How are you, sweetie?"

"I am good, mom," Still full of food in his mouth. "How was your dinner last night with Mr. Hoa?"

Phuong sits down next to Michael. She puts some sugar and cream into her coffee and drinks. "It was fine. We ate, we had some booze, and we talked. That was all."

"He is a good man, mom."

Phuong gets choked.

"Are you ok, mom?" Michael asked.

"No," Phuong coughed a little bit. "Just choking," She tries to maintain herself. Breathe in, breathe out. "Darling, why did you say Mr. Hoa is a good man? You just met him recently."

"I just see that, mom," Michael cleans his mouth. "He is nice, kind, and lovely. He seems to be like that kind of person."

"Seems to be, you said?" Phuong asks.

"Yes, mom. I want him to take me to that ice cream store we visited last time. It was perfect."

Phuong laughs. "Ok, ok, ok."

"Michael, why don't you get prepared so your mom can take you to school?" Mrs. Nhu says.

"Yes, grandma." Then, Michael rushes outside the kitchen to get ready for school.

In the kitchen, Mrs. Nhu looks at Phuong with a look of a mom that had a teenage girl who was in love. "Tell me everything about last night later. I want to hear."

Phuong chuckles. "Mom, there was nothing. We had dinner. That was it."

Mrs. Nhu stands up and brings all the dishes and cups on the table to the sink. She turned back and threw Phuong a smile. "Darling, I am your mother, and I can tell what is happening. Now, go!" Then, she turns on the water and starts washing the dishes.

Phuong is bewildered by what her mother says. Is Phuong blush? She goes to the living room and looks at the mirror on the wall. It shows clearly that she blushes. But why?

After Phuong drops Michael off, she goes to the hospital to work. The girls at the receptionist stand up and say hello to Phuong. She comes by the desk to check the schedule for today.

"Good morning, girls!" Phuong says.

"Good morning, doctor," Malia, one of the girls, says. "How are you today?"

"I am doing well," Phuong says. "How about you?"

"I am ok," Malia says. Suddenly, she leans forward and whispers to Phuong so the other girls will not listen to what Malia says, although the other girl is on the phone. "How was your date last night?"

Date? Phuong would not call it a date. Just a simple dinner. Why do people keep assuming that Phuong and Hoa are on a date? That pisses her off.

But that is not all.

The only thing Phuong is scared of and hates the most in this hospital is the walls. Phuong always considers every wall of this hospital has ears. Nothing coming from everyone's mouth is safe. The gossip and the rumors can spread fast, even faster than viruses, or even worse than those moms at Michael's school. For example, the divorce of Phuong and Adam got spread out just one day after everything was done. One day after the divorce,

Phuong did not go to work because she did not have the mood to think of working. Of course, she did not tell anyone about the divorce. And yet, she had received so many text messages from her colleagues to encourage, to share, to express their feelings, and blah blah blah. The privacy of Phuong started to be limited for some reasons. Now, the dinner between Hoa and Phuong has turned into a date, and by some anonymous sources, they had known Phuong had gone out.

"What are you talking about?" Phuong asks while her hands are in her pocket and her left hand is holding the stress ball, which is her favorite toy, tight.

Malia chuckles. "Everyone knows you went out last night with a guy. So how is he?"

"Oh God," Phuong leaves immediately with anger.

Phuong goes to her office. She turns on the light and gets frozen for a few seconds. There is a bouquet of red roses on her desk. She walks fast to her desk. There is a note on the flowers. Phuong opens the letter and reads.

Good morning, Phuong.

First, I wanted to apologize for my action last night. I did not know what I was thinking at that moment. I should not have kissed you like that. That was so inappropriate and stupid. I have caused you confusion and shock. Second, to apologize, I bought you this bouquet, and I love you will like this. Like a rose, you are always beautiful.

So sorry,
Hoa.

Phuong understood why Malia asked her like that and why this hospital might have known about the story between Phuong and Hoa. Everything makes sense. Phuong sits down and reads the note one more time. Then, she opens the drawer, puts the letter inside, and closes it.

Looking at those red roses, they are so beautiful and so elegant. It had been a long time since Phuong did not have anyone give her a red rose. The last person is Adam.

She is a middle-aged woman who has been through many things in life, so she knows this bouquet is not simply an apologetic gift. It is something else. Something that she believes Hoa would not let go of so quickly like that.

After the shift in the hospital, Phuong goes straight home. Adam picks Michael up today because he wants to take Michael to the zoo this weekend. Later that night, Mrs. Nhu and Phuong talk. Phuong is peeling the apple. Mrs. Nhu sits down with two cups of herbal tea.

"Thanks, mom," Phuong says. "Eat some apples, mom. It is perfect for your high blood pressure."

"Ok, dear," Mrs. Nhu takes a bite. "It is a delicious apple. Now," Mrs. Nhu clears her throat. "Tell me about your dinner last night with Hoa."

Phuong chuckles. "Well, it is just a normal dinner, mom. It is not a date as everyone else thinks. Hoa and I are just friends."

"All right, I won't tell it as a date anymore. What do you think of him?"

Phuong holds her teacup tightly so she can feel the hotness of the tea. "He is nice and generous. He has a lovely smile." Phuong could have said more about Hoa, but no. If she continues to say good things about him, her mom will think she has fallen in love with Hoa.

"You know, uhm," Mrs. Nhu takes a sip of tea. "I think Hoa loves you."

Phuong looks at her mother. "What are you talking about?"

"Darling, I am your mother, and I look at people well. I can tell whether they are in love or not. And I think Hoa loves you. You and Adam were history. It had been done for years. Don't you think it is time to open your heart to move on? Life is too short, darling so instead of being so hateful, try to love more and give more. That makes life more precious and lively," Mrs. Nhu stands up with her herbal tea. She puts one hand on Phuong's shoulder. "Give him a chance. And remember to take me to the supermarket at nine tomorrow."

Phuong kisses her mother's hand. "Ok, Mom. Good night."

"That is a lovely bouquet," Mrs. Nhu points at the red rose bouquet on the table. "He has artistic eyes."

Then, Mrs. Nhu leaves the kitchen.

Even Mrs. Nhu can see that Hoa has a crush on Phuong, but why doesn't she see that? Maybe her mother is right, and her heart has not opened yet. It is still closed and never be easy to open back.

So, this weekend, Phuong has more time to review her patient's records, which she is not fond of since her son is not around. Usually, she will sit down with some of her colleagues to review together. But this weekend, they are all busy; some have surgeries for patients.

A few hours pass by, and Phuong starts to get tired. She looks at the clock. It is 9 p.m., and her eyes want to shut down immediately. She went to the kitchen and made herself a cup of coffee. While waiting for the coffee from the coffee maker, Phuong looks at the rose bouquet on the dining table. She must admit that she cannot take her eyes off the bouquet. Her fingers run through each rose. She smiles. Something pleasing is happening inside her.

The following day, because Phuong stayed awake late last night, she woke up late. It is about 11 a.m. *Shit!* Today she is supposed to take her mother to the supermarket. She must have taken Mrs. Nhu at 9 a.m. After finishing everything, Phuong rushes downstairs. Suddenly, Hoa is there with her mother in the living room. She gets stunned. Her mouth is shut close, and her eyes are bewildered.

Hoa stands up. "Good morning Phuong. How are you?"

Phuong still cannot open her mouth.

Mrs. Nhu looks at Phuong and frowns. "Phuong, don't stand like a statue like that."

Phuong returns to the earth. Phuong turns her look to Mrs. Nhu and clears her throat. "Mom, Uhm, I am sorry for waking up late. Let me take you to the supermarket."

Mrs. Nhu laughs and waves her hands. "Never mind. Hoa took me this morning. I did not want to wake you up because you stayed up late last night. Thanks to Hoa, he is free today." Mrs. Nhu turns to Hoa. "Thank you so much, dear."

"There is nothing, Mrs. Nhu. Whenever you need."

"Well, I will go to the kitchen to prepare lunch. I will let you two talk."

Mrs. Nhu leaves the living room, which makes Phuong feel more awkward, and does not know what to do. Hoa sits there and waits for Phuong to sit down. Finally, Phuong takes a deep breath and sits in front of Hoa.

"Thank you for taking my mom to the supermarket," Phuong says with a smile.

Hoa leans back on the couch. He crosses his legs and places one hand on the couch's back. He chuckles. "And?"

Phuong is curious. "And what?"

"Come on. You know what I am talking about."

The bouquet of roses. That must be the thing he is trying to bring up. That is true. Since Phuong found the bouquet in her office, she has yet to call or text Hoa to say thank you. Maybe she forgets or is too overwhelmed to say thank you to him.

"Oh, thank you for your bouquet," Phuong says. "It is so lovely."

Hoa claps his hands. "There you go, and you're welcome. I am glad that you like it."

Phuong laughs out loud. She stands up. "Who said that I like your bouquet?"

"You."

"I didn't say the bouquet is lovely nor mention anything about loving it."

Phuong comes near the minibar near the fireplace, her favorite place in this house. Since the day Phuong moved into her mother's house and one part because she was desperate after getting divorced, she has bought so much alcohol and drunk like an alcoholic.

There was a time she turned on the music out loud, drank many bottles, and accidentally hit Michael because he asked her one homework question. Michael, at that moment, just looked at her surprisingly without blinking. He was terrified by the way Phuong looked. Her eyes were so evil. She held her son's arms tightly.

"DON'T YOU EVER INTERRUPT ME WHEN I AM ALONE, OK?" Phuong talked to Michael with a different voice then she screamed. "NOW, GOOOOO!"

Later on, she realized what she had done so far was so wrong, and she tried to rehab. Phuong still drank, but not a lot like it used to.

"Do you want anything to drink?" Phuong says as she opens the mini-fridge under the minibar and takes out an ice tray.

"At this time?" Hoa looks at his watch. "It is only 11:30, and I want to get drunk already?"

"Yup," Phuong pours herself a glass of brandy. "Consider it as a mouthwash for you."

"All right then, when in Rome. I will have a glass of wine if you have."

"At your service," Phuong opens a wine bottle and pours it out. She brings the glass to Hoa and hands it to him. "It is French wine. One of my friends bought it for me on her business trip to Paris."

Hoa takes a sip of wine. "It is an excellent wine."

Phuong takes a sip of brandy. "Of course it is."

"So," Hoa clears his throat. "Why don't you like my bouquet? It is a gorgeous bouquet."

"It is just lovely and fits with my house for decoration. I was thinking about buying some flowers for my house to make it more lively and refreshing. Luckily, you bought it for me. So I did not have to spend too much money buying it." Phuong raises her glass. "Thank you for that." Then, she drinks.

"Cheer," Hoa raises his glass too. "Listen, uhm, about what happened the other night, and I want to say sorry about that. I didn't mean to react like that and make you feel uncomfortable. It was just an emotional outburst. I hope you understand."

Phuong scoffs. "I have forgotten about that night already. So you don't need to feel guilty about it," Phuong rolls her glass around. "The other day, my son talked about you."

"About me? What did he say?"

"He said you are a very good man and wanted you to take him to ice cream in the last shop we visited."

"Really?"

"Yes. He seems to like you a lot. What did you do to him and my mom that love and worship you like God?"

Hoa laughs. "That went a little bit too far. Anyway, if Michael wants to have ice cream in that shop, I will take him there."

Phuong nods slightly. "Thank you so much. I will tell him." Noticing that Hoa's glass is empty. "Do you want more wine?"

"Sure." Hoa hands Phuong his glass.

Phuong comes back to give Hoa the glass. Suddenly, she gets tripped. Damn the carpet. And the wine pours over Hoa. His white polo gets stained.

"Holy shit," Phuong hurries, cleaning his polo with the tissues on the table. "I am sorry, Hoa."

Hoa does not get angry. Instead, he chuckles. "That's all right. I am planning to buy a new polo anyway."

"I am so careless," Phuong continues wiping the shirt even though it is useless. "Let me buy you a new shirt."

Phuong realizes she is so close to Hoa that she can smell his cologne. She looks up and meets Hoa's eyes. They are both silent. Hoa puts his arms around Phuong and kisses her lips.

Phuong rounds her arms on Hoa's neck and kisses him too.

"I love you, Phuong," Hoa says as he looks into her eyes.

"Are you sure?" Phuong asks. "I am not as good as you think and much older than you."

"That's not what I care about. All I care about is you."

Now, no more messing around. Phuong has fallen in love with Hoa. It can be a new beginning for her, where she does not even need to mind the past.

Mrs. Nhu comes to the living room to call them in for lunch and catches them kissing. But she does not interrupt them. She smiles and returns to the kitchen.

CHAPTER 8

Ha

As a lawyer who has been in charge of divorce, there are times Ha had to deal with domestic violence and abuse cases. When she sees the victims with many marks and pain on their bodies, Ha swears to herself that she has to win the case and prosecute those criminals by any chance.

But at work, it is different than at home.

The last time Ha got beaten was in her high school by Five Fab Gal. Since then, no one has ever touched her.

And yet, she just received a slap from her husband.

Her left cheek is burning, and her head is throbbing. All she could hear is a buzzing sound. Thomas keeps screaming into Ha's face.

Mr. Tan, from behind, pulls Thomas out to protect Ha. He pulls hard, and Thomas falls. Then, he lifts Ha gently.

"Are you ok?" Mr. Tan asks, and he carries her to the chair.

Ha sits down on the chair. She breathes hard. Thomas stands up and tries to rush into Ha again, but Mr. Tan shouts at him.

"That's enough. Sit the fuck down. Don't you dare to lay your fingers on her again," Then, he turns to Ha? "You good?"

Ha nods slightly. "I am a fine dad."

She meets the deadly eyes of the scariest person in the room. Mrs. Linh, is sitting across the room comfortably in her chair. Her eyes show a predator's evilness and sharpness, which is about to slay the prey.

"I don't know what is happening here. But I know one thing I don't deserve to be beaten like that." Ha says.

"You deserve to be beaten up for what you did." Mrs. An interrupts. Her voice sounds irritated. She can shut the fuck up immediately. If that is about the family business, she should stay the fuck out of that. What a bitch!

"All right, enough," The voice comes from Mrs. Linh is finally spoken. She is still sitting there and turns her cold look to Ha. "Ha, what is the relationship between you and Adam?"

Ha gets startled. Her hands are shaken, and her lips can not even move. All suddenly, the memories of her and Adam comes back. Their sweetest times, their dinners, and their wild sex. It is so strange. In just a moment, everything is being exposed.

"Cat got your tongue?" Mrs. An asks with a sarcastic voice.

"Why don't you shut the fuck up?" Ha shouts out.

Mrs. An and everyone in the room get wide eyes opened.

Mrs. An stands up. "What did you say to me? How dare are you telling me to shut up?" Then, she turns to Mrs. Linh. "You hear what she just said? She is so rude!"

Mrs. Linh raises her hands to tell Mrs. An to stop talking. She returns to Ha. "What is your relationship with Adam? Don't you dare to say there is nothing between you and him because I know you are lying?"

"So you have known everything. I have nothing to hide from all of you," Ha takes all the bravery that she had inside her to speak up because there is nothing to lose right now. She sighs. "Yes, I was in the affair with Adam."

Thomas, who is still not stopping getting angry, shouts. "You fucking WHORE! How could you do that to me, huh? How could you betray me like that?"

Ha keeps silent and her head down.

Mrs. Linh stands up and comes near Thomas to smooth and calm him. "Be an easy dear. You don't need to react like that. She'd confessed the whole truth so let her finish it," Then, she turns to Ha. "Ha, for all these years, you are lying to this family? How could you do that to Thomas and this family? It is such ashamed."

Mr. Tan looks down at Ha and puts his hand on her left shoulder. "Ha, tell us the truth." Ha looks up. "That's ok. You have me."

Ha comes back to Mrs. Linh. "Yes, I had an affair with Adam. But this affair had ended six months ago. Now, there is nothing between Adam and me."

"We don't believe you," Mrs. An says. She stands up and shows her phone to Ha. "I took these pictures in the afternoon when I caught you with Adam at the cemetery. And I had followed you from the hospital since I saw you talking to Phuong, and I believe Phuong already knew about this."

Ha, looks at all the photos. Her heart suddenly beats faster, and she feels like it would jump out of her heart. Mrs. Linh stands up and crosses her arms. She gives a cold chuckle with a sarcastic voice.

"Like mother like daughter."

Woah, they have touched the fire ant cave. Ha finally gets angry. She knows what Mrs. Linh means. There is one thing forbidden in Ha's life. No one can touch her mother. If they do, she will not leave it alone, even the family member. But Ha still tries to keep her anger inside her. She holds her fist tight.

"What?" Ha asks with a loud voice. "What did you just say?"

"Like mother like daughter," Mrs. Linh repeats. "Or maybe you are better than your mom. How big are your mouth and your pussy?"

Ha points her finger at Mrs. Linh. "You've gone too far. Take that back NOW."

"Am I not telling the truth?" Mrs. Linh scoffs. "Everyone who lived in Saigon before 1975 knew about your mother. Trang "Cave." A famous call girl stood on every street and waited to satisfy someone for money. You are her daughter, and there is no doubt that you have the same personality as her. I can see that you want to keep the tradition of being a hooker. Bend down and suck other men's dick and pleasure them for money. I could see your real person the first time I met you. You are nothing than a low-class bitch under cover of a lawyer."

Mrs. Linh has unleashed the sleeping monster inside Ha, which she has been hiding for a long time because she wants to be nice in her husband's family's eyes. Ha kicks the wooden table, and it hits Mrs. Linh's legs. She feels so painful and falls to the floor. She jumps into Mrs. Linh and slaps her, then pulls her hair.

„YOU FUCKING OLD CUNT!" Ha shouts

Mrs. Linh screams out loud.

Thomas pulls Ha out and beats her. He punches her face, kicks her stomach, and almost chokes her to death by strangling her. Then, he held her hair and slammed her head on the edge of the wooden table. A crack on her forehead, and blood starts to fall. Luckily, it is a small cut.

"You fucking bitch," Thomas cries. "How dare you hurt my mother like that?"

Mr. Tan runs in to stop Thomas. With all his strength, he punches Thomas in the face (Mrs. Tan used to have a black belt). Thomas' nose bleeds badly. And he pushes Thomas hard, and his head hits the side table next to the couch. The flower vase drops and breaks. Luckily, there is no serious injury.

Mr. Tan carries Ha up to the chair. He looks at the cut on Ha's head. Quickly, he runs to the kitchen to get first aid. He cleans the cut on her head and bandages it.

"How are you feeling?" Mr. Tan asks.

"I'm good," Ha says weakly. "Thanks, Dad."

On the other side, Mrs. An tries to calm Mrs. Linh after being hurt in the leg. She turns to Mr. Tan.

"Look at what your daughter-in-law has done to your wife and this family. She deserves to be taught a lesson like that. Why do you stop your son?" Mrs. An says with all the hateful words.

"Get the fuck out of my house," Mr. Tan yells into Mrs. An's face. "This is none of your business. Get out now!"

Mrs. An looks surprised and shocks. "What? Why do you want to kick me out? I am the person who knew your daughter-in-law was having an affair. If someone needs to be out of this house, it will be her. Not me. You should thank me."

"Thank you for what? For sticking your noses inside this shit? You've told us enough. Now, get the fuck out of my house." Mr. Tan says firmly.

Mr. Tan is her brother, and how can he take a side against her sister like that? But looking at the anger on Mr. Tan's face, she feels so scared, as she always does whenever she is in front of him. Her life is still dependent on Mr. Tan and Mrs. Linh. So she quietly leaves the house.

The house is quiet again. It is as if there is a break between two matches. Thomas wipes the blood on his nose and stands up to sit next to his mother. Now in this house, two sides are fighting each other.

"Why did you stop me?" Thomas points at Ha. "This is my wife. She did bad things, and I had to straighten her out. You should stay away from my business, Dad. By the way, she betrayed this family and failed you too. You still want to protect her?" His voice raises. "What is the matter with you?"

"You should ask yourself that question." Mr. Tan says. "If I did not stop, you would have killed her."

There is no interruption from Mrs. Linh. She agrees with their actions of Thomas. She keeps quiet. Mr. Tan sees the tension in this room so severe, and Ha is exhausted and in pain. He tends to carry Ha back to her room to rest. If necessary, he would take her to the hospital. But Mrs. Linh stops him immediately.

"Things have not been done yet." Mrs. Linh says. "She had to be here to explain her affair. Until then, she could not leave this room."

Mr. Tan feels the ridiculousness in the voice of his wife. How can she be so cold like that? Ha is a human, not a thing that they can do whatever they want.

"No," Mr. Tan shouts. "She will go to her room. If you want to talk, we will talk when she gets better. Look at her. Your precious son had just beaten her badly in front of you. Don't you feel anything at all? What is the matter with you?"

"The matter is that she has put a big shame on this family. Her dirty behavior is ruining the reputation of this family." Mrs. Linh points at Ha while she is confronting her husband. "Thomas loves her with all of his heart, cares for her, trusts her, and wants to have a child. But no, she is so selfish to appreciate the love of Thomas for all these years. She betrayed him and this family. Do you ever think about our son's feelings?"

"Thomas' feeling? What a good way to say!" Mr. Tan laughs ironically. "Fuck his feeling and maybe fuck your feeling. It would be best if you listened to her explanation before judging. I am all tired of the way you have treated her in this family. I know that you hated her in the first place because of who she is. What has she done to you that you hated her so much? She has tried to gain love from you and find sympathy from her mother-in-law when she can't have a child. You...»

Suddenly, Ha pulls the sleeve of Mr. Tan. He looks down. "Dad, that's ok. If she wants to straighten everything out, let's do it!"

"But you're weak. Let me take you to your room and rest. I will handle everything here."

"Thanks, Dad. I still can continue." Ha points at her tote bag on the floor and asks Mr. Tan to bring her tote bag here. "Can you please take out the pink folder inside my bag?"

Mr. Tan takes the folder out. It says one word. "*HOPE*" is handwritten, and under that word is a list of days and a "*failed*" word next to each. He opens the folder. It is all the reports of all the time she goes to the hospital to conceive, to do medical examinations.

There is a choke in Mr. Tan's voice. "Ha, this is….»

"Yes, dad. I am sorry," Ha begins to say. "I have tried so many times, spent money because I want to have a child. Doctors said the ability to have a child like mine is tiny, but it doesn't stop me from having hope in my life. Whenever I saw a child, my desire to have one increased, and I felt desperate and useless. Sometimes I wanted to give up because I felt so tired but thinking about keeping this marriage and having love from my mother-in-law pushed me to try harder. And I want to give you a grandchild, Dad. I truly am. Now, I can't take it anymore.

"I have tried to seek sympathy from my husband." She turns to Thomas. "You are not like you used to be. When we were dating, you told me that whatever happened in our lives, you would never leave me and stay beside me. But it was all over when we got married. Or it just lay from you to own me. You've changed completely. I felt abandoned. You stood with your mom when there was something happened to me. You turned cold because we don't have a child. At those moments, I felt so lonely. I cried a lot. You never knew or felt that I needed you beside me. I did not want to fight because I didn't want your mother to judge me. I know it is weird and inappropriate to say this, but luckily, I found Adam, who loved me, cared for me and had sympathy for me. He made me feel I wanted to continue living in this world. He made me feel special, and he is better than you in bed, Thomas. He has done everything a husband could do for his wife. And I love him. Yes, I fucking love him."

She looks to Mrs. Linh," You are the worst mother ever. You never love me and have sympathy for me. How could you treat me like that? Before you became a mother-in-law, you used to be a daughter-in-law like me. Instead of being a bitch to me, you could have understood and loved me like your daughter. But I guess you can never do it. I bet that now that I can't have a child, you will want to kick me out and tell Thomas to marry someone else. Honestly, I have been waiting for that moment because I don't give a shit anymore. It will release me from this hell house. I did not know what I did to make you hate me like that. Not only that, you've been despairing me for many times you've expected to have a grandson. I know that you are still following the old tradition of this family. I must have a son to heritage. Fuck that tradition. Fuck all the prejudices. And fuck who made that rule." Ha laughs hysterically. "You know what, now I feel so happy because finally, I have my vengeance on you. You will never have a grandson as long as I am still in this family and after I walk out. You have failed to keep that tradition. I can laugh at your face right now. In my eyes, you are nothing than a low-class common bitch with all of hypocrites and morality."

Mrs. Linh and Thomas are stunned at what Ha just said. They could not believe that Ha would say those words one day; somehow, it was true.

No one says anything.

Ha continues. "This is it. Those were all the things I wanted to say. I am glad you knew about my affair, so I can leave this house because I can no longer live here where my husband doesn't love me anymore, and a mother-in-law hates me so much. I have to leave. This house, this house is rotten to the core. There is nothing to fix or save. I have to save myself from this family."

Then, Ha takes off her wedding ring and throws it on the floor. She gets her tote bag and takes it off.

"See," Ha turns back, looking at Mrs. Linh and Thomas. "You don't even stop me. I understand."

Mr. Tan follows her to the door. "Wait," Ha looks back. "Please, don't go. You still have me in this house."

Ha holds Mr. Tan's both hands and kisses him. "Dad, I love you. You are the only person in this house who loves and cares for me. You are like my father to me, and I will never forget you. But I have to go, dad. Enough is enough."

Mr. Tan bursts into tears. "You are like my daughter to me, too, and I am sorry for what happened to you."

"No, no, You don't have any faults. I always appreciate what you have done for me," They hug each other. "Goodbye, dad."

"Where will you go?" Mr. Tan asks.

"Somewhere peaceful."

Ha starts the car and drives away. Mr. Tan watches the car driving. He looks to the sky, prays to the Buddha and ancestors to look after Ha, and keeps her safe.

Ha arrives at the location that she wants to come to. She knocks on the door. Someone opened the door.

"Hey!" That person said.

"I love you, Adam. I will never leave you again, and please don't leave me. Everything is over now." Ha says.

She needs someone to be with at this moment.

"I won't and I never leave you." Adam welcomes Ha inside the house and kisses her.

He looks at the bruise on Ha's face. "What happened?"

Ha bursts out crying out loud without saying anything. Adam can somehow understand what happened to her. He keeps her in his arms and kisses her.

The door shuts.

PART 2

CHAPTER 9

Phuong

On one Tuesday night, Adam unexpectedly dropped Michael at Phuong's house. Phuong was surprised because that day was not the day Adam stayed at her house. Adam explained that he had a business need to do and would be pretty busy for the next few days. Michael, of course, believed his dad. But Phuong knew there was no business. It was just an excuse for Adam to do something by himself.

"I won't buy that." Phuong crossed her arms.

"What are you talking about?" Adam asked.

"There is no business at all, right? It is just an excuse for you to do everything you want. For example, fuck some girls."

Adam chuckled. "How funny! You know what? You are such a selfish and manipulative bitch. We got divorced. I have my own life to live. I do whatever I want to do. You don't know about my business, so please don't make ridiculous assumptions like that. It is so fucking annoying. You don't know shit. Besides," Adam cleared his throat. "I heard that you just turned out to be a cougar."

"What?" Phuong got startled. "Who told you that?"

"Michael told me everything. He said you are seeing somebody else, and he is afraid your lover would ruin everything in the family. I thought we had a deal to keep this secret from Michael until he was older. You've broken it already?"

"I have not. We are…friends."

"Come on; you don't need to lie to me. I got it. You've moved on. But to be honest, it is too naked and created thinking that you betrayed me to be with another man."

Ok, Adam just *made* a point. He wanted to blame Phuong for ending this marriage, and he would become the victim. He would inject every horrible thing about Phuong and Hoa into his mind of Michael. He would brainwash Michael with all of the good things he did. And the worst thing is that Michael would no longer listen to Phuong or believe in what she says.

When the whole affair thing happened, Michael was not there. Phuong was the only person seeing everything. Of course, after the divorce, Phuong could have broken the agreement between her and Adam, which keeps this secret from Michael until he is old enough to understand, and she will spit out the truth. She could have gained more love from Michael, and Michael would belong to her forever. Adam would lose everything, which is a price he had to pay. After all, Adam is the root of all of these things. If he did not do it, this family would not have been shifted at all.

Now, she wishes she has done what Hoa told her.

Too late for that.

"It seems like we are both fuckers," Adam continued. "We can't control ourselves in front of the temptations." Adam looked at his watch. "I have to go now. Good luck with your new lover! Bye."

Phuong watched after Adam. "You know what?" Adam turned. "Yes, we cannot control ourselves in front of temptation, but I am more different than you. I know that temptation is good for me and does not make me feel regretful. And you fell into the temptation that destroyed everything. Do you understand?"

Adam smiled and clapped his hands. "Bravo. Good saying. Maybe what you said is true. But remember that temptation is never a good thing, and we must know how to control it before it turns to regret."

Then, he left.

Phuong got inside the house. She went to Adam's room, where he was playing with his iPad. Phuong sat down next to him. She put down the iPad.

"Mom, I am playing." Michael groaned.

"I know. Talk to me for a second." Phuong put the iPad next to her. "You told your dad about Mr. Hoa, didn't you?"

"Yes, mom. I've told him about that."

"Why?"

"Because I want dad to know. I never hide anything. It is so unfair for him when I have another dad in the house."

Phuong chuckled. "Another dad? What are you talking about?"

"You love Mr. Hoa and will leave my dad and marry him. Then, he will be my stepdad. I cannot meet my real dad again; the worst thing is that I have to change my last name. And you won't love me anymore."

"Sweetie," Phuong rubbed Michael's head. "I always love you no matter what. I will never leave you. You knew it. Mr. Hoa is a nice man, and he is kind to you. We are just friends. There is nothing between us."

"No," Michael shoved Phuong's hands. "You lie to me. I will never welcome him into my life. Yes, he is nice to me, but to be my life, I will never accept, Mom. No one can replace dad inside me. I don't want to listen anymore. Give me back my iPad and leave me alone."

„Michael, I…..»

"GIVE ME BACK MY IPAD!" Michael screamed.

"All right, dear, here you go." Phuong handed him the iPad. Michael pulled it back to him and returned to his game.

Return to her room, Phuong sat down in front of her make-up desk. She brushed her brown hair, which Hoa's cousin had dyed for her a week ago. Suddenly, she threw the brush into the mirror angrily.

Phuong finally found her new love in the arms of Hoa. He usually takes her out for dinner or boba, or sometimes they go on traveling. Time with Hoa makes Phuong feel like she was reborn again. No more haunted past, no more misery, no more string attached to her old relationship. And yet, her biggest concern is that Michael does not accept Hoa. Even if he knows Phuong and Adam are divorced, Michael will never take Hoa. He just declared. Adam has built himself as an icon in Michael's eyes and brainwashed Michael with all the best of Adam.

Her relationship with Hoa is being jeopardized. She loves him, but Michael doesn't, and if they think about a different relationship, it will be a big challenge. She does not want to lose Hoa, but she also does not want to lose Michael. She understands that the distance between her and Michael is far now. Once Hoa steps into Phuong's life, Michael may never want to be with her again. So Phuong promises herself if, in that situation, she would tell Michael the truth to pull Michael back to her.

It is Phuong's birthday. Hoa wants to make her a surprise birthday party at Mrs. Nhu's house. He discussed it with Mrs. Nhu, and she thought it was a great idea. Hoa told Michael about this. Outside, Michael agreed. But inside, he is preparing something else.

When Phuong and Adam were still together, Adam always cooked her favorite food on her birthday and came with many expensive gifts. From jewelry to technology devices. Or even a car. It was so memorable. Adam and Phuong were watching a "The Oprah Winfrey Show" episode, in which Oprah gave every audience a car. "You're getting a car! You're getting a car! You're getting a car! Everybody's getting a car!" That moment inspired Adam immediately. One week later, Adam gave her a small box on Phuong's birthday. It was no decoration. It was an ordinary box with a bow on it. Phuong opened the box, and she reacted exactly like the audience in The Oprah Winfrey Show in that episode.

"You're getting a car! You're getting a CAR!" Adam screamed out loud.

Phuong always loved that surprise gift. Time went by, and Phuong hoped that one day Adam could buy her a Tesla. But it never came. They divorced.

Phuong has a surgeon on her birthday, giving Hoa some time to decorate the house. Michael is not going to school today, so he stays home to help Hoa. Even though he does not want to do it, the theme of this year's birthday is black and white. Phuong loves watching black-and-white movies because Hoa introduced her to the world of films. He usually watches film noir movies and some golden-age movies in Hollywood. Her favorite movie is Double Indemnity. She loves the plot, the characters, and the dangers of Phyllis Dietrichson. She hopes she is dangerous as her. After she divorced, she sometimes hated Adam so much that she wanted to kill him.

Knowing his girlfriend's favorite, Hoa prints out all the posters of famous noir movies hanging all the living, black and white balloons as a dome, and in the middle of the crown, a backdrop that said "Happy Birthday Phuong! Straight Down The Line", precisely like what Phyllis said; champagne on ice; birthday cake mixed of black and white chocolate. Mrs. Nhu walks into the living room and is amazed by Hoa's creativity.

"I am impressed," She hands Hoa a glass of iced tea. "Phuong will love it."

"Thank you," Hoa drinks the iced tea. "I hope so." Hoa looks at his watch. "Oh, I have to pick up something. I'll be right back."

"Come back for lunch, ok?" Mrs. Nhu reminds Hoa.

"I will." Then he leaves the house.

Mrs. Nhu turns to Michael, who is playing his Nintendo Switch. "Did you help him anything?"

"Yes, I did." His eyes are still sticking to the game.

"Michael, how many times have I told you that when you talk to someone, look at them and talk? I don't like you talking to me like that. That is so rude and disrespectful. Do you understand?"

"Yes, Grandma." No change at all.

Mrs. Nhu grabs his Nintendo Switch from Michael. "That's enough."

Michael gets angry. "Grandma, what are you doing? I am playing. That is so rude, Grandma."

Mrs. Nhu chuckles. "Rude? How dare are you telling me that? This is the only way for you to look at and talk."

"I hate you," Michael shouted and ran to the stair. He turned back. "I hate you. I hate mom. I hate Hoa. Nobody cared about how I felt in this house. I want my dad. I want my dad. I WANT MY DAD!" Then, he runs upstairs and slams the door hard.

"Michael! Michael!" Mrs. Nhu sighs in desperation. She looks at the Nintendo Switch, which appears as a continuing game. Mrs. Nhu does not understand what he is playing. She tosses it onto the sofa and returns to the kitchen. She is wondering why Michael reacted like that. He is never liked that before. It is so strange.

One hour later, Hoa comes back with a package. He goes to the kitchen, where Mrs. Nhu is sitting sadly.

"What happens, Mrs. Nhu?" Hoa asks.

"Oh, you're back," Mrs. Nhu smiles. "Nah, there was nothing. I was thinking about some stuff. What are you having on your hand?"

"I ordered a box of macaroons. Phuong always loves eating this." Then,

Hoa puts the box inside the fridge. He comes back to the table and sits down. He looks around. "Where is Michael?"

Mrs. Nhu stands up and pours out the soup from the pot into a bowl. "Michael told me that he was not hungry."

"Really? Let me go and get him down."

Mrs. Nhu waves her hands. "Don't be bothered! When he feels hungry, he will come."

"I have a feeling that Michael doesn't like me. Maybe he doesn't want me in this house."

"Michael is just a child. There are so many things that he has not known yet," Mrs. Nhu says. "Don't worry! I think he will like you."

After finishing her shift in the hospital, Phuong goes outside. All the nurses, doctors, and patients are standing in the hall to cheer Phuong. They all say "Happy birthday," which makes Phuong surprised. The confetti pops up. They secretly plan to give her a surprise party. A nurse walks to Phuong with a chocolate cake. They start singing happy birthday. Phuong blows out the candles, and they clap.

The head nurse comes up and speaks. "This is a surprise party for all of us. On behalf of all the doctors, nurses, and patients here, I want to wish you a great birthday and wish you to have all the happiness in your life and be successful in your job. Thank you for being here with all of us."

Phuong puts her hands on her heart. She gets so emotional. "Oh my God, you guys. I don't know what to say. Uhm," Phuong is bursting to tears. "It is my pleasure to be with all of you and help everyone here get better. I am so glad. Thank you so much for everything."

Everyone raises their glasses. They are all apple cider. "To Phuong." One of the doctors says. Then, they all say together. "To Phuong."

The party goes well, and after that, everyone returns to work. Phuong sits quietly on the bench. Rachel sees her and comes near Phuong. She sits down.

"Hey, what happens? You don't like this party?"

Phuong chuckles. "No, I love this party. I am so happy to have you guys as my colleague. Always care for each other."

"So why does your face look so sad?" Rachel asks.

"I know it sounds weird, but..." Phuong sighs and finishes her apple cider in the paper cup. "I feel old. So old. I am in the 40th club right now."

"Are you thinking about your relationship with Hoa?"

Phuong nods slightly. Rachel continues. "Yes, I know. It is awkward. But listen, after all these years, you have been sad and suffered from your last marriage. Now, you have somebody who loves you. Don't you think it is the time for you to come to him?"

"It is not about the age gap, Rachel. I don't mind people calling me a cougar. But..." Phuong goes silent.

"But what?"

"It's Michael. Michael will not accept Hoa. He doesn't want him to replace Adam. I feel so confused right now."

Rachel holds Phuong's hands. "So what are you going to do? You will tell him about you and Adam. I mean, it is the only way."

Phuong sighs. "I don't know. I have no idea how to talk to him about that. I don't want to hurt him."

"I know it sounds cruel. But you and Adam have hurt him already."

Phuong looks straight into Rachel's eyes. "What?"

Rachel laughs. "Isn't it obvious? Come on, why in the world haven't you told him the whole truth? If I were you, I would have told my children that we got divorced and whose fault it was. Just tell Michael the truth about his father. There is nothing more to hide. Don't let this ruin your new happiness! Explain to Michael why you and Adam got divorced, and then talk well about Hoa. Just like that, Michael will accept Hoa."

"You think so?"

"Yes. You love Hoa, and he loves you, too. Then why the hell can't you tell Michael the whole truth? The more you keep, the more Michael will hate Hoa and even hate you. You had suffered from your last marriage, where you gave so much love and trust to Adam, and he failed you with his cheating. I won't say he did not love you initially, but his love for you was not enough. You worked it out that failed marriage that had died long ago. Hoa is a different man who cares for your feelings, loves you, and fulfills the hole inside your heart. He is a good person, and it is time for you to begin a new chapter with him. I have a good sense about him."

"What if Michael doesn't believe in what I said, and what if this love is another failure?"

Rachel shakes her head. "He will believe you because you have evidence. The video of Adam having sex with that woman."

"Ewww, I won't show that to him. He is still young."

"Then try to explain to him as well as possible. Ask your mom to support you. Michael will be convinced. Trust me. Besides, this love will be a successful one. I promise. You lost your youth with a guy like Adam. Now, let Hoa takes care of you for the rest of your life. Besides, you have been through a failed marriage with Adam, and I think you have full experience keeping your husband," Both laugh. "I think you will be happy."

"Awww," Phuong hugs Rachel. "What will I do without you? I think you should become a psychologist."

Rachel finishes her cup of apple cider. "I wish I could, but my strict parents don't want me to read their minds. They got scared."

Phuong looks at her watch. It is time for her to go home. "I have to go right now. My mom said she would make me a birthday dinner."

"Ok, enjoy your birthday."

Phuong leaves the hospital. On the way home, Phuong is thinking about Hoa. A man with whom she recently fell in love. Maybe Rachel is right. Hoa is her true love after Adam. Even Rachel believes it is time for Phuong to tell Michael the truth. It is time.

Phuong parks the car and gets into the house. When she opens the door, Hoa shoots out the confetti. BAM. Phuong gets goosebumps and screams.

"Surprised!" Michael, Hoa, and Mrs. Nhu shout at the same time.

"Oh my God," She does the same reaction as in the hospital previously. "Another surprise?"

Mrs. Nhu, Hoa, and Michael look bewildered. Hoa asks. "What are you talking about?"

Phuong drops her gift bag and her tote bag on the couch. She smiles. "I just had a surprised party in the hospital from my colleagues and my patients." She looks at the decoration of her favorite film. Phuong feels so happy. "This is so lovely. This is my favorite movie. You made all of these?"

"I just did the decoration with the help of Michael, and your mother cooked all of this delicious food," Hoa says.

Mrs. Nhu hugs her daughter and kisses her left cheek. "Happy birthday, dear! Time had gone so fast, and I still remember the day I carried you in my arms. You were so little. Now, you are exactly like how I expected. I am so proud of you, babe."

"Thank you, mom! For everything! I love you too. I am so blessed to be your daughter."

Michael is standing next to Phuong to wait for his turn. "Happy birthday, mom I made a gift for you, and I hope you love it."

"Babe," Phuong opens the box, and it pops out. It is an explosion box with all the cute handmade stuff and contains memories with photos. "This is so lovely. Come here!"

"I love you, mommy," Michael says.

"I love you more." Phuong kisses Michael's forehead.

Hoa stands behind Phuong. She turns back. "I have double gifts for you. One will be revealed when you go to your bedroom right now. And the second one... well, you know what they say. Keep the best for last." Hoa says.

"Ohhh. Sounds mystery."

They can kiss, but Michael is in the room, and they don't want to make a scene. Then, Phuong left the living room and went to her bedroom. She sees a red silk dress on the bed when she walks in. She looks at it. It is so gorgeous. Phuong immediately puts it on after she takes off her clothes. She looks in the mirror. Woah, she cannot believe that at the age of 40, she can still have a slim body. There is a feeling inside her when she puts it on—a feeling of being a queen. Phuong sits down in front of her makeup table. Put on some powder and red lipstick. She is brushing her long brown hair. Now, she looks like a queen.

All hail the queen.

Everyone is sitting in the living room and waiting for Phuong. She walks down the stair, and they follow her steps. Hoa stands up immediately. He gives out his hand. Phuong holds his.

"You look beautiful in this dress. So fancy." Hoa gives the compliment.

"I can't expect that you have good eyes like that."

Michael claps his hands. "You look so beautiful, mom. I love it."

"Thank you, sweetie. Mr. Hoa bought it for me."

Immediately, the smile on Michael's face turned off. "I see." Then, he ignores it.

"All right," Mrs. Nhu said. "Let's take pictures and have dinner. Things are getting cold."

Phuong gets to the backdrop and poses. Then, she takes with her mother, Michael, and Hoa. But before she can take a photo with Hoa, there is a knock on the door.

"I'll get it," Michael quickly comes to the door and opens it. "Daddy, you've come. I am waiting for you," He jumps into Adam immediately. "Why did you come so late?"

Mrs. Nhu, Hoa, and Phuong are stunned by the appearance of Adam.

"I was a little busy," Adam says, and he holds Michael's hand and comes inside the house. He sees all the eyes of hatred and uncomfortable from people who do not want him here. Indeed, no one wants him to be here. Especially Phuong.

Phuong smiles awkwardly. "Michael, what is all about this?"

Michael answers innocently, even though he has planned everything. "I called dad here. It is your birthday, and I don't want dad to miss it. Besides, I want our family to be together on this special day," Then, he turned to Adam. "Dad, come on! Let's take pictures with mom and me."

"Sweetie, I...." Phuong says.

"Mom, hurry up. I want to take pictures with you and dad."

Phuong looks at Hoa. He does not say anything and slightly nods. Adam stands in front of the backdrop with Michael. Phuong looks at them and shakes her head.

"No," Phuong says firmly.

"What, mom?"

"I said NO," Phuong yells.

"Why?"

Phuong turns her look to Hoa. He is looking at her and waiting for Phuong to answer. Since the first dinner they had together, Hoa has advised Phuong to tell Michael the whole truth many times. All Phuong's responses were "I will do it," "Yes, I did it already," and "Michael is still young, and I think I will be careful when I talk to him about it."

Hoa believes her and does not want to doubt his girlfriend. And today, he has found out nothing is confirmed. Phuong has not talked to Michael about the divorce. Hoa intends to build a good bond between himself and Michael so that he can have a different look at Hoa. But Phuong does not give him that chance by keeping silent on her divorce. Everything makes sense now. That's why Phuong does not want to show love or kiss Hoa in front of Michael because of this.

Hoa sighs and looks away.

"Michael, I am so disappointed in you," Phuong shouts. "I could not believe that you did that to me."

"What did I do to you? I simply want dad to be here at your birthday. We are a family, Mom. And a family should be together like at this moment."

"WE ARE NOT FAMILY. STOP SAYING THAT!"

The shout of Phuong makes the whole room quiet. Everyone stares at her with frightened eyes. Phuong walks to the minibar and pours herself a cup of Whiskey. She knocks it off and slams the glass hard on the table.

"We divorced," Phuong says. "Your dad and I are no longer together. We lie to you and go behind you to make you believe we are still together. We do that because we love you and don't want to hurt your feelings. We want to wait until you are old enough to tell you the truth. And I never think today is that day. I am so sorry for everything."

Michael frowns. He looks at his mother than his dad and his grandma. "You said that both of you did that because you love me. That's funny because if you guys loved me, you would have never done it behind my back. All I want is a happy family. Seeing you guys apart makes me feel lonely. But I trust my parents. After all, it was just a lie. You guys divorced, and all I am living is the fake life you made up."

But Michael changes his attitude toward his mother. His eyes turn sharp as if he hates his mother so much.

"Mom, for all these years, dad was alone in that house, and he is always beside me and took care of me. And you, all you care about is him," Michael points at Hoa. "You love him, and he is your everything right now. He is the person who destroys this family. He stepped into your life and replaced everything. I will never accept him in this house." Then, he turns back to Phuong. "I must be the person who disappointed you. I hate you. I HATE YOU."

Phuong cannot take it anymore. "ENOUGH!" She screams. "Shut up!

Just shut up." She wipes her face. "Do you ever wonder why your dad and I got divorced? I always want to tell you the truth. But you are too young to understand, and I don't want to hurt your feeling. You told me that I don't love you? Babe, I love you more than anything, and that will never change. You told me that your dad has been alone all along?" Phuong laughs hysterically. "That is so funny. He is never alone, which was why we divorced." Phuong turned to Adam. "Your dad cheated on me. He lied to you and me. He took another woman to our home and fucked her on my bed, and maybe they did that in your room too.

"All of my life, I always loved your dad, and I thought he and I could be together for the rest of our life like we used to take the vows. But no. Your dad betrayed you and me. In your eyes, he is always the best because he has bought you many kinds of stuff. Do you know what for? To get your attention and your sympathy for him. He knew that he would lose you, and soon, you stood for him when you found out the truth. Your dad never loves you...."

"Shut up," Adam shouts. "It is not true. I always love Michael."

"Fuck you," Phuong does not care that Michael might hear her nasty words. "You must be the person who shut up. Do you know why I took Michael back to my house and lived with me? Because that woman had moved into your house. That's right! I saw everything. How great it is!"

Adam stands still. His mouth cannot even move.

"What? Cat got your tongue?" Phuong continues. "You don't want Michael to see it because your perfect image will be gone in the eyes of Michael."

Phuong knees down and holds Michael's arms. She looks straight into his eyes. "Michael, babe, I am so sorry to tell you this. But I can't hold it anymore. You've heard everything about the real person of your dad. Your perfect daddy! And I am a bad mom? No, you should know one thing: I never leave you or never even think for myself even one. I have been suffering from the pains your dad caused me, but I still hold into you as my courage and hope to move on. Now I have found my new love, a good man who loves you and me. I hope that you will accept him. Please, Michael. It is time to see everything clearly and know what is right and wrong. Please!"

Michael walks toward his dad. Adam meets his eyes. "Dad, is everything like what mom said?"

Adam swallows his saliva and sighs. "Michael, listen, I….»

"Answer me. Yes or no?"

"Yes, it is true. I am sorry. You have full right to get angry at me, but there is one true thing I always love you. I never buy your happiness with all of those things. I did that because that is the love a father can give his son. It is true love."

"But you betrayed mom and me." Michael points at everyone in the room. "All of you hide everything from me and treat me in lies. I live in lies and secrets. I hate all of you guys."

He runs upstairs, and all they hear is a slam of the door, just like in the afternoon. Michael must love slamming doors.

The door opens, and a person walks in. Everyone looks at that person. "YOU!" Phuong says.

When Adam dropped Michael off that Tuesday night, he forgot to put the medicine inside Michael's backpack. The following day, Phuong drove to Adam's house, where she did not return. She arrived and saw a car in the driveway next to Adam's. Probably, Adam had taken a girl home to fuck last night. Phuong shook her head.

"What an asshole!"

Even though they got divorced, Adam has not changed the door lock. Maybe he was lazy. Phuong opened the door with her old key. Inside the house, it was tranquil. Phuong walked into the kitchen to find Adam, but he was not there. Well, she just needed the medicine.

Phuong went over every corner of the living room, kitchen, and even the office, but there was nothing. Phuong went upstairs. She got immediately into Michael's room. She was surprised by the tidiness of his room because usually, Michael barely cleaned his room; Phuong was the person who cleaned for him. She had not come back to his room for a long time. Still the wallpaper of The Incredible, his favorite animated film; the twin bed and the desk, which Adam bought from Pottery Barn. Nothing changed. Everything was still in the same place.

The medicine was on his desk. Phuong grabbed it and left. In the hall, Phuong suddenly heard talking between Adam and someone else. The voice of that person sounds familiar to Phuong. She had heard somewhere.

She slowly walked to the room at the end of the hall, which used to be her room with Adam.

"I miss you in bed, Ha," Adam said.

Phuong gasped. She was shocked that Ha had moved in with Adam.

"I miss your penis too. You are still strong." Ha said.

She walked downstairs and went straight to the door. Sitting in the car, Phuong thought Ha was here right now, meaning she had left Thomas and planned to move on with Adam. Phuong would never let Michael live in one house with that woman.

That bitch would never be welcomed in that house as long as Michael is in that house.

CHAPTER 10

Ha

"I miss you in bed, Ha," Adam says as he kisses and sniffs Ha's boobs. Ha scrubs his head. Her fingers run through his hair. There is some gray hair on his head. But still, she could smell the Head and Shoulder shampoo, his favorite. It always attracts Ha every time. And his cologne.

"I miss your penis, too," Ha says. "It is still strong."

Adam looks up. "The little boy has been put to rest for a long time. Of course, it had to be strong. I did not use any viagra to make it hard. You are the best pill for me, babe."

"Awww," Ha lifts Adam's head and kisses him. "I love you."

"I love you more," Adam says. He puts his hand down on Ha's private part. He grabs her vagina and squeezes it. Ha moans in happiness, and she gets another orgasm. "What do you think we do another round?"

Adam releases his hand. Ha gasps and returns to usual. "Save it for tonight. I have to go to work. I don't want people in the firm to have any suspicion about me."

"It won't take long, baby."

"No," Ha pushes Adam to one side. She puts the pillow to cover Adam's penis because it will turn her on if she looks at it. "A quick sex will never satisfy me."

Ha gets out of bed. Naked. Adam sees some bruises on her body. He could not believe that asshole had done it to her. Yesterday, when seeing Ha with a face of desperation and misery and bruises, even though Ha did not say what happened the first time, Adam still could understand what happened. He helped her to rub some oil and Neosporin.

He was a strong man, yet he had dropped tears when doing it. Ha shared the story, and she told him not to mention it again. "Enough is enough," she said.

Adam reaches for the cigarette pack, takes out one, puts in his mouth, and lights it up. "It works it me, babe." Adam releases the smoke.

"Save it for tonight," Ha puts on her bathrobe. "By the way, since when you start smoking cigarettes. I only saw you vaping before."

"Vaping is for a child. Smoking is for a real man. Don't you see I look cool when I smoke cigarettes?"

"Ha ha ha," Ha says with an ironic voice. "Very funny. Yes, it is cool," She takes the cigarette off Adam's mouth. "Be cool until you sit behind the chicken and eat fruits with your grandparents."

"Hey, hey, what the hell does that mean?"

Ha walks to the bathroom and speaks out. "It is a phrase from Vietnamese people. It means you die."

Adam gets out of bed and puts on his underwear. "Where did you hear about that?"

"One of my friends," Ha puts on some lipstick. "Babe, you should learn more Vietnamese. There are so many good things about Vietnamese culture."

From behind, Adam holds her belly and kisses her neck. "Speaking of which, what do you think about vacationing in Vietnam? It will be great."

"That is a great idea." Ha puts on the foundation. "I have not been back to Vietnam for a long time."

Adam keeps kissing. Ha feels so satisfied, but Adam annoys her a little bit, preventing her from doing her makeup. Yes, it is so good because she misses the sense of a man. Ha turns around and kisses Adam. Then, she let go.

"Babe, I miss your pancake and your roast coffee. Would you mind making me some?"

"Pancake?" Adam says.

It has been a long time since he did not make any pancakes, even if Michael is at home. His son loves sausage egg McMuffin at McDonald's more than his pancake. Before Ha, Phuong was the only one who loved his pancake the most. Now, in front of their request of Ha, Adam is still determining whether he can make pancakes as good as they used to be.

He accepts the request immediately. "At your service, madam." He bows and leaves the room.

Ha looks at him through the mirror, and she smiles. But it stops immediately when she takes off the bathrobe. She sees the bruises on her body in the mirror. Tear starts to burst out from her eyes. She collapses down to the floor and covers her face to cry. She tries her best not to make any noise or ruin the makeup. She has done a great job putting some concealer on her face to cover the bruises her face.

The burst-out only lasts for a few seconds. Then, she sniffs and stands up again.

"It's over," She says to her reflection in the mirror. "No more pain. No more suffering. No more hiding."

Ha forces herself a smile to be stronger. She knows one thing for sure now and will not need to return to that hell house again.

Ha realizes that before she left that hell house, she did not bring any belongings. The clothes from yesterday smell wrong and have some bloodstains on them. That motherfucker, she thinks. But she has no choice. After finishing her job at the firm, Ha would throw these clothes away and buy a new ones. Maybe Adam would buy it for her.

Divorce. Divorce is the most important thing she needs to do in the next few days. Finish it once and for all.

In the kitchen, Adam has done the first batch. The smell of the pancake makes Ha cannot stop herself from eating all the pancakes that Adam made today. She is famished.

"Smell so good, babe," Ha gives a compliment. She walks to the coffee maker and pours herself a cup of coffee. "It is exactly the thing I've missed."

Adam smiles. "It has been a long time since I have not made pancakes. I don't know if I still have the skill or not."

Ha opens the cupboard next to the fridge, where Adam puts cream and sugar. It was Phuong who was the real housewife of the family. She is a very organized woman. Everything must be in order when she touches it. Ha still remembers everything in this house and where they are being kept. She cannot believe that Adam can still manage to keep everything organized after the divorce. She put some cream inside her coffee and stirred it up.

"Try it." Adam hands her the syrup.

Ha pours the syrup on the pancakes and takes a bite. She groans in happiness. "Oh my goddess, I have found heaven. It is so fucking delicious."

"For real?"

"For real." Ha takes another bite. She says with a mouthful of pancake. "I love you so much."

Adam laughs. He turns off the stove and brings the plate to Ha's place. He sits next to her. His fingers run over her hair. Just like that, Adam keeps staring at Ha while she is eating like a bird. Ha turns to Adam.

"What?"

"Nothing" Adam slowly takes his hands back.

Ha finishes her dish. Adam offers her his dish, but Ha denies it. She is so full. She drinks her coffee and looks at her Apple Watch. It is 8:00.

"I have to go now. What are you doing today?"

"Well, doing some stuff and checking on my new merchandise for selling. What about you and I going out to have dinner tonight?"

Ha fixes her hair. "That sounds good! Where?"

"I don't know. Let me go and check. Vietnamese, ok?"

"Sure."

"I will look up. Then, I will send it to you."

"Ok, honey." Ha comes to Adam and kisses him on his lips. "See you later!"

"Oh wait," Adam calls her back. Ha turns. "I will buy your new clothes. You can't go to a restaurant wearing this. Same size?"

Ha smiles. A little dream comes true. "Never change, babe."

Then, Ha leaves the house to go to the firm.

Walking inside the firm, everyone is looking at Ha and starts whispering. Ha looks back at them, and she begins to feel something went wrong. She gets into the office and sits down. It's weird when they stare at her.

Oh God, Ha thinks. *Maybe they have known about the affair. Gossip in the Vietnamese community is the scariest thing ever. Just one post on the*

Vietnamese in America group on Facebook, they can know everything. Fuck that shit!

Mrs. Linh is a member of that group.

There is a knock on the door.

"Come in," Ha says.

A man with a white Ralph Lauren shirt, blue tie, and black jeans comes in. It is Tony Nguyen, one of Ha's colleagues.

"Good morning, Ha! How are you today?" He says. He places a coffee cup on Ha's desk. "For you!"

"Awww," Ha smiles. "Thank you, Tony."

Tony Phan is a charming guy with a face of a Mister Global. He used to be an assistant of Ha during his time as an intern here. And now he has passed over her to become one of the trusted lawyers in the firm. Every case that he is in charge of always succeeds. There are some times Ha feels jealous of this guy. But Tony is a good guy and never shows arrogance to everyone in the firm. When he gets stuck, he always comes to Ha to seek advice. When it comes to Ha's birthday, he throws a small party for her. When there is a successful case, he always invites everyone in the firm to eat in a fancy restaurant and dedicates himself to Ha.

With him, the success of him is the success of the firm. Charming, friendly, and sweet, Tony must have a girlfriend. But no, he had none. Some girls in the firm like him. Tony ignores them. He treats them as colleagues.

Tony's private life is still a considerable hidden number.

"Do you know why everyone looked at me like that?" Ha asks.

"Oh, about that. Because of your mood today."

"My mood?"

"Kinda positive. They hardly saw you smile before. What went wrong?"

Yes, it is true. Ha does not notice that there is a good mood on her face.

"Really?" Ha asks. "That is.... strange."

Tony sits down on the chair in front of Ha's desk. He leans back. "Strange as hell, of course. By the way," He clears his throat. "I just finished collecting all the evidence for Evan's case. We will go to the court two days later. That bastard's family made a scene at the court the other day after his bail was denied. He deserved it."

"I've heard about that," Ha takes a sip of coffee. "What a mess at the court. I also heard that the victim's family brought the picture of their late daughter to court. It is a nice move because it can provoke the anger and the frustration inside them."

"Take a look at this."

Tony hands her his phone. Ha puts on her glasses to see. It is a photo of the victim's body provided by the police department. The victim has suffered from domestic violence by her husband. Most of his actions came from alcohol. There were multiple bruises, wounds, and scars on her. The main reason that leads to her death is that her husband pushed her down from stairs and her head hit the staircase. She died later after that because of a cerebral hemorrhage.

Ha is the person in charge of this case. But she wants to give it to Tony because Tony can crush the defendant and gain justice for the victim's family.

"That motherfucker," Tony grins his teeth.

Ha looks at Tony and smiles because she knows she has put this case into the right person's hands.

"I hate any man who abuses their wives or family members. Those bastards should be punished and punished hard. They use their powers to abuse others. They never realize how lucky they are."

"You should bring what you just said to the court. It will touch the soul of Judge Gary."

"Maybe I should," Tony stands up and fix his tie. "Well, I should get back to work. Do you want to have lunch today? My treat."

"Awww, on what's the occasion?"

"You smile."

"All right. What a big deal, hah! I'll see you later."

Tony gets out of Ha's office. Ha returns to her work. Suddenly, something pops up inside Ha's mind. Something's pretty cool and funny. Tony never likes abusive men. He cannot bear seeing any woman or child beaten up badly. In his short career, he has been dealing with many cases like that, and mostly he won. There is one thing that everyone in the court fear of him and loves him, which is his way of delivering the case.

First, he would tell the victims stories of how they live and what they have been through. His dramatic way of interpreting could make anyone cry, even the judge.

Second, he would change his tone to be angry to tell what the defendant did to the victims. He screams, yells, cries, and even curses. There is a time when the judge warns him, but it seems no one can stop him from what he does.

Third, he ends his argument well and suggests sentencing to the jury and the judge. When he starts his career, he usually carefully notes every experience he has with Ha and his colleagues. Then, he writes a script of what he should say.

Finally, he performs. Now, at a new level, he can do everything by himself.

What just popped up in Ha's mind is why she doesn't Ha ask Tony to become her lawyer in her divorce from Thomas. Ha would ask him to do it at lunch. Of course, he will accept my offer, Ha thinks.

At 12, Ha gets to the lady's room to do some make-up and check herself again. Then, she goes to Tony's office. She knocks. But there is so answer. So, she opens the door and walks in. There is a peppermint sense in his room. So relaxing.

Ha sits on the chair in front of Tony's desk to wait for Tony. She is so excited to have lunch with him and asks him to do what she wants.

Tony's phone rings. At first, Ha does not care. But for the second time, it rings again. It may be necessary. She looks at it. It does not say any name. Ha sees the phone number so familiar. She must have seen this number somewhere, as if she had a deja vu. The caller stops. A moment later, there is a text message coming. She looks at it.

"Hey babe, I tried to call you, but you did not answer. Maybe you are busy. I just booked a room at the All Seasons hotel. Room 405. See you then at 5 p.m. I told my old husband and my son that I was going out of town to visit my friend. We can have the whole night together, babe."

This is...funny. Tony has a girlfriend. Ha feels so rude when going over Tony's phone. It is none of her business. Tony can love anyone he wants. But she cannot believe Tony's type is so weird and unique. There are many young girls, yet he chooses to love a married woman. Nobody can expect anything from anyone. Ha places the phone back on the desk where it used to be. She returns to the couch. Even though she has told herself not to pay attention to Tony's personal life, she cannot get that phone number out of her mind.

So familiar, she thinks.

Ha immediately unlocks her phone. She looks over every name in her contact list. For the love of God, there are so many names on the list. How the hell can she know which one is that number? She uses the search bar to search for the owner of that phone number. She types in, and the result shocks her, almost making her drop the phone.

It is her mother-in-law's phone number. Mrs. Linh's phone number.

Ha covers her mouth with her hand. Her heart beats faster. She cannot believe that Mrs. Linh is having an affair with her colleague. Tony opens the door that startles Ha.

"Hey," Tony says. "When did you get in? So sorry for letting you wait for so long."

Ha smiles. Or pretends to smile. "I just got in. Shall we go?"

"Sure. Let me grab my phone and my jacket."

Tony looks at his phone and smiles. Then, he puts it into his pocket, grabs his jacket, and they leave.

Tony's smile shows Ha that he is really in love with Mrs. Linh. Ha is worrying about this relationship. It is not ok at all and unhealthy.

They go to have lunch at Denny's right across the street. Tony orders himself steaks and French fries with coke. Ha has chicken sandwiches with a vanilla shake.

"What do you think of Evan's case?" Tony asked.

Ha is not paying attention to the conversation. She is stirring her milkshake with the straw.

"Ha? Ha!" Tony calls.

"What?" Her soul finally returns to her body.

"What happened to you?"

"Oh, nothing. I am a little tired. What did you ask before again?"

Tony chuckles. "I asked what you think of Evan's case."

"Well, you talked to me about it before. I think he is guilty. His violent behavior is also being reported by so many people who used to be with him. Besides, his wife had so much insurance money. The greed inside him had raised. He killed her for the money then he used the money to live with his mistress. As you know, a young girl always looks for her sugar daddy. After they stole all of their money, they will walk away without turning back."

"That is the motive. His mother-in-law asked me to do anything that could put in jail forever or put him in the death chamber. She had been suffering so much."

"It is easy to understand. There is nothing more painful for a mother than losing a child. In court, don't lose your temper. Just stick with what you had prepared and focus on the witnesses who take the stand. Their words may be true. When I met Chelsea, Evan's wife's cousin will be the person who lies."

Tony looks bewildered. "Why?"

"I suspect that Evan's mistress is Chelsea. Since the police questioned her, she has always tried to protect Evan and talked shit about the victim."

"I can see that. Do you think Chelsea is his partner in crime?"

"We are not sure about that. But after he is sentenced, you should advise the victim's family to prosecute Chelsea."

"I will. Thank you for that."

The food is coming out. They eat and talk. Ha stares at Tony eating. The question mark about Tony's relationship with Mrs. Linh has come back.

"Tony," Ha finally asks. "What is your type?"

Tony swallows the piece of steak which he is chewing. He wipes his mouth and chuckles. "Why do you ask that?"

"Well, I want to know more about my colleague. You know that you are mysterious in your private life, right?"

"It is private, so why do I have to share? Do you have someone for me? Or are you in love with me?"

Ha gets goosebumps. He has touched her secret, which no one in the firm knows about. "Hell no. There are some girls in the firm who, I think, have a crush on you. I am a woman, and I have a special sense."

Tony takes a sip of his drink. His fingers cross together and begin. "Well, since you are insisted, I think I will tell you some of my personal life."

Ha's eyes are wide open as if she is a child who will be given candy or her parents will buy them new toys. "Shoot it."

"I am not gay; let's start with that. There are so many people in the firm who spread out the rumor that I am gay. I am straight. But…Uhm…."

"But what?"

There is a blush on his face. Ha can expect what he is going to say. It is never easy to say about that. Just spit it out, Tony, Ha thinks. *I am one step closer to bust you having an affair with my mother-in-law. Don't worry! I won't blame you.*

"I have an issue with my life," Tony says. His eyes look down at the empty plate. "You know what, I can't share this. It is too embarrassing."

Shit, Ha thinks. "Come on. Don't be such a child like that," Ha says. A little push. "You are a big monster that everyone scares at the court. Where is that monster? Remember, there is nothing to be afraid of saying when you are a lawyer. That is the most important lesson ever."

"All right, you're right. So, fasten your seatbelt," Tony announces. "I am a pilot."

"What?" Ha shouts. It makes everyone around look at their boot. Ha does not care. Tony looks around and smiles shyly.

"What the hell are you talking about?" Ha lows her voice. "What do you mean by that?"

"It is a Vietnamese phrase. Don't you know about that?"

Ha shakes her head.

"I am not an actual pilot or flying an actual plane. I fly older women. A cougar, you know. I don't know why they call a cougar a pilot. I heard that from one of my friends. They said young pilots fly old ladies' planes. I am that pilot, and my type is old ladies. Gosh, I am so embarrassed when I tell you this."

Ha's mouth drops open wide. So this is it. Tony has admitted that he loves old ladies. And his lover is Mrs. Linh. But she needs him to confirm that Mrs. Linh is his lover. His plane.

"Tony, it is normal. Everyone has their type. There is nothing to be ashamed of. So, do you have anyone with you?".

"Yes. But this is not the time you know about her. I can only share that information with you. And please don't tell anyone about this."

Ha smiles. Inside her, she smiles evilly because now she knows her mother-in-law's secret, and she will use it against her. "Your secret is safe with me. Let me pay for this lunch for you."

"Come on. You don't have to do it."

"Let me do it."

After lunch, Ha comes back to her office. There are some cases she needs to review. But she does not open or see it. She keeps staring at it and thinks of something else. It is the relationship between Mrs. Linh and Tony. He admits the whole thing. It is strange.

What did Tony see in that woman? Ha thinks.

For all these years, Ha always thinks Mrs. Linh is a loyal wife and never does anything behind her husband's back. Of course, Ha hates her mother-in-law so much because of how she treats her. Also, her mother-in-law hates Ha so much.

Only yesterday, there was a big fight in that house between family members about Ha's affair with Adam. Thomas beat her up like a dog; Mrs. Linh threw her sassy and crucial words into Ha's face, and Ha fought back; Mr. An kept pumping in many unacceptable words to Mrs. Linh, and her father-in-law, Mr. Tan, protected Ha. It had happened so fast, and in Ha's mind, she could not even think everything had ended so soon, even though she wanted it to happen. But not in that way.

A person with all the nice things and the exemplary can do such a shameful thing as that. It is a big fucking lie. She dislikes her daughter-in-law for her misfit in the family. Well, the mother-in-law is a whore now. She dislikes Ha because of not giving her a grandson. Now, she will never have one. She dislikes Ha because of her lack of responsibility as a daughter-in-law should do when she stays in her husband's family. Now, it is all fucking fake masks when Mrs. Linh just tried to cover it with her perfect performance as a wife, a mother, and a mother-in-law. The real person of Mrs. Linh was this. A cheater. A hypocrite. A slut. A deep-fake.

If that is what Ha thought about her mother-in-law, she would have thought about herself again. The whole affair with Adam has made her become a whore too. Her mother used to be a prostitute back in Saigon. She used to have sex with many men to provide for her daughter and her family. But is that a bad thing?

In some cases, it is understandable because a mother would do anything to raise her child and not let her child live in misery. On the other hand, this job would hurt her child, and maybe it would affect that child's future. And it did. Ha had an affair with Adam, her friend's husband and son-in-law of her mother's friend. How bad can it be? When Ha thinks about that, she tells herself that she has disappointed her mother. A full-time lawyer and a part-time slut. But there is nothing wrong or sinful about that because her action can be understandable compared to what she has been through. And one more that Ha can please herself is that she lived true-self without regrets.

Ha looks at her watch. She would create a play, a perfect play for her husband and her father. Let people see the *actual* person of Mrs. Linh!

Ha leaves the firm 15 minutes early with the excuse of having a headache. She is going to the hotel where Mrs. Linh and Tony will meet. Ha is going to do it; Ha is going expose the truth, and Ha is going to take this opportunity to think on the positive side. The whole affair of her mother-in-law and Tony will be her vengeance for all these years she had to live in hell and yesterday's family feud.

If you think you can be over me and trounce me like that, Ha thinks. *Well, think again, mother. I have the Ace in my hands now.*

At. 4:30 p.m., she arrives All Season hotel. It is a standard hotel. But it looks so fancy and so luxurious. Ha does some research in the lobby, and this hotel is rated 7.9 on Trivago. It is a good score for a standard hotel like this. Ha reads every review. Bad, yes; Good, yes; Excellent, a few; Terrible, somewhat; Great, many. What makes Ha surprised is one review. "This hotel is so great for having an affair with your lover. The receptionist will advise you which room you can stay in if you go with your lover who is not your wife or your husband. Just say 'I have cookies' to the receptionist or type on the search bar of the hotel website, then they will tell you what to do. Highly recommend this hotel."

This is so fucking sick, Ha thinks. Suddenly, a black guy wearing a white suit comes to her. Ha does not notice.

"Madam?" He says.

Ha gets startled. She almost drops her phone. She looks up. There is a sense of cologne coming out of him. It is attractive.

"Are you a guest here?" He asks.

"Uhm, not actually," Ha says, but she does not know what to say next.

"So, what are you doing here?"

"I, uhm." Ha gets stuck. She takes a look around. Tony walks into the hotel to the reception desk. He may ask the reception girl about the room, Mrs. Linh. Then, he goes to the elevator.

"Hello?" The man snaps his fingers to Ha's face. "If you are not a guest of this hotel, please leave. Or else I have to call security."

There was an idea that popped into her mind. When she almost gets what she wants, something or someone will tell her what to do. She will direct a drama. Ha gently opens her purse and takes out some cash. She counts. It is $300, and she puts the rest back into the bag.

"What is your name, sir?" Ha asks.

"Excuse me?"

"I just want to know your name." Before he answers or says something, Ha sees his name tag. "Frank, huh?"

Frank does not answer after Ha says his name.

"Well, Frank, I have a little job for you."

The elevator stops on the 4th floor. Ha walks out and looks for room 405. The room is at the end of the hall. He smiles. Then she leaves for the balcony. Her hands were placed on the rail. It has been a long time since Ha did not have a peaceful moment like this. She is looking at the city when the sun is set. It suddenly is so beautiful. This is what Ha always wants—enjoying the sunset and the sunrise peacefully. Ha lids a cigarette and smokes.

Her cell phone rings. She answers.

"Everything is ready. They are here."

"Thank you, Frank. You have been so helpful."

Ha hangs up the phone. She takes the last smoke and bruises it to a plant pot nearby. She is about to come inside. But she hears noises coming out from the hall. It is the yell from her father-in-law.

"It's showtime," Ha says. Then, she walks inside.

Frank is standing outside. The door of room 405 opens. He is watching the whole drama play.

"I must say this is the most interesting show I have ever watched," Frank told Ha as she gave him the rest of the money.

"It is not something we cannot see every day, hah?"

"Indeed." Frank turns to Ha. "I wish I could stay to see more, but I have to return to my shift. Whatever they did to you in that house that made you do this, I think it is so painful, and I am glad you got out. Take care."

Ha is touched by the words coming from Frank. She hugs him. "Thank you for doing this for me."

She has made the right decision when asking Frank for a little job—calling her father-in-law and her going-to-be ex-husband to watch this play. Moreover, she wants Frank to tell her father-in-law more dramatically that Mrs. Linh is having sex wildly with her young lover, and they are doing it joyfully, that Mrs. Linh always comes here. It is a pain that no one can heal if that person is not strong enough like Ha.

Hearing this room's yelling, screaming, and crying can make Ha satisfied and happy. She finally walks inside as if she is the mastermind of all the schemes from a movie. There should be music playing to make her entrance more grant.

Mr. Tan is shouting in Mrs. Linh's face. She is in bed, and her body is covered with the bedsheet. Next to her is Tony.

"You are a fucking whore. You're old, and you make all of these jokes, huh? Aren't you ashamed at all?"

Mrs. Linh keeps silent. What else can she say right now? Sorry? There is no chance that sorry could save her life. A woman with all of the traditional thoughts, with all the personality of an elegant lady, with respect from everyone. Now, she is nothing like a cunt who loved her job. The humiliation of her today would never be washed away. You deserve that, mother, Ha thinks. Thomas is standing in the corner of the room and doing nothing.

Mrs. Linh notices Ha is there. "You!" She speaks.

Then, everyone turns their looks at her.

"Ha, what are you doing here?" Mr. Tan asks.

"I am the person to know about this affair, dad. I told Frank to tell you about this."

"When did you know about this?" Mr. Tan asks.

"Just this morning. And just like you, I am shocked too."

"Do you know about this man?"

"No, I don't. But I know one thing for sure that this relationship has been happening for a long time before." Then, she turns to Mrs. Linh.

"What you said yesterday to outrage me for my affair, I think you should keep some for yourself too. You and I are nothing different."

Mrs. Linh bursts out crying. Her hands cross to beg. "Honey, please, I am wrong. I am so sorry. Please!"

"If there is nothing else to say, I leave. Please, shut the door and have conversations." Ha says and smiles, satisfied.

Ha leaves the room. Thomas runs after her.

"Ha, wait," Thomas holds her hand back. "I am so sorry. I know I mistreated you and did not care about your feelings. Now, I know about my mom, and she can no longer tell me what to do now. You are the only one I love, and I think I can still make it up to you, and we can be one family again." Thomas begins to cry.

Ha jerks her hand back. "Aww, that's so cute! But, fuck you. Never in my life have I seen you cry. Did you just read those words from a novel?" She laughs. "Everything is over. I am sick of you and your mom. I wish that you could say that before. I wish you could one time stand up for me in that house. It's over, Thomas. My lawyer will contact you soon. Bye."

Despite Thomas begging her to stay, Ha walks away without giving a damn about him. What has ended, let it stay like that.

In the car, Ha suddenly cries. She slaps the wheel many times and screams.

"Why are you crying?" Ha asks herself. "You must laugh. You must be happy. This is exactly what you want." She wipes the tear on her face and starts the car.

When she is ready to leave, Tony knocks on her car. Geez, he is like trash. He has lost all of the handsomeness in him. Mr. Tan has beaten him up badly.

Ha rolls down the window. She chuckles. "Are you happy?"

"Why?" Tony asks disappointedly. He must feel regret that he told Ha about this story. "Why did you do that to me? And how do you know about the whole thing between her and me?"

Ha turns off her car and gets out. "I saw the number on your phone this morning when I came into your office. It is my mom's phone number. I did not want to get into your private life, but there is something you should know about why I did it."

Ha grabs her purse. She gets out the makeup wipe and takes out one sheet. She wipes the makeup on her face in front of Tony. It shows some bruises on her face. Tony is frozen. He is shocked when seeing Ha's face.

"Oh my God, what happened to you?" Tony asks.

"This is why I did it," She points at her face. "Look what they have done to me. There are more on my body. My husband beat me up because he found out about my affair with another man, and my mother-in-law talked into my face with insulting words. She touched my mother. I will talk to you about that later. For all these years, I have lived in hell, Tony. You will never understand." Ha places her hand on Tony's left shoulder. "I don't blame you for what you did with my mother-in-law. You are just an outsider. Find somebody that is perfect for you. Ok? See you tomorrow at the firm."

Ha gets back into the car. Tony looks down at the car. "Ha, wait. You won't tell anyone about this, will you?"

"Don't worry! Your secret is safe with me." Ha says. "Oh, by the way, can you do me a favor?"

"Anything."

"Be my lawyer for my divorce. You trust only yourself. You are a good lawyer."

Then, Ha takes off.

Ha returns to Adam, where right now with her is the most peaceful place for her. She cannot wait to tell Adam what happened today. It's as if every good thing has come back to her.

Adam and Ha will have dinner tonight. Ha is so excited for tonight. At 7 p.m., Adam is sitting in the living room and drinking some alcohol. Ha, from behind, grabs him by the neck.

"Miss me?" Ha asks as she kisses Adam's head.

"Yes, I do," Adam says, but his tone is not so excited.

Ha sits on Adam's lap. "Babe, what happens? Is something wrong?"

"Not really. Michael just called me an hour ago. Do you know what day it is?"

Ha shakes her head.

"It is Phuong's birthday. And Michael calls me to come and join the birthday. At first, I denied it, but Michael was crying, and he insisted that I had to come. He has yet to learn about the divorce. I know we have dinner tonight. And I…»

Ha kisses on Adam's lips. "Go, babe. It will mean a lot to Michael. We can move the dinner to another day. There is still plenty of time."

Adam looks at Ha. "Are you sure? I don't want to upset you."

"And you don't want to upset Michael either, babe. Go."

"All right." Ha leaves Adam's lap for Adam to stand up. "I'll go." He embraces Ha's belly and kisses her. "I love you."

"I love you too."

Adam tends to leave the living room. But he stops. There is something that strikes him. "You know what. Maybe you and I will have dinner tonight. Come with me!"

Ha looks bewilder. "What are you talking about?"

"Phuong and I divorced. We were over. Then, I will only stay for a short time. I just came and said her happy birthday and left."

"What about Michael?"

"I will make an excuse. He will understand. Besides, you are the only one that I care about. I won't leave you alone."

"Oh, Adam." Ha hugs Adam. Adam lifts her and carries her upstairs. Just like a newly married couple.

At 8:00 p.m., Adam and Ha arrive Phuong's house. Ha never thinks she will return to this house one day. The house never changes.

She looks up to the second window to the left of the house. It was Phuong's room when she was in high school. Ha wonders whether Phuong is still in that room or not.

Back then, when Ha and Phuong were in high school, Ha often came here to play with Phuong every day after school or even slept over. They helped each other with homework, cooked, gossiped about boys at school, did makeup, and did all kinds of things that young girls did. Mrs. Nhu was so nice to her before. She even told Ha to call her mom because Ha and Mrs. Trang were like family members to Mrs. Nhu.

After everything, Ha is so ashamed when she thinks about coming here to visit Mrs. Nhu even though she desperately wants to see her. She must be so disappointed in Ha a lot. And so is Mrs. Trang, her mother.

"I will come back soon, ok?" Adam says.

"Take time."

Adam gets out of the car and comes into the house.

A few moments later, she hears the fight coming from the house. She walks out of the car and comes close to the home. But she does not go in there. She hears the fighting and the argument from Phuong, where she exposes the truth about Adam. Ha covers her mouth with her hands. Phuong's words start to get more crucial and more complex. Phuong is ready to tell everything. Then, Michael confronts his father, which is like a knife stabbed into Adam's heart and her heart. Before, she feels regrets after she had an affair with Adam. But now, everything with her is over. It's time to meet Phuong and Mrs. Nhu. Time to tell the story from her point of view.

Ha opens the door and comes in.

"You!" Phuong says when she sees her. Everyone looks at Ha just like her husband's family looked at her when Ha came in the middle of the drama this afternoon.

CHAPTER 11

Phuong and Ha

Every year, when it came to Thanksgiving, Adam and Phuong usually hosted the party and invited friends and family to come. Adam would cook the turkey and every food, baked cherry cake, became a bartender and decorated the table. Meanwhile, Phuong went shopping to buy stuff for her husband and helped him decorate. It was not exactly a tradition in their house. It was just an excuse for everyone to meet and get drunk: fun but tiring aftermath.

A week before Thanksgiving, Phuong and Adam went to Costco to buy food and drinks to prepare. They met Ha and Thomas were going shopping too. Phuong saw Ha, and she got excited. It had been a while since they had yet to meet each other. They hugged, and their husbands just watched them hugging.

"Oh my god, how are you?" Phuong said

"I am doing good. You look terrific." Ha said, even though she did not know what else to say.

Phuong looked at Thomas. "Hey Thomas, how have you been?"

"Hey, Phuong," Thomas shook her hand. "I am fine."

"How is the restaurant?"

"It is not my restaurant, but I am a sous chef now."

"Good for you! You are the best at cooking." Phuong turned to Ha and shoved her elbow to Ha. "We are lucky women to have a husband who is the best cook, right?"

"Babe," Adam finally said. "You're embarrassing me. Thomas is a great cook. I am just an average cook. How can I compare to him?" To Thomas. "You are the best, Tommy."

"It's Thomas. I don't like people calling me Tommy or Tom."

Adam felt more embarrassed but also felt weird. When he was in high school, he had a friend named Thomas and called him Tommy all the way. There was nothing. This guy was so severe.

"I am sorry. My husband did not know about that." Phuong hit her husband on his left shoulder. "Babe, be careful about what you say!"

"What are you guys shopping for?" Ha asked to change the subject.

"Well, Thanksgiving is coming. Adam and I go buying stuff to cook and decorate too." Suddenly, there is an idea popped up inside Phuong's mind.

"Hey, why don't you come to our Thanksgiving dinner? It will be great. We only invite a few people: just a few friends and my family. Adam's family can't enjoy themselves with us this year because they are on vacation. Please, don't say no."

"I'd love to. But," Ha turned to Thomas. "I don't know about Thomas. What do you think?"

She knew Thomas did not want to be disturbed on his day off. Besides, Thomas' family did not celebrate Thanksgiving because they were all traditional and old thoughts.

Thomas said. "We will be there. We'd love to join the dinner."

"Great. I will send you the invitation. See you on that day. Bye, guys!" They said goodbye and left.

"Babe, are you sure?" Ha asked Thomas.

"Yeah, it will be fun. It is my day off, and I want some fun."

Ha nodded her head. Maybe he wanted to relax. Let him rest in his way. But they did not know what would happen at that Thanksgiving dinner. Things were about to change forever.

Mrs. Linh woke up early that morning. She dressed up nicely and put on her expensive perfume. Ha went downstairs to make herself a cup of coffee. Today, Thomas and her would visit Ha's mother's grave. Thanksgiving with Ha was the opportunity to pay respect to all the people that she owed.

On the other hand, Thomas just wanted to spend his day at home and playing games. He hated to be annoyed on his day off. He wanted to rest and join Phuong and Adam's Thanksgiving dinner. But to keep his wife's mouth shut, he agreed to visit her mother's grave.

Ha saw her mother-in-law dressed up nicely. She felt so unusual. Mrs. Linh put on her lipstick and then fixed her dress.

"Mom, you look pretty today. Where are you heading to?"

"I am going to see a friend of mine. She just came back to town. So I want to spend a day with her."

"Is that so? I hope you will have a good time with your friend."

"I will."

Ha tended to go to the kitchen, and Mrs. Linh called her back.

"Ha, where are you and Thomas going today?" Mrs. Linh asked.

Ha smiled. "He and I will visit my mother's grave today. I want to bring her fresh flower and…."

"Do you know today is Thomas' day off?" Mrs. Linh jumped in Ha's mouth. "Why don't you leave him to rest? For God's sake, it is one hour's drive from here. If you want, you can go by yourself. Besides, I remember your mother's death anniversary was two months ago, and you missed her already?"

Ha felt disappointed and sad after what Mrs. Linh said.

Mrs. Trang was her mother. Her only mother. It was the duty of a daughter to be grateful to her mother. It was the love of a daughter giving to her mother. It was the respect of a daughter to pay for her mother. Ha was all alone after the death of her mother.

She remembered that after the funeral, Ha was depressed and always in a bad mood. She did not want to do anything. She held her mother's picture and cried all day and all night. Thomas heard her crying, and he could not sleep. He moved to another room. If he loved his wife, he must be there to comfort her, encourage her, and help her overcome the pain. But no, he just ignored her. One simple reason was that he did not like his mother-in-law because she always lectured him about being a perfect husband and keeping the family happy every time they met. She annoyed him. She said those things because she wanted him to be a good husband to her daughter. She understood what Ha had been going through in that family. With the same thought as Thomas that Ha was annoying the whole family with her crying, Mrs. Linh went into Ha's room to yell at her.

"Dead people could not come back to life. What are you crying for?

It has been days since your mother passed away. You are making Thomas, me, and your father uncomfortable with your sobbing. If you want to cry, go outside. Don't disturb people here!"

Mrs. Linh did not even say a nice word to Ha. She stopped on the way out. She turned her head—about 90 degrees. "Your mother is not the person you should grieve. You have Thomas, your husband; he is the only person you should care for and love. After you leave your mother to get married, you no longer belong to your mother. You belong to us. Stop crying for a person who is longer here."

Mrs. Linh had gone too far with what she had just said. After the door close, Ha grabbed the glass next to her and threw it at the wall. It broke into pieces. Then, she put the pillow over her face and screamed.

"I think I can visit my mom for a moment. I miss her, and besides, it has been a while since my husband did not come and visit her. My mom loved Thomas when she was alive." Ha said, although her handheld was tight.

"You are only good at making other people tired. Go home early for Thomas to rest!"

"Yes, mom"

Mrs. Linh left the house.

"*Dit*," Ha cried. It means *fuck* in English.

It was 5 p.m. Everything was ready.

The table was covered with a red sheet. In the center of the table, Phuong put a boutique of red roses she got from her garden and decorated it by herself. On this particular occasion like this, Phuong was so generous to display her favorite china, which she bought from Vietnam on her trip with her mother. They were so expensive because they came from a village in the North called "Bat Trang." And the drinkware, she used glasses imported from Italy. And silverware too. Phuong was so selective in using her stuff.

5:30, the guests started to come in. There were members of parent associations at Michael's school. Rachel came too because she was single and her family was not here with her. With Phuong, Rachel was like a sister to her. Each of them brought something. Some brought wines; some brought dessert. They all threw those stuff on the table in the living room. Adam pumped up the bouncing house for the children and his son to play without interrupting adults doing their business. Alcohol and adult stuff, of course. And also, they did not want the children to hear them curse.

Phuong was cutting the roasted beef. Rachel came in with two glasses of wine. She handed Phuong one.

"Those women over there make me sick to my stomach," Rachel said and pointed to a group of women standing, drinking, and eating next to the glass door on the way to the backyard. Those women were the lords of gossip in school.

"What happened?" Phuong took a sip of wine.

"All they talk about is school, children, and their husbands. I talk to them, and I don't have any fucking clue what they are saying."

"Me, either!"

"It looked very delicious," Rachel gave the compliment. "Adam is such a great cook."

"Thanks," Phuong took another sip of wine. She sighed. "Can you believe it? I spent hours decorating the dining room and the table, yet no one sat down and ate. Or using my china. They all use a paper plate."

Rachel laughed. She picked up a piece of roast beef with her hand and put it inside her mouth. "This one is good." She chewed and swallowed. "It is lucky for you. You don't need to wash those later."

"But..."

"Shut up," Rachel said. "This is your party. Cheer up and be nice."

"All right."

"Wait," Rachel realized something. "Where is your mom?"

Phuong wiped her hand with the white cloth on the table. "She will be here soon. She came out to see her friends. They had a meeting. I don't know." Phuong carried the tray of roasted beef. "Would you mind bringing the paper plate, please?"

Phuong carried the tray, and Rachel brought the plates, following her. They placed them on the table where those women were standing around.

"Enjoy, ladies," Phuong said.

They said thank you to Phuong and continued their conversation. Phuong and Rachel came to the dining room, and together, they enjoyed the food from Phuong's china collection.

Thomas came out of the bathroom after taking a shower. Ha was standing in front of the mirror to look over the black dress she bought in Bloomingdales the other day. She spun around for Thomas to see.

"What do you think, babe?" Ha asked delightfully.

But Thomas was not paying attention to her. He was busy choosing the perfect shirt for himself.

"Babe, look at me."

"WHAT?" Thomas got angry. He finally looked at Ha. "For the love of God, you are coming to a Thanksgiving dinner. Not a funeral. You look like a widow. Now, stop showing me your ass and help me to choose the shirt for tonight."

A husband who did not give a damn about his wife's ass. What kind of husband was that? Ha had been loving wearing black clothes for years. Other colors seemed so bright with her and did not honor her body. She had tried so hard not to get her belly getting fat. She understood that if she had the luck to have a child, she would get bigger and accept the truth. But not right now. Not a single chance.

Ha walked to her husband. Looking inside the closet, she took a blue navy polo from Ralph Lauren and tossed it hard into Thomas' face. She got irritated.

Thomas caught and frowned. "Hey, what is that attitude?" Thomas raised his voice.

Ha did not say anything. She slowly wore her diamond earrings. Then, she grabbed her purse from her make-up table and went to the door.

She turned back. "Hurry up, babe! We are late for the Thanksgiving dinner. That polo can help to hide your fat belly. You're welcome. I'll wait for you in the living room."

Ha turned the knob and left.

At about 6:00, Ha and Thomas arrived at Phuong's house. At the same time, Mrs. Nhu returned from meeting with her friends. Ha got out of the car. Mrs. Nhu was walking toward her with a young man. Ha was delighted when she met Mrs. Nhu, a close friend of Mrs. Trang when she was alive.

"Hi, Mom," Ha shouted.

"Oh, Ha." Mrs. Nhu walked faster and hugged Ha when she came to her. "Sweetie, how are you? It has been a long time since I have not met you. I miss you so much."

"I miss you too," Ha said. She held Mrs. Nhu's arms. "I am so busy that I don't have time to do anything else. I often wanted to visit you, but I could not find one second. I am so sorry."

Mrs. Nhu waved her hand. "That's ok, dear. I can understand. It is because we don't have that fate to meet. Now, we do. I was so excited when Phuong invited you to the dinner" Mrs. Nhu turned her look to Thomas. "This must be Thomas."

"Oh yes," Ha let go of Mrs. Nhu, and she put her hands around Thomas, who did not hold out hands to grab Ha's belly. "My husband, Thomas." To Thomas. "Babe, this is Mrs. Nhu. You remember her, right?"

Thomas smiled. "Yes, I remember." To Mrs. Nhu. "How do you do?"

"I am doing fine. How are your parents?"

"They are still ok."

"That is perfect. At this age, we don't want anything but good health."

"I agree."

The young man behind Mrs. Nhu was still standing and saw the three of them having a small reunion. He put his hands inside his coat's pocket. Ha looked at the young man. She asked Mrs. Nhu who it was. Mrs. Nhu turned back and introduced the young man. He was Hoa, a son of her friends. He was a senior in a university in journalism major. Hoa got an internship for a local newspaper and, after graduating, he would work there.

After Mrs. Nhu introduced Hoa, they all went inside the house.

A few guests had left because they were busy with Black Friday, a momentous event with them. Hearing the door, Phuong walked out of the dining room, where she was enjoying her china with Rachel and some girls.

Phuong came out with a cheer on her face. She had a few drinks and was probably a little bit drunk. Her right hand was still holding a glass of red wine. She hugged Ha tight.

"You guys had come. I am so glad." Phuong said. "Why did you come so late?"

"Uhm," Ha said. "I had some....»

"Thomas, hey." Phuong let go of Ha without letting her finish the sentence. She hugged Thomas. "Welcome to my house."

Suddenly, Phuong was overjoyed, and she spilled some wine behind Thomas and hit on Hoa's t-shirt. Mrs. Nhu shook her head.

"PHUONG!" Mrs. Nhu said in a high voice. "What are you doing?"

Instead of getting panicked and finding something to wipe off the wine spill, Phuong laughed out loud.

"Oh, come on. There is nothing so serious, Mom." Phuong said and turned to Hoa, whom she did not have any idea who he was. "I will get you a shirt of my husband. No worry. If you want, I can give you the phone number of the best laundry store in the town." Turning to Mrs. Nhu again. "Mom, why don't you get a shirt for him, and I will take Ha and Thomas to the kitchen."

"What?" Mrs. Nhu said.

Hoa smiled. "That's fine. I don't....."

"Anyway," Phuong turned to her notable guests. "Come on in. The food is getting cold. But my husband can make it warmer."

Ha, and Thomas followed Phuong to the kitchen. Mrs. Nhu and Hoa were left alone in the hall. Mrs. Nhu sighed.

"Sometimes I just wished my daughter could calm herself down." Mrs. Nhu said.

"I think she is fine. She is just getting excited." Hoa said.

Mrs. Nhu took Hoa upstairs to find him a shirt to wear.

In the kitchen, Adam was making himself a drink. His friends had left an hour ago. Phuong, Thomas, and Ha came in.

"Babe, Ha, and Thomas are here," Phuong said.

Adam put down his drink. "Hey, you guys."

"Hi, Adam," Ha said.

"Hi," Adam said.

"Please, enjoy the food," Phuong said I'll hope you love it."

Thomas and Ha looked at the food, where there were not so many. But still, they looked delicious. They ate and talked in the dining room—a cozy and full dinner.

At 7:30, Rachel had to leave because she was also crazy about the Black Friday sale. The rest were staying in the dining room and talking about all kinds of stuff about this world. From politics to entertainment. From trending events to daily life. Everyone except Adam left the room half hour ago. Ha felt so bored because she had no idea what they were talking about. It was Ha who did not use any social media platform, who did not update any news from the outside world than the laws of the U.S. Her husband, on the other hand, knew all the things in this world because he worked in the restaurant where he was around with tons of gossip people.

Ha had for herself an excuse. "Can I use your restroom?"

Phuong said. "Sure. It is on the second floor." Phuong turned to everyone at the table. "Can you believe this house does not even have a bathroom on the first floor? No wonder why it is cheaper than other houses in the neighborhood." Then, she turned back to Ha. "Do you need me to show you?"

Ha waved her hand. "That's fine. I can look for it by myself."

Ha left the dining room to go upstairs.

In the dining room, Phuong and the rest were still talking. She saw there was no more wine on the table, as well as no food.

"Let me get more wine and dessert." She said, even though she was so drunk right now. "I have fruits, and then we have to continue the topic with Trump."

"Babe, I don't think you should drink more. Besides, it is kind of late. Thomas and Ha are probably tired." Mrs. Nhu said.

"Oh no, I am fine," Thomas said. "I don't mind. It has been a long time since I have not had so much fun like this."

"That's the spirit!" Ha tapped on Thomas' left shoulder. "I will get some more. Excuse me!"

"I will help you." Hoa offered.

"Sure," Phuong said.

Mrs. Nhu and Thomas were the only two in the dining room. Mrs. Nhu smiled.

"My daughter is always like that. She never knows how to stop herself."

"She is the best hostess ever. I think she had handled this dinner pretty well."

"That is very nice of you to say so." Mrs. Nhu said. "Oh, by the way, since I am talking to the most famous chef, maybe you can share some secret recipes with me if you don't mind."

"Well," Thomas said. "Normally, I won't share any recipes with anyone. But I can make some exceptions today because I am sitting in front of a beautiful woman like you."

"Oh, you," Mrs. Nhu was embarrassed but liked it. She wanted people who told her beautiful. Then, she asked him how to make this food or that food. They share and talk about food.

Meanwhile, in the kitchen, Hoa was helping Phuong with the fruits. Phuong was looking at the wine case to choose the wine.

"Have you chosen the good wine yet?" Hoa asked while she was cutting the apple.

"I don't know." She said. "Everything is so good to me. I want to pour all of them inside a pitch and drink them all."

They both laughed. Ha picked a bottle of French red wine and showed it to Hoa. He nodded slightly. She put the wine down on the table. She was impressed by the way Hoa decorated the fruit dish. It was in a phoenix shape.

"You have an excellent hand in decorating." Phuong praised.

"Thanks. One of my friends taught me that." Hoa wiped his hands.

"Can you help me to open this bottle?" Phuong handed him the cork screwer.

"Sure."

Phuong looked at Hoa twisting the cork screwer. She started to catch stories to talk to him.

"How do you know my mother?" Phuong asked.

Hoa smiled. "She was one of my mom's friends. I think they have known for a long time."

Phuong nodded. Hoa finally opened the wine. Phuong poured out some wine into the glass. She drank. And poured Hoa a glass.

"Are you still in college right now?"

"Senior year."

"What major?"

"Journalism.»

"You must be good at English, hah? I hate English and other social subjects back in the day. I only loved to study science."

"That's why you are a doctor right now."

"Yes," Phuong said. "But thanks to hating English, I met a guy who is now my husband. He helped me a lot in that fucking subject back then."

"You must love him a lot."

"Every single piece of him."

They took another sip of wine and poured more without remembering they must bring the wine and fruits to the dining room where Mrs. Nhu and Thomas were talking about food.

"Do you have a lover?" Phuong asked.

"No, I don't."

"Really?" Phuong was surprised because with a pretty face like Hoa, and the voice was so sweet. North Vietnam accent. "Are you kidding me?"

"I won't lie to you."

"Woah, you must be very selective."

"Or I am lazy to look for a girl."

They laughed.

"You have a North Vietnam accent. Are your parents from the North?"

Hoa shrugged. "I don't know. I guessed so."

"You don't live with your parents?"

"Yes, I do. But..." Hoa paused.

Phuong looked at him. "But, what?"

"But I don't live with my real parents. I was adopted."

"Oh, sorry to hear about that."

"That's fine! I don't..."

"So anyway," Phuong cut him off. She was so drunk. "Have another drink. Your glass is empty."

She poured another drink for herself and ran Hoa another one. Hoa pretended to drink; then, he poured another glass when Phuong did not notice. He felt a little awkward with what was happening right now. He got stuck with a drunk lady.

"Where is your son?". Hoa just asked randomly, and it did not relate to the kitchen.

"He went to his friend's house for a sleepover," Phuong said. "He was here previously. Why?"

"Nothing. I am just curious."

Then, there was silence. They fell into an awkward situation. What to say right now? Suddenly, something popped into Phuong's mind.

"Do you want to see my collection?" Phuong asked Hoa.

"What collection?" Hoa asked.

"My china collection."

"Sure."

They walked to the living room. Phuong turned on the light of the shelf, which contained all the china dishes, bowls, and teacups inside, and they were locked. Hoa was amazed by this collection. He had heard about china stuff before, but this was the first time he could see them in real life.

"They are so beautiful!" Hoa said.

"Thank you so much." Phuong opened the shelf. "I got all of them on the trip to Vietnam. They are from Bat Trang, a village in North Vietnam."

"Why do you love them so much?"

Phuong took out a dish with a dragon and a phoenix pattern. Both were flying around the moon in the center of the world. She handed it to Hoa.

"Look at this. This is one of my favorites." Phuong said. "Do you know why?"

Hoa shook his head.

"Dragon and Phoenix in Fengshui mean the combination of yin-yang, happy marriage, good fortune, and peaceful life. It is like my family right now. It reminds me of what I have today because I am living a life without any regrets. I have a husband who loves me; I have a son who is good and nice; I have a mother who always cares for me. I am blessed with everything, and I am forever grateful. When I feel down and irritated, I look at this dish or other china stuff on this shelf."

Hoa smiled. "You are so lucky. I wish I could find love for myself soon."

"When the time comes, you will have. Let me tell you something," Phuong sat on the couch next to the shelf. "I don't mean to lecture you here. If you can understand what I will say, it will be great. If you don't, maybe I am too drunk."

"Don't worry. I am always listening."

"My relationship with Adam was up and down all the time. We fought, we argued, and we dissed each other. There was a time I wanted to leave him, you know. I want to rescue myself from this relationship. I want to go somewhere far away. I want to have some time for myself to think.

But then there was something that kept me staying. My son, Michael. I realized that we still have Michael. We love him with all of our hearts. Michael is like an invisible string that attaches both Adam and me. Then, we find ways to solve the problems and be happy again. You know, I need Adam, and I love him. Our fates belong to each other. I cannot leave him, or he cannot leave me.

"What I am trying to say is when fate is being sent to us, whether you want it or not, you still have to accept it. It will go even if you try to make it stay when fate is over. So you don't need to worry about the love of your life. It will come soon. When it comes, and you are not ready, believe me, you will be so shocked and so tired. So, you must always be ready." Phuong gave out her hand. "Pull me up."

Hoa pulled Phuong up. She stood but was not steady. She almost felt. "Woah," Hoa exclaimed. "Are you ok? Do you need me to take you to your room?"

"No, I am good," Phuong said, and she grabbed Hoa's shoulders. Her head was placed on Hoa's chest. "You will find yourself the true love."

Hoa got goosebumps. He did not know what was happening. Phuong then did not say anything or respond. Hoa looked at Phuong. She was passed out. Maybe she was too drunk. Hoa put Phuong down on the couch. He ran his fingers through her hair to see her face. He sighed.

"Sleep well," Hoa said. He put the china back where it belonged, closed the shelf, and turned off the light.

Hoa returned to the dining room. Mrs. Nhu and Thomas were still discussing food recipes and writing them down on the note.

"Mrs. Nhu," Hoa said. Mrs. Nhu looked at him. "I have to take off right now."

Mrs. Nhu stood up. "You leave? Why don't you stay longer?"

"I would love to, but I have important things to do tomorrow."

"Oh, I see. Thank you for taking me here and coming here today. I hope you enjoyed the dinner." Mrs. Nhu said. "Oh, what am I saying? I am not the host. My daughter and my son-in-law must be the people who say that. Where is she anyway?"

"She passed out in the living room."

"Oh my God," Mrs. Nhu covered her mouth with her hands. "Is she ok?"

"She's fine," Hoa said. "She was too drunk. Maybe later, Adam can bring her to the room."

"I can never understand her." Mrs. Nhu said in a disappointed voice. "Why she always sobbed like that?"

"That's ok, Mrs. Nhu. Today is Thanksgiving. She should have fun a little bit." Hoa checked his phone and said goodbye to Mrs. Nhu and Thomas. Then, he took off.

Ha put on some lipstick and her foundation. *"What a stupid dinner,"* Ha said to herself. Then, Ha came out of the bathroom. She usually was not a curious person who wanted to go to the house of someone to look around because it was so weird and impolite. But this was Phuong's house, and Phuong was her best friend (if she thought that way). They had a beautiful place. Ha could take around to see how this house was decorated. Then, she could apply it to her home. Of course, everything must be gone through the acceptance of the evil queen in the house. Mrs. Linh.

Ha walked into Michael's room. The whole room was covered with blue color and white cloud details. It was like a big blue sky. The ceiling had a giant sun in the middle. The room looked neat, creative, and childish. But it was a big mess when she came in. Toys were all over the floor, blankets and pillows were not folded, and clothes were thrown everywhere in this room. Ha could not understand why it could happen in this house. And yet, it gave Ha a sense of sadness because she had not had a child. She always wanted to decorate her child's room one day, all by herself. But until now, she had nothing. Thinking on the positive side, this room gave her hope. A hope to have a child soon.

She continued her journey. Now, she walked straight to the room at the end of the hall. She pushed the door to come. The first thing that came directly to her was the sense of space. The lavender. It made her feel so relaxed and so sensations. She walked around the room to see, and the thing that caught her eye the most was Phuong's makeup table. She wanted to see what kind of makeup or skincare brands Phuong used. It was nothing so special. Phuong just used brands exactly like what Ha was using at home. But different functions.

"Let's get out of here," Ha said.

But when she tended to leave, she heard the music coming from somewhere. Ha tried to look for it and found out the music was coming from the balcony behind the curtain. That was strange! She did not hear the music in the first place when she walked in.

Ha walked to the balcony, and Adam sat on a chair, smoking and chilling.

"Hi," Ha said to Adam.

It startled him a little. As a quick reflex, Adam bruised the cigarette into the glass ashtray placed on the little table next to him. He stood up.

"Please, don't tell my wife about this! She hates when I smoke and will kill me if she finds out." Adam said.

Ha laughed. "Well," She started to come up with an idea to play with him a little bit. "What will you do to pay me off to keep this secret?"

Adam scratched his head. This was the first time he got into a difficult situation like this. He was always the person who controlled the game. Being caught in the middle of the fun could never make him feel comfortable. He felt annoyed in many different ways. He first masturbated when he was 16 and was caught by his mother as she came in to tell him the dinner was ready. He then smoked pot and was caught by his father. Damn, he hated that so much. He had escaped the feed to be alone here to smoke.

Adam knew he could not reason with Ha over this whole thing because she was a lawyer.

"I don't know," Adam shrugged. "What do you want?"

Ha smiled and pointed at the cigarette pack on the table. "Give me one."

Adam looked at where she pointed. He picked up and popped out a cigarette. Ha took it by her mouth. Adam lighted up.

"You smoke too?" Adam asked.

"Not in a while." Ha leaned forward onto the marble balcony. "Why aren't you downstairs with everyone?"

Adam groaned. "I hate those parties."

"Why? You've cooked so well."

"Because I have to. My wife always loves big parties. She always invites many people to join. More people, more fun. I hate to be around so many people like that."

"Me neither."

The cold breeze covered the night, but it was cool. Stars were shining, and the moon was bright.

"It is such a lovely night. It is not the night you can always enjoy." Ha blew out a line of smoke.

Adam looked at Ha curiously. He did not feel the same as Ha felt. He just sighed.

"I don't see that," Adam said.

Ha turned to Adam. "You are such an emotionless person. Let's be real. How long have you not felt the beauty of life?"

Adam looked bewildered. "What do you mean?"

Ha smoked in and exhaled the smoke. "Like this. Smoking and enjoying the night. It was relaxing and escaping the reality of life. It is a gift, you know. You're married, and sometimes..." Ha got close to Adam, pressed her finger to Adam's chest, and said in a low voice. "You feel trapped inside a cage and want to get out. Your heart is trapped."

Adam sat up straight and looked at Ha. He seemed like he had understood what she had just said. "Continue."

"Continue what?"

"What you are saying," Adam said. He put down the cigarette on the ashtray. "You said we were trapped inside the cage and wanted to get out. What do you do to get out? Do you fight? Or do you wait to be released?"

It was a funny question, yet, it was very tricky too. She was fighting or being released. Her marriage life had been a shit hole because Mrs. Linh's prejudice and hatred were over her and the ignorance of Thomas for her. She felt isolated in that house. She could never do anything that she wanted. She did not have a voice or her opinion. Sometimes, she reflected on her life before she got married. How great it was! How wonderful it was! How glorious it was!

Now, she was nothing like a little maid inside the hands of devious owners. Once she messed up, the owners would punish her in all the ways they could. Indeed, Ha had scars on her. Not physically. But inside her soul. Her friends used to say, "Girl, you should go and check in with a medium because some dangerous spells might have voodooed you,"; or "If you leave a life like that, please, get a divorce." Ha just laughed about getting over it. She could not do anything else but be submissive. She thought about her marriage because she hoped it would work out. If saying she fought for her freedom was right in some parts. She had tried. She wanted to return to her mother-in-law, using all her strength to fight back. But fuck me, why didn't she have the gut to do it?

Waiting to be released might be the only way.

"I have no idea," Ha said.

"But you just said…."

"I know. But I don't know what to do in that situation." Ha blew out some smoke. Her cigarette was halfway done.

Adam did not usually talk to someone about their feelings because it so sucked and so weeping. He hated it. But Adam could sense something in Ha. Something was terrible, taboo, and unhappy. She needed someone to talk to.

"Is there something wrong with you?" Adam asked as he stood up.

Ha sighed. She looked at the night sky with shining stars and a bright moon. The moon's light shined down, and it could reveal anything—even the most profound secret. Confess, Ha, confess. The moon was the judge, and Adam here was the jury.

Her hands had some dropped tears. She wept and wiped it with her hand. Adam stood up and got next to her. He smoothed her.

"Hey, hey. Are you ok?" Adam asked.

Ha cried out loud. She put her head into Adam's chest as if he were a close person she could trust. Adam's hands were up, and he got frozen. Ha placed her hands on his chest at the same time.

"What life am I living right now? I don't feel happy at all with my life. I feel empty."

Adam still needed to figure out what he had to do next. Please, he thought, don't do this. You have to stop. All right, he had no choice. He hugged her back. Tight. Just like that, Ha stopped crying. She looked up. Adam's face was like a male Greek statue. It was so perfect and so charming.

"Kiss me," Ha said (*whether she was drunk or not*).

"What?" Seriously, what the fuck was going on? In just a second, Ha had lost her mind already. Adam was uncomfortable. He let Ha out of him. She chuckled. "Oh, no, no, no. I can't do this. I'm afraid that's not right."

Ha did not care. She came back to Adam. She put her arms around

Adam's neck. She kissed him on the lips. A few seconds later, she let him out. She smiled. "That is what I need."

Ha embraced herself. Suddenly, she realized that she was a little overreacting. Not a little, so much overreacting. "Oh my God, what have I done? I am so sorry. I should go."

But no. Adam pulled her hand back and kissed her. Oh damn! This whole weird situation had turned worse. And just like that, they kissed. They kissed as if they had never kissed in their lives. They kissed as if Thomas and Phuong had never existed. They kissed as if that was the last thing they could do on this earth. They spun around, and finally, they stopped at the chair. Ha stopped. She looked at Adam, and for a moment, she could feel the love, the warmth, and the happiness all over again. For Adam, he could find himself again when he was with Ha.

Both had had feelings for each other since then. They began the relationship without feeling guilty. The affair was burning up fast and hot. From the hotels to Adam's house. They finally could live true-self when they fucked. The experience could have lasted longer. There was a saying, "A needle in the bag would come out."

It was out.

Being caught in the middle of the affair had made Ha and Adam shameful. But no regrets. Ha chose to be quiet and left. Phuong was sitting in the living room. She had not cried yet because that was Phuong. A strong woman. She never called for something that was not worth her tear. She saved it for the perfect time.

Adam walked into the living room. He went to the minibar and poured himself a glass of brandy. He sat down in front of Phuong, who was looking down, her fingers crossed to hold her head. Adam enjoyed the drink while looking at his wife. What an asshole! Cheating behind your wife, and he acted as if nothing had happened. This was the man that Phuong got married to. A liar. A dick. A cheater.

"Are you going to say something?" Adam said, although he knew whatever he said right now was meaningless. "If you are not going to say anything, I will say. Yes. I love Ha. I am sorry for letting you see that. You have the full right to be angry with me. But before you do it, I want to say Ha has no faults in this whole thing. I had felt on her first, and we hooked up."

Just stop right there. The more he said, the more he could show how he treated his wife. It was Ha who kissed him first, and then they hooked up. So Ha was a slut in this situation. A husband stealer. No, one word in Vietnamese can be used in this situation. A new term that Vietnamese teenagers think of. Tuesday, meaning the third person jumps into a relationship and messes up everything. It is like a parasite (deadly parasite).

Phuong turned up her head. She threw her handbag hard, which hit her china collection shelf. Luckily, it was shaken a little bit but not dropped anything inside.

"How could you do this to me? I love you, and I trust you," Phuong said. "I never do anything to make you sad. I always try to be a good wife and a good mother. Everything I did is because of you, yet you sleep with her? What the fuck is wrong with you? You sick fuck!"

Adam put down the glass on the table. He stood up. "You want to know why? Fine. Here's why. It is because of you. You are the reason why I did what I did."

"Me?" Phuong stood up and pointed at herself. "Why?"

"Yes, it is you. You know what you did?" Adam wiped his face and pointed his finger at Phuong. "You ignored me. You don't love me like you used to. You work all the time, you go out with your colleagues and party with them, you host every party for no reason, and I am always the person who is behind your shadow. You don't even care about what I think or how I feel. Whenever I want you to spend a day, a night, or just one hour with me, you always say I am busy, have a job, and have to join my friend. Do you know how lonely I am when I sleep, and no wife is lying next to me? Or do you know how desperate I am when you treat me like a normal husband? It hurts, Phuong. Of course, I understand that because you are the dean, you have to be with them. I am just a normal guy who works normal jobs," Adam sighed. "I need you to be my wife. MY WIFE. Not anyone's wife. You are perfect; you are respected; you are outstanding. And I am lost in your world. I don't even know who I am in this world anymore. I need to be released from it. Ha is there for me when I need someone, and she is the one who rescued me. And I love her. When I am with her, I feel safe; I feel love; I feel I am reborn again. She gives me things that I want and things that I lose. I need her."

I need her. That sounded awful, coming from the mouth of a cheating husband. His wife was here in front of him and was shocked after she discovered the affair and caught them. It had added more to Phuong's rage. She sniffed and sobbed. The tear had finally come down and run through her cheek. "Why don't you tell me before? Why do you keep all these secrets and then reveal them to me today?"

"Were you there to listen to me?"

"I could have been there for you to listen. I could have been a better wife if you had told me. If you had told me, I could have stopped you from being an asshole. I am still your wife, Michael's mother. I deserve to know everything from my husband." Phuong yelled out loud.

"Don't you hear yourself a little bit?" Adam said as he picked up his glass to finish the rest of the brandy. "You are being contradicted by what you said. You don't even give me time to talk to you. Not a single second."

"Ok, I admit I did not care for you like I used to. I can try, you know. I can try to be a better wife and love you more. With all the hustle and bustle outside, I have no choice but to join that flow. You think I don't want to quit it to come home with you and Michael to have dinner with you or watch movies together, or normally have a good time with my husband. I want it so much. I am craving that. But I can't. If I sacrifice my job for my own happiness, who will be there to save all the patients waiting for me? Who will be there to lead my team to operate the surgery? I can't do that, Adam. You know it more than anyone. That is what I hope. Hoping my husband can understand me without thinking bad about me." She paused to sob. "But I was wrong when I think like that. Do you know what the best stress cure for me is? This home is where a husband cooks for me and makes me happy; there is a son who always laughs and is good at school. I do care for this family, Adam. I care in my way. And yet, you blamed me for everything. Marriage is about understanding and compromising. You cannot expect me or us like we used to be when we were a newlywed couple. That's selfish, Adam. You betrayed me." Phuong came near Adam and banded onto his chest multiple times. "YOU BETRAYED ME, YOU FUCKING ASSHOLE. How could you do that to me? How could you?"

Phuong screamed, cried, and broke down. She slowly fell to Adam's feet. Adam was upset too. He was thinking how selfish he was and how terrible he was when he did not understand his wife for so many years married.

Regret. It was not correct because the love for Phuong had died, died a long time that Adam could not remember when. Adam understood what his wife had felt for all these years. It was not the same as he thought. It was a huge difference. Adam thought for himself only, his feeling. Phuong cared for this family, for this marriage, and feared it might be lost. Now, it was true. It had rotten to the core when the whole affair began.

Did Adam not say anything? Because what else could he say right now?

Outside, the rain kept pouring hard. It was like the end of a relationship that used to be happy and thought to last forever. In the future, the rain would follow the flow of water on the road and drain down to the sewage. Adam looked at his watch. It was 2:30. It was time to pick up Michael. Today, Phuong must pick him up because they will see the doctor today.

"Listen, we both made mistakes in life. We fucked up hard. But I still have Michael. So, think for him." Adam cleared his throat. "I will pick him up and take him to the doctor. I can see that you don't want to do it." He got out of the living room. But he stopped in front of the door and said without turning back. "If you want, I won't come home tonight. I will stay in a motel. The house is yours."

Then, Adam took off.

The whole house was quiet again. Phuong was alone on the floor. The tears had stopped. She stood up slowly and walked to the minibar. Yes, she needed a drink right now. She must get drunk to forget. But how could she do that? It still appeared inside her head and spun around. It was like mocking her, telling her how stupid she was when she did not know how to keep her husband, how idiot she was when she let her husband put a giant horn on her head like that. They fucked on her bed. They might fucked everywhere in this house. Even the chair that she was sitting on. They might have laughed at Phuong out loud for her stupidity and naivety. Adam had felt the hot and sexy body of Ha, and Ha had touched his penis and did a blowjob to him. Oh, yes, yes! They had made a big play in front of her to tell Phuong that she was a big fucking loser. HAHAHAHAHA!

"STOP IT," Phuong screamed, and in an instant rage, she threw the glass into the china shelf. The glasses on the shelf broke and fell on the floor. The china dishes and china tableware together were falling and breaking. Some were still on the shelf.

Her favorite china dish with the pattern of Phoenix and Dragon flying around the moon had broken. The Dragon piece was on one side, and the Phoenix piece was on another side. But the moon had broken in half. This marriage had broken into pieces without gluing back.

CHAPTER 12

Ha and Phuong

Moving around to different places was something that Phuong got used to with it. One of the reasons Phuong and her mother moved around a lot was the rent cost. For some reason, it always went up, and once it went up, they would not be able to pay. Mrs. Nhu worked in the restaurant 6 days a week and Phuong worked at a swap meet on the weekend. And yet, it was still not enough for them to pay the rent, only enough for eating or buying essential stuff for the family.

Finding a cheap house to rent was always tricky because mostly when the advertisements in the newspaper came out, everyone would jump onto the phone, dial, and call. Some people got lucky in the first place and got the house. Some people aren't fortunate. For example, Mrs. Nhu had called so many landlords with an affordable house, but they only said. "I'm sorry. Someone has already rented it." Of course, she felt sad, but she never gave up hope.

One day, while working in the restaurant, one of her co-workers was having a break. She read the newspaper and immediately saw there was a house for rent. She ran directly into the kitchen and told Mrs. Nhu to call. Mrs. Nhu did it, and just like a miracle, the house was still available. She left her job behind and drove immediately to that house. The landlord of that house was lovely and understood the circumstance of Mrs. Nhu and her daughter. He decided to lower the rent a little bit for them and told them that they needed anything, so don't hesitate to ask him.

Two weeks later, Mrs. Nhu and Phuong settled in a new place. Parallel with that, Phuong had to move to another high school. At first, moving around made Phuong feel so annoyed because she had to meet new people in new schools, which tortured her every time. But soon, she found out she had to deal with that, and finally, she learned how to accept it.

In this new school, on her first day, she went to an English class. Since she was new to the type, her English teacher, Mr. West, asked her to introduce herself in front of the course. Oh my God, she despaired it so much. So, she stood up, but her head was down. She was afraid to look at everyone's eyes who were looking at her like some new piece had been found in a tiny voice. "Hello, my name is Phuong. I...I...I am new to this school. I just moved to this city w-w-with my mom. Thank you!" Then, she quickly came back to her seat and stayed quiet. Mr. West is surprised because he has not asked anything about her or told her that she could return to her heart. But he still had the class to teach, so he ignored it.

When Mr. West was teaching, a student came in with a note in his hands. He gives Mr. West and leaves. He looked at the message. It said, "PHUONG NGUYEN COMES TO K-12 TO DO THE PLACEMENT TEST". So, every new student to the school, especially if English was their second language, must take the placement test to put the students in the classes that fit them. Phuong had submitted her education report from her previous school, but they still required her to do the placement test. She had done the test for English, and because her overall score was ok, not the best and they placed her into this class where she learned about literature (Shakespeare, Anglo-Saxon). Phuong got into many difficulties that she had to overcome.

Now she had to do the Math test. Mr. West tells her to come to K-12 to do the test. She packed up and came to Mr. West to take the note. He asked her whether she knew where K-12 was. She shook her head. Mr. West smiled. "That's ok! I will send somebody to go with you, ok?". She nodded slightly.

Mr. West called a girl sitting in the second row discussing work with her friends. "Ha, can you take Phuong to K-12, please?"

That was Ha, a girl with red hair. Ha looked up. "Right now? But I am doing work with my friends."

"It won't take long.",

"Ok, Mr. West." Ha stood up. She walked to Phuong, and she went with her to K-12.

On the way to K-12, they didn't talk about anything, making Ha uncomfortable. She looked at Phuong, who looked so weird and so shy. She only looked down. Her long hair covered her face. Ha took a deep breath and started the conversation.

"When did you come to the U.S.?"

No answer.

What the fuck? Is this girl deaf or something? Ha thought. She asked Phuong again. Louder. But no, Phuong did not answer. Phuong was not deaf. She was just too shy to reply. Her mouth was being sewn together. Phuong did not know the girl next to her was a big sister who, on the one hand, had taken down the most famous group in this school. People who hated her will fear her. People who liked her would consider her a good friend or a queen. The thing that Phuong did not answer made Ha herself stronger.

Ha walked in front of her and stopped. Phuong overlooked that, and she hit Ha. Phuong tried to walk away, but Ha stopped her. Ha held Phuong's shoulders and looked straight into Phuong's face.

"That is so disrespectful!" Ha confronted Phuong. "When I ask you, or anyone asks you something, look at them, open your fucking mouth, and talk. Do you understand?"

Ha did not know that what she said had made Phuong more anxious, and she was ready to cry. Ha looked at Phuong's face, which was blushing, and tears were about to come out of her eyes. She had no idea how to make a person stop crying or another way to say she hated being in drama.

"Oh God," Ha exclaimed. "All right, I am sorry. Let's go to K-12."

When they arrived, Ha showed Phuong the way in, and then Ha left. On returning to class, Ha could not wait to tell her friends about this weird girl.

In the 5th period, Phuong had a P.E. class. She walked into the locker room. The room was loud. The girls were talking and cursing at each other. Phuong did not like it at all. She preferred quiet. So there it was the office of the P.E. teacher. The office was open, but Phuong still knocked on the door to show him politely.

The teacher was sitting on her hands; she was holding the "Rosemary's

Baby" book by Ira Levin and reading it. Because she had the book covering her face, Phuong could not see what she looked like. But the teacher was so focused that she did not notice the appearance of Phuong there.

Knocking over three times but finding nothing, Phuong decided to walk inside. She banged on the wooden desk, and immediately, the teacher dropped the book on the floor as if the police ordered the suspect to put down the gun. Phuong chuckled a little bit. The teacher breathed heavily and brought herself back to normal.

She smiled. "Hi there," she said, "I am so sorry I did not see you there and let you see me reading....this book."

With Phuong, it was nothing. "That's fine! I don't mind about that", Phuong said, "Do you like the book?"

The teacher bent down and picked up the book. "Well, I am just curious about the book, so I bought it. It turns out it is good. So," The teacher sat still on the chair. She put her hands on the table and intertwined her fingers. "How can I help you today?"

Phuong looked at the schedule to see the name of the teacher. Joyce Gavin. "Yes, I am the new student. My name is Phuong Nguyen. Are you Mrs. Joyce Gavin?"

"I'm sorry, what?" Joyce asked because she did not understand what Phuong was saying in this tiny voice. It was like she had not opened her mouth to talk. "Can you repeat, please?"

"I am a new student here," Phuong improved a little.

Joyce smiled. "That's better! Welcome to my class," Joyce said as she raised his hands as if she wanted to hug John. "You just moved here?"

"Yes," Phuong said, "I moved here yesterday with my mom."

"Yesterday? And today you've gone to school already? That's amazing!" Joyce pushed out her chair and stood up. "Mostly, they will spend time settling down, and one week later, they can begin to go to work or school."

Phuong did not say anything.

Joyce walked to the drawer next to the window heading to the locker room. She opened the drawer. "You know," Joyce continued. "Students and teachers here are super nice. You can befriend them in this school. I can promise that. They will help you out." Joyce takes out a package in a plastic bag. It is a P.E. uniform. "What size are you, Phuong?"

"Small," Phuong said.

Sam looked at the package. It was Medium. "We don't have Small. Maybe Medium can fit you. Is it ok?" Joyce handed Phuong the box.

"It is fine," Phuong said, "It fits me."

"Good. By the way, do you have a locker with you today?" Joyce asked. Phuong shook her head. "Not yet."

Joyce turned to the drawer, took out a locker, and handed it to Phuong. "Take that. I give it to you."

Phuong was surprised. "Uh... Thank you." In a small voice, of course. Phuong looked at it and turned back to Joyce. "Are you sure?" She was still confused.

"Yeah, take it," Joyce said. She came to the door to the locker room. "Consider it as my welcome gift to you." Joyce waved her left hand briefly to instruct Phuong to come with her. "Let me show you your locker, and then we can start the class. I don't want to be late for class. So hurry up."

Joyce walked Phuong through the locker room. The students saw Joyce and said, "Hello Coach"; "How do you do, Coach?"; "Hi Coach!"

Joyce turned left to the last locker row. "By the way, I coach the soccer team, and all the students call that. If you don't like to call me coach, that's fine! Just call me Mrs. Gavin. I don't push my students. So don't worry about that."

They stopped at a locker—number 231. The vault was covered with black and a little rusty. "This will be your locker; of course, you've already had the lock. Use it and remember the code. I won't remember it for you. Don't forget that!" Joyce said. "Change your clothes and be ready. The class will start in about 15 minutes."

"Yes," Phuong said.

Joyce left Phuong and went away. Phuong opened the lock and looked at the code. 358. "Turning the first number three around clockwise. Then turning the second number counterclockwise. Finally, turning the last number clockwise one more time." Bingo. The lock opened. Phuong changed her clothes and began the P.E. class.

On the basketball field, on the ground, there were numbers, and each student would stand in the number of themselves. As fate settled for them, Phuong had to stand next to Ha, an annoying girl who bullied her this morning. Inside Phuong, there was a rage that she wanted to stay away from this girl as soon as possible. But damn it, her last name was the same as Ha; besides, she and Ha were the only Vietnamese students in this class. Back in the day, the Vietnamese community's growth was different from now. Seeing Phuong, Ha crossed her arms and clicked her tongue to show her disappointment in this new girl.

The class began. Today, Joyce wanted her students to choose. They could play basketball, jump rope, or walk around the football stadium. Whatever they wanted to do must relate to sport and no laziness. Ha would go and play basketball with her friends. Phuong might leave the basketball field to walk around the football stadium. Alone. She would appreciate every opportunity to be alone. Maybe she wanted to think about something.

As Ha saw Phuong like that, she felt pity for Phuong. It was straightforward to understand that she was new to the school and must be lonely. Phuong reminded Ha of whom she used to be—being bullied, being despaired, being nothing. Ha did not want Phuong to be in the same circumstance as she used to be. If Phuong could be like her (be strong), Ha could befriend Phuong and help her survive in this school. Or was she trying to help Phuong not to be outcasted here?

Ha decided to leave the basketball to go with Phuong. She ran to catch up with Phuong.

Meanwhile, Phuong was walking, enjoying the beautiful day with the blue sky and sunshine above. She did not think this was the P.E. class. It was like walking in the park. Suddenly, from behind, there was a call from somebody. Phuong turned back. It was Ha. Phuong immediately walked faster to avoid this annoying girl. But she was too slow. Ha grabbed Phuong's shoulder. Angrily, Phuong pushed Ha away.

"What is wrong with you?" Phuong cried. "Why are you keep following me? Just leave me alone."

Ha breathed heavily of the tiredness. Then, she brought herself back to normal and stood up straight. "Woah, you can speak. That is impressive! We thought that you were deaf or mute."

Phuong did not say anything.

"Listen," Ha continued. "I want to talk to you and befriend you. That's all."

"Why do you want to befriend me?" Phuong said. "I am not the kind of person that you want to befriend. I want to be alone."

Ha laughed out loud. "If you act like that, you won't survive in this school. To tell you, Vietnamese students in this school aren't a lot, and many hate us. You need a friend here too....»

Phuong looked bewildered. Ha does not continue. Instead, Ha shrugged. "You know..."

"Know what?" Phuong asked.

"To protect you."

"Why?"

"Believe me; they love targeting innocent girls like you in this school."

Phuong was shaking when she heard the word "targeting." It was not the first time she had heard of this topic. In her previous schools, she had seen many Vietnamese students being bullied. In words, yes. By violence, yes. By harassing, yes. And it all led to suicide.

Mrs. Nhu always reminded her never to touch anyone in the school, to ignore them and be on her own. But Phuong was still scared that she would be targeted like others one day.

Ha could see the scare inside Phuong's eyes. She tabbed on Phuong's left shoulder. "Can I walk with you? You can decide whether you want to befriend me or not. The choice is yours. But truly, I want to befriend you."

"Why do you want to befriend me?" Phuong asked firmly.

"I don't know. I want to befriend a Vietnamese. I play mostly American and Mexican. I think it would be great to hang out with you because we are Vietnamese and can understand each other more easily."

Phuong smiled. For the first time, she could smile in a new place. And someone talked to her to make her smile. Then, they walked around the football field for the rest of the period. It had begun friendship between Ha and Phuong.

CHAPTER 13

Phuong and Ha

"You," Phuong points and says. "What the fuck are you doing here?"

Adam walks fast to Ha. He holds her hand. "Why are you coming in here?"

She smiles. "I just want to end this." Ha let go of Adam's hands and comes to Mrs. Nhu, standing with her fingers crossed together.

She faces Ha.

"Mom," Ha says.

Ha still wants to call Mrs. Nhu "mom" because Mrs. Nhu is still like her second mother, no matter what.

When Ha's mother passed away, Mrs. Nhu was the only person who stayed with Ha till the end after everyone left the funeral as the coffin touched the ground. Her husband's family left early, especially Mrs. Linh and Thomas, the most heartless people in the world.

Mrs. Nhu held Ha in her arms and comforted her. Ha cried out loud on Mrs. Nhu's shoulder. She slowly stroked Ha's hair with her hand. She said. "That's ok! Cry out loud. Cry to stop the pain. Cry to make you more comfortable. But it would be best if you held strong when the tear is dry to move on. I swear your mom does not want to see you like this. She always wants you to be strong, proud, and happy. If you are happy, your mother would be happy in the other world too."

With those words, Ha could overcome her mother's death. Mrs. Nhu is always there for Ha.

"I really miss you," Ha says, holding Mrs. Nhu's hands. "I know I have done so many things that disappointed you, made you hate me and broke your heart. I had acted stupidly, and I'd turned myself into a person whom no one, including my late mother, could not recognize. Maybe I failed her too. I often wanted to come here to see you but did not have the guts to do it because I was too ashamed to stand in front of you. After I heard the fight coming from the house, I thought it was time," Ha lets go of Mrs. Nhu's hands and turns to everyone else in the room "to end all the feuds and hate among us. What we had done so far caused a terrible consequence to Michael. We had torn him apart when he did not do anything wrong. I....»

"Why don't you shut the fuck up?' Phuong interrupts Ha. " Who the fuck do you think you are here to lecture us about the mistake, huh? It would be best if you remembered that you are the root of every bad omen in my family. You caused everything, and you'd destroyed everything that I had built so far. Do you know how much pain I suffered for a long time? I'd never done anything to harm you or betray you. I will always love you as a friend. No, not a friend. A sister to me." Phuong put her hands on her chest. "And yet, you failed me. I felt betrayed. You went behind my back to fuck my ex-husband. WHY?" Phuong screams. "Why did you do that to me? I hate you. I despair you. Get out of my house now!" Phuong pounds multiple times on Ha's chest.

Ha does not move a bit. She lets Phuong do whatever she wants to do. Phuong has been waiting to do this for a long time ago. But now, when Phuong has a chance to do it, and she does it, why are there tears coming out of her eyes? She cries out loud. Hoa goes into getting Phuong out. Adam also embraces Ha and takes her to the clear place in the living room.

Mrs. Nhu sees everything happening in the room; she is sad. She quietly sits down on the couch. Her face shows disappointment because she never thinks that one day she can witness her ex-son-in-law and her daughter, between her future son-in-law and Ha, in the room. For all her life, she has wanted nothing more than happy for her children. She wants to see them growing up, having more grandchildren, and taking care of them. Mrs. Nhu has sacrificed so many things since she was in this country with nothing inside her hands. Now, at the age that Vietnamese people call "near the ground, far away from the sky," she only sees Phuong, her only daughter, be happy for just a few years, and then it is over in front of her eyes. She has witnessed Phuong's pain after the divorce. But she feels more disappointed when the mistress of Adam is Ha, whom she loves as her daughter and permits to call her "mom."

Sitting alone on the chair, watching them fighting, she cannot hold her tears. She looks up to the ceiling, where there is a chandelier. But it is not the chandelier that she is looking at. She looks at what is above it—Michael's bedroom. What Ha just said to Mrs. Nhu is right. They have caused terrible consequences when Michael is the person who indeed suffers the pain because of what the adults did. And Hoa said about a bitter truth that Phuong and Adam do not even care what Michael thinks or how he feels in life. They only care about themselves and their new happiness. But they don't even realize that their true happiness appears in front of their eyes. It is Michael all along. When Phuong and Adam think they did everything for Michael, they want to buy him and make him choose the side he will be on. They have been fighting to have his love. After the divorce, they never genuinely love Michael because of their hatred for each other. Now, they have new passions for themselves, and Michael is officially abandoned.

Mrs. Nhu agrees with Ha that everything has to stop immediately. No more fighting. No more hate. No more misunderstanding. She quietly leaves the room to go somewhere.

If anyone ever goes to some women's boxing fight, the tension in the room is exactly like that. The heavy boxers: Ha and Phuong are fighting to get the championship place. At this time, Phuong has more benefit in the fight because she shows her "furious anger" toward Ha. And besides, Ha doesn't mind fighting back because she thinks she deserves it. Phuong, with a fury that stays inside her for such a long time, it may be time to let it out. Just like Ha did to her husband's family before. And because she has used all of her power in the biggest fight of her life and a little energy left to expose her mother-in-law's scandalous affair, Ha feels tired right now. She wants everything to end so she can start a new beginning with Adam.

"Stop it! All of you!" There is a voice coming from somewhere that is not so loud, but inside that voice, there's some tiredness. That is Mrs. Nhu, turning the game around to become the central game controller. "You guys are nothing more than a big mess. For the love of God, you are all adults, yet you're acting like a child. Can you even think of being a role model for your children? For Michael?" Then, they turn to Michael standing next to Mrs. Nhu. His face is blushing, and his eyes are red. He has been crying.

Crying for his life. Crying for the selfishness of his parents. Crying for being outcasted. Crying for….

Phuong turns to Adam. "Are you happy now? This is what you caused our son. He had to see what he did not have to see."

Mrs. Nhu tells her to stop talking and listen to her, but Phuong does not even care.

Adam scoffs. "Why don't you blame yourself too? We divorced, but you left him to be with your boyfriend. I should have fought for the full custody of him"

"What? Now you want to bring the custody up to me, huh?" Phuong talks louder. "Right, ok. If he lived with you, perhaps, he would have learned how to betray his lover in the future to fuck with another person."

"Excuse me?" Adam says. "How dare you talk to me like that? I will never teach my son like that." He points his finger to her face. "Don't even start the fire." Adam suddenly laughs out loud. "Oh, right, I almost forgot. Today is your birthday. Your fucking birthday. How many boozes have you taken so far? Perhaps, 10 to 20 bottles? You are fucking alcoholic, Phuong. You can never be rehabbed from that. You're always drunk, and you beat our son when wasted. Probably, Michael would have learned that fucking negative habit from you too. What kind of mother is that? So don't tell me that I am a bad FATHER!"

"You motherfucker!" Phuong jumps in and shoves Adam falling. She hardly pulls his shirt and pounds her fists into his chest as she did to Ha recently. But harder. It will be a horrible crime scene if Phuong holds a sharp knife. "Shut the fuck up. You cheated on me. You are the fucking liar and a fucking pig. I'll kill you. I'LL FUCKING KILL YOU!"

Hoa, one more time, had to jump in to stop Phuong. "Babe, please, don't do it." With the accumulation of strength and anger, Hoa pulled Phuong out.

On the other side, Ha also helps Adam to stand up.

"For God's sake, YOU ARE STILL MICHAEL'S PARENTS!" The shouting from Hoa gets Michael's attention. He looks at Hoa, standing in the middle of Adam and Phuong.

Hoa continues. "From the beginning, both of you acted in front of

Michael to make him believe that he is still happy and has his parents. You've made a mistake from that moment." Hoa turns to Phuong. "Babe, I've told you my personal story about my childhood experience of an unhappy family. I advised you to tell Michael the truth as soon as possible, but you did not listen to me." He puts his hands on his chest. "When I saw Michael for the first time, and your mother shared your story, I knew immediately that," Hoa swings his arms around, meaning to include Adam. "if the lies continued, Michael would have ended up like me. Sooner or later, you tell me. Today, Michael had to witness this disgusting scene and the consequences that both of you had built. Looking at him now, how do you feel? Regret? Shameful?"

Hoa sighs. He walks to Michael and kneels. He holds Michael's arms. "Michael, I know you don't like me because I've stepped into your mother's life, and you think I have taken away your dad's place. I've not had that thought to replace anyone in your life. I love your mom, and I love you. I did everything not because I wanted your love or attention but because I care for you. I can see myself when I was a kid inside you, and I knew I had to save this child's life from not being like I used to be. You are a strong boy and have the bravery to go through everything in life. Including the trauma of tonight or any other obstacles in your life. Be strong, ok?" Then, he kisses Michael's forehead as if Hoa is Michael's biological father, even though the little boy is frozen and cannot open his mouth.

Michael looks at Hoa and just slightly nods. Hoa smiles and stands up. To Mrs. Nhu. "See you later, then." He returns to Phuong. He does not say anything, and then he leaves. Phuong runs after him.

"Wait, why are you leaving?" Phuong calls.

Hoa stops and turns back. "I am not ready for you, babe. Obviously."

"What are you talking about?"

"You have not forgotten your past yet. Looking at you, still full of hate, you have not been ready to move on."

"I moved on, babe. How could I be with you right now if I was not?"

"You are lying to me, lying to yourself. Don't you see what you did in that room previously? If you truly moved on, you would not have reacted like that in front of your son."

"I was angry because of their appearances, which triggered my anger.

You know that I want to confront them and you... You told me to tell Michael the truth. I did. What else do you want?"

"You told Michael the truth TONIGHT, not before, as I told you. Why didn't you listen to me and be honest to yourself, for God's sake," Hoa chuckles? "Besides, it is not what I want. It is about what's best for you.

"Listen, I love you so much. I truly do. All of the time we are together, I always hope I can take you out of that pond of misery where you'd lost yourself for so long. What you had been through, what you had been suffering, how your life had been rolling in the deep. I can understand, and I am always there for you to help you go through it. I thought you were finally yourself again. But I was wrong. Nothing is called 'love' and 'forgiveness' in your mind and heart. You smile, and you act to be happy. It is just a facade of something rotten inside already, babe. Deeply inside you," Hoa places his right hand on Phuong"s left chest. "Your heart is shallow and empty."

Hoa pauses because he can see Phuong begins to cry. Hoa's eyes are a little red right now. He tries not to drop any tears. He continues. "I think we should take a break here for you to find yourself again and be normal. Today is too much for you or everybody else. Take time to think, digest all the animosities, and know what you truly want in this life. If you cannot find yourself when you are in love with me, try to think about Michael. He is your only hope in this life." Hoa lifted Phuong's chin. He looked at her face. "Bye, Phuong."

Hoa walks away despite Phuong calling him back and screaming. The car drives away.

Phuong collapses on the cement floor with details of rock. The sky is where there are millions of shining stars and a full moon. The breeze is cool, and together have made tonight a beautiful night. Nobody has ever expected that things would be poorly ruined on this night, and most importantly, Phuong and Hoa have taken a break. They are on a break like Ross and Rachel.

Regret now is a new term added into Phuong's life with anger and hatred. A perfect equation to make life rotten and turn into hell. There is no sign of light in that. The soul does not want to open to the better things or for someone to save it. It is completely closed and isolates itself from the outside world. When the equation is completed eating one's soul, death may be the only choice.

After what Hoa says to her, Phuong realizes she still holds too much hatred. It is just a sense when she thinks she is ready to move on with Hoa. An immense sense blindfolded her true feeling. Nothing more than that. Does she ever love him? Or does she use him to fill up the empty hold inside her heart that Adam used to break? What about Michael? Does she ever think for him or love him as a mother to a son, or she wants to compete with Adam to get his attention and his favorite? When seeing Ha and Adam, she still wants to destroy them, to make them pay for what they did to her. It may be the only thing that can make Phuong happy and continue with her happiness. Phuong can do it, but why didn't she do it when she had the chance? When she caught both of them on the bed, Phuong did not beat up Ha. When she meets Adam, she can only yell at or insult him with the coldest words. And today, when Ha and Phuong finally faced off, Phuong could only pound on Ha's chest without pushing her down and beating her up like she always thought about. It is because of her nature. She wanted something else. Phuong is a doctor, and her job is to save lives and love patients. She cries and feels impotent when she cannot keep a life during surgery, or a patient dies in front of her when they come to the emergency room. She is delighted when a patient or their family comes and shows gratitude to her. Happiness with her is seeing Michael growing up every day, enjoying her mother's cooking, and being with Hoa, her new love and a new beginning. That is Phuong's heart, which only fills with love and compassion. But she did not realize it until now. Ha and Adam, yes, they've caused the pain, but their love for each other is real. They don't even care about Phuong's hatred of them or know that Phuong hates them so much. They ignore and stay together.

Sitting on the sidewalk of her house, many regrets come through Phuong's mind like a movie. Hoa has gone, and if she wants to get him back, she will do something to end and "divorce" the past. She doesn't know what to do, but she knows one thing for sure sitting here would not help anything.

Phuong stands up and gets back to the house. Inside, she sees Mrs. Nhu, Michael, Adam, and Ha together in the living room. Adam is sitting next to Michael, and they are eating the birthday cake, which Phuong supposes to cut and eat first. Ha is sitting next to Mrs. Nhu and talking to her. Ha is holding Mrs. Nhu's hands. Their eyes look at each other affectionately. All of them are doing things together for the first time as if nothing has happened.

Michael sees Phuong first. He calls. "Mommy, come and eat the cake with us."

Everyone turns to look at Phuong, who is still shocked without know what the fuck is happening here.

Mrs. Nhu smiles. "Come in, dear. We are waiting for you."

Phuong nods slightly and walks to them.

Everyone takes their eyes on Phuong when she runs after Hoa. They all feel that it is a sign that something terrible will happen. Break up, perhaps. Ha tends to follow Phuong but Mrs. Nhu tells her not to do it. Let Phuong be alone with Hoa and let them work it out. It is not Ha's business nor Mrs. Nhu's business.

Mrs. Nhu continues. "Both of you have something to do right now."

Ha looks at her. "Yes, mom. Just end it tonight."

Adam does not know what Mrs. Nhu is talking about. "To do what?"

Both Ha and Mrs. Nhu sigh, and both talk at the same time. "IT'S MICHAEL!"

Adam exclaims. "Oh," even though he has not understood anything yet. How comes he is so stupid like that? After the past hours with all the drama, it is time for the four to talk to Michael about everything. Phuong can speak to him later. But a person, who started the ending of a "happy" family, needs to speak up first, explain to Michael, and say sorry to him.

They sit down on the couch. People would have believed they were a happy family if they were in a restaurant. Michael sits next to Mrs. Nhu. Ha and Adam sits on one side.

"I'll go first." Mrs. Nhu says. "I have been waiting for so long to confront both of you. What you have done to my daughter and my grandson is unforgivable. I was so mad, even despaired you both." Mrs. Nhu turns her look to Adam. "Never in my life could I believe that one day my son-in-law, whom I loved and had the trust in him, would have betrayed his wife without any shame. I am disappointed in you."

Adam keeps his head down. He does not feel shame because he would not have had an affair with Ha if he did. He loves her for real. But he has a big regret for his mother-in-law. He has not talked to her since the matter broke out. He knows that Mrs. Nhu cares about him and never even doubts him.

The day Adam and Phuong married, Mrs. Nhu, came to the dressing room to talk to Adam, which he never forgot. "To be honest, at first and until this moment, I still have doubts about your honesty and your love for Phuong. I do not trust you completely. But this is my daughter's life. She has made her final choice, which is you. She is happy with you, and you have changed her life. Now, I can't interfere with her life anymore. Her life, her decision. Listen, even though I am still having doubts about you. But I hope you will prove me wrong from this moment. I hope you will love her with all of your heart; I hope you will never break her heart; I hope you and Phuong will be happy for the rest of your life. You have my blessing." Then, they hugged each other for the first time. Adam promised Mrs. Nhu to do precisely what she'd expected. And he did. Soon, Adam gained the trust and love of Mrs. Nhu.

The trust and the love thought it would last forever. He broke both into pieces.

"I am so sorry, mom." Adam finally opens his mouth. He meets Mrs. Nhu's eyes. "I know what I did is unforgivable, as you said. I have failed you and your trust in me. The love I gave to Phuong since the day we dated and after we married was real. I loved her with all of my heart. I did not pretend or act to love her and gain your trust. That is the thing that you don't need to worry about. Never a day in my marriage could I think of a day Phuong and I would get divorced. That is something crazy and ridiculous to think about. But things that will happen must come. The fate between Phuong and me could only last that long. I understand your feeling right now, and you have the right to hate me. But I hope you won't resent Ha. It was not her fault. Everything is my fault. Blame me, don't blame her."

Adam gets out of his seat. He comes to Michael and kneels. His hands hold Michael's arms. Mrs. Nhu and Ha look at Adam. "Mikey, I know you are very disappointed in your mom and me. We've lied to you and acted happy in front of you. All things we've done are to win your love. We are such terrible and selfish parents. I am sorry, Mikey. You can blame everything on me because I caused everything. But don't hate your mother! Your mother loves you so much. She cares for you; she raises you better than me, and I trust her. Your mother is the best person in your life, and you will never find anyone who loves you more than her. I...»

Mrs. Nhu clears her throat.

"And your grandmother, too." Adam continues. "I love you too, but I believe I have not loved you as your mother does. I competed with your mother for what? For your love? Do I ever love you in my life? I am such a bad father, and you don't deserve to have a father like me. I feel regret about that. But deep inside me right now, I hope I can do anything to fill the hole of disappointment and emptiness inside your heart right now. I love you, Michael. I love you. I hope you can forgive me."

Nobody says anything at the moment.

Michael starts to drop some tears. He looks down, his fingers crossed together. Then, he takes the strength to look at his father's face. Michael does not know how much, in his words, is true.

Adam has lied to everyone in this house, including him. The image of a father, whom Michael always idolizes, has crumbled and shattered in front of him after he knew the ugly truth. He regrets that he does not understand his mother's love for him before, even though there are some of them just acting. But still, Phuong takes care of Michael and spends her time with him more than Adam does, and he only buys his expensive toys, Play Station, iPad, and many more. But he is spending time with him a little. Of course, Michael loves those things. But it can never replace the love of a father.

On the other hand, Hoa always spends time with Michael, takes him out, teaches him to study, tells him many fascinating stories about Vietnamese history from the beginning, and raises pride in being Vietnamese in Michael.

Those actions Adam has not done even once. And yet, Michael always wants to kick Hoa out of his life. Now, everything is clear as daylight. Michael understands everything, and he will make a choice.

"Mr. Hoa was always there for me when I needed him. He hung out with me, took me to the park, and bought me my favorite treat: ice cream. I hate him so much because I thought he tried to replace you with me. But now I know what he has done is because he had seen the things that you and mom were doing lately, and he wanted to make sure that I was not alone by being there for me." Michael says. "You and mom abandoned me. All you cared about is yourself, your selfish purpose to have my favorite." Michael stands up. "What about me? Am I dead in your eyes? Now, after every lie and play you acted, you and mom chose this moment to tell me. How lucky I am! What you just said sounded so nice, like a movie script. Maybe later, mom comes in and says the same thing." Michael sighs. "Tell me, what am I supposed to do?" He turned to Ha and Mrs. Nhu to ask. "What am I supposed to do now?" He bursts out crying.

Adam hugs his son. His voice starts to crack because he is sobbing. "You are my son, and I love you. I am sorry for everything, Mikey. Now, I hope you can give me a chance to offset every loss that mommy and I caused you; give me a chance to be the father you've always wanted. Please, Michael!"

Whether what Adam says is sincere, he cannot change the past and the sin he committed against his son. But the person, who needs to understand and make the final decision, is Michael. It is like standing at a crossroads without knowing where to go. Facing his father's face right now, inside the hate and the disappointment, there is still a spark of compassion.

Michael snorts. "I don't know whether the decision I am about to make is right. But you are my father. No matter what happens, I still love and forgive you. Grandma taught me that we must learn how to forgive to make peace inside me. I want to have the peace in me," Michael takes a deep breath and breathes out. "Will you love again for real? Like a father to his son?"

Adam smiles. "Of course, Mikey, of course." Then, they hugged each other. "I love you, Mikey."

Mrs. Nhu looks at them and smiles. Ha feels happy because they can finally solve this smoothly.

Adam releases Michael and introduces Ha to Michael as his new girlfriend. Ha comes to Michael and shakes his hands. She believes that Michael is not ready to take a hug from her yet. He shakes back and smiles. He knows that right now, he accepts the appearance of Hoa in his mother's life, and he can learn how to get his father's girlfriend even though it is difficult and takes some time.

Mrs. Nhu turns to Ha, and she holds her hands. "Now, it is your turn. Do you want to say something?"

"I don't know what to say because whatever I say right now is unimportant and not worth it. I am the person who ruins everything here." Ha said honestly.

"That's ok. Just tell us what you want to say. Everything is clear right now." Mrs. Nhu says.

"Tell her about your marriage with Thomas and your life under that house," Adam suggests.

Ha does not feel comfortable sharing this with anyone except Adam. She does not want to seek sympathy from other people. She used to be a different person before—a strong girl. But for years, she had lost it. She wants to find that strength again to escape the swamp of desperation. She does not like to hear things like "Stay strong," "Everything will be all right," and "I can understand your feeling," which are the worst sayings ever. They don't understand shit at all. They don't live in her shoes, and how the hell on earth can they know what Ha has been through? When somebody says that to her, she tells them to stop from the outside, but in her mind, she says, "Fuck off." Her life is desperate enough, and she wants to leave everything behind. She does not want to dig up the past and the pains. Before Adam, her mother was the only person she could share with until cancer took her away.

Now, she has a chance to meet Mrs. Nhu again, who is also a mother to her. There is nothing to be ashamed of or afraid to share with a mother.

Ha nods and begins to tell her story. Inside her mind, she wishes Mrs. Nhu would not show her sympathy for her to cry for her. She wants to speak up to make her soul peaceful again. After sharing the whole story, Mrs. Nhu does not say anything. She nods slightly. She turns to Adam and says. "Ha, is my daughter too. I love her as much as I love Phuong. You have known her story and what she has been through. It is too much pain. Her heart needs to be healed; if she takes another pain, she will surely die. She has chosen you to be her new love because she trusts and loves you. So, as I did before your marriage with Phuong, I will ask you to love her with all of your heart, not to break her heart, to be happy with her. Can you do it? I will not let Ha be with you if you can't."

Adam stood up and came to Ha. He takes her hands, and Ha stands up. He kisses her. She smiles.

"I love you," Adam says.

"I love you, too."

Then, they all sit down and talk happily, like a delighted family. Adam cuts the cake without waiting for Phuong and eats with Michael. Ha and Mrs. Nhu talk and Phuong comes in. All of them put their eyes on Phuong, who is showing sadness and desperation on her face.

"Come in, dear. We are waiting for you." Mrs. Nhu says.

The atmosphere inside the room is strangely cozy, as if she has walked into another land. She thought there would be a war here, but no, they are close together. It could be better because what happened outside between her and Hoa is enough pain and pressure for one night. Of course, she would never believe that her birthday would be the day to end everything and end in such a good way that she can never forget for sure.

Phuong is exhausted. She walks to her mother like a little girl and cries on her lap.

Back in the day, when she came home from school with a red face because some students at school were mocking her, Phuong found only safe and more confident in her mother's arms. It healed her immediately. Mrs. Nhu used to say that many other parents had told their children before. "If you failed in your life or any bad thing happened to you, you'll always have a home to return to. This is where you were born, and this is where you're. We are waiting for you."

"What happened, dear?" Mrs. Nhu asks, and her hand runs through Phuong's hair.

"We broke up."

All gasp and get surprised. Traditional South art is called "Cai luong," like music in Vietnam. The rhythm of "Cai luong" has been the life of many South Vietnamese people for many decades. There is a short music lyric in a musical in which people would sing those lyrics when something unexpected or unusual happens. "Just hearing that as a thunder hit beside my ears."

"Oh, no! Why?" Mrs. Nhu holds Phuong's hands to lift her.

"I did not do the thing I was supposed to do a long time ago. And Hoa got upset. Then, we broke up." Phuong sits down on the couch.

"Is it about moving on?"

Phuong turns to Mrs. Nhu with wide-opened eyes. "How do you know?"

"Because that is what I told him to help you."

Phuong remains silent. Mrs. Nhu continues.

"For years, you have been suffering from the pain of your previous marriage. Even though you said that you finally moved on with Adam. Babe, I am your mother, and I know deep inside you that you still have hate for him. It is growing up inside you with a hope that one day, you will lay vengeance upon him. I never deny how much you love Michael and what you did means good for him. But soon, I realized that you laid revenge on him by winning his favorite and making him love you more than Adam. Luckily, well, Hoa is there. I talked to him about you, and he offered to help. At first, I just thought that he helped you because he understood my feeling. But soon, it does not only stop there. He told me that he loves you. I was stunned and did not know what to do. The gap between you and Hoa is too big. Besides, I did not know whether you are ready to move on, and..." There is a pause. Mrs. Nhu sighs. "And is he the next right person for you? I don't want my daughter to suffer any other pain. One is enough. But soon, I can see the love he has given to you is real and sincere. That is what I feel. He is nice to you, to me, and Michael. Hoa is a good man I can trust once more to let him love you. It is sad to hear you and him broke up. I don't mean to blame you. But," Mrs. Nhu shakes her head slightly. "you are wrong this time, darling."

Phuong's hands cover her face.

"Now it is over. It is best to let things settle down for a while and find a way to talk to him. It has not been the end yet. Trust me. He still loves you, and deep inside, you finally love him."

Phuong looks at her mother. "It will never happen, mom. It is the end. Period. He will never come back."

"Why are you so sure?"

"Because he is a strong viewpoint person. He will never change his mind."

"Ah," Mrs. Nhu says. "That means you have not understood him, dear.

You need time to digest everything and get to know your lover." Mrs. Nhu turns to Ha. "Do you have anything to say to Phuong?"

Ha looks at Mrs. Nhu. "I...I...I don't know what I should say or not because of what just happened?"

"Just spit it out, Ha," Phuong says. "You started everything and now end it."

Ha stands up and sits next to Phuong. "I am truly sorry for everything. I failed you and your mother. I always consider you my sister, and a sister would never do anything behind her back. Sometimes I remember when we hung out, we helped each other with homework, and you were always tired of explaining stuff. We even gossiped about boys in school. Remember when you and I had the same crush on Timmy, the football captain with a sunshine smile and hazelnut hair? We fought to have his attention. You were too shy to make him like you, and I did all kinds of stuff to make him like me. Eventually, you won. I did not know how you could do it. I was pissed off, and until now, I still hate you for that. And I..."

Suddenly, Phuong chuckles. Then she laughs. "Do you know why Timmy liked me more than he liked you? Because Timmy told me you were annoying and he only preferred a quiet girl like me. So I won."

"Annoying?" Ha raises her voice. "The hell I was annoying. I was pretty and nice and got all the elements to get a boy to love me."

"Not with that attitude!"

Everyone in the room laughed. Ha smiles. "So you do remember every memory between you and me?"

"Of course I do. How can I forget them?" Phuong says. "I hated you, Ha. I could never believe my best friend could steal my husband like that. My heart was broken, and I even cursed you not to be happy with your marriage. And it turns out my curse is true."

"What are you talking about?"

"I knew about your health and the ability to have a child."

"How?"

"Remember the time you and I met each other in the hospital? That was the time I knew about you. I asked the nurse who followed you to give you the recommendation paper, and she told me the story. At that moment, I decided to forgive you. It is not the punishment that I felt satisfied with. I am a doctor. Even though they are my enemies, I can never feel happy when someone suffers from pain. And with you, I can't even think of hating you more. Sometimes I wanted to talk to you, but my ego was too big to do such a thing. So, I stopped."

"If you forgave her, why did you jump on her to beat her today?" Adam cut into the conversation.

Phuong looks at him. "Because you and her ruined my birthday party. And you are eating my cake. Fuck you."

Adam stands up. "Watch your mouth. Mikey is sitting here."

Phuong continues her fight with Adam. As usual. "Oh, please, don't act like he has not heard a bad word. He...»

Phuong starts to realize that what she has said is unacceptable. It is like a child listening to the wrong words from their parent, a regular thing. She looks at Michael, whom she and Adam hurt. She does not know if what she has done for Michael is her true love or if she is playing with him. She feels regret. Doesn't she learn anything? She fights with Adam again, and she supposes to make peace with him and let things go. This is not what Hoa wants or what Michael wants.

She covers her mouth with a gasp.

"Oh my God, darling," She says as she approaches Michael. "I did not mean to say that to you. I am sorry. I love you and have done so many bad things to you. I should have loved you like a real mother to her son, not jeopardized your feeling like that. Oh, I am such a terrible mother. I am not deserved to be your mother. Why did I compete with your father when I could have loved you with my heart?" She screams. She stands up. "I am a—a monster." She turns to Adam, then Ha. "When both of you are ready to move on, I still hold the hate inside me, and I've lost myself. I never realized I was having a new beginning with Hoa. He loves me. When I thought I was in love with him, it was wrong. I was—just using him to fill the void in my heart. How could I have done that to him? What is wrong with me?" Phuong collapses and cries out loud. "I need a drink." She stands up and runs fast to the mini bar in the corner of the living room. She opens Jack Daniel's bottle and drinks like a bottle of water.

Seeing that, Adam comes in and takes away Jack Daniel's bottle. But Phuong pushes him out. Adam grabs her wrist holding the bottle, and squeezes it hard. Phuong feels hurt, and lets go of the bottle. It drops and breaks. Adam holds Phuong tight. They sink to the floor. Phuong is crying in Adam's arms.

Adam cocks his head to her head. "Don't do this." He whispers. "Don't blame yourself. You've done nothing wrong. It was me all the time. I caused this to you and Michael. You still have Michael as your mental support. Don't let him see you or us like this anymore. He has the whole future in front of him. Time to let him feel happy again."

Phuong looks at him and wants to say something. But she can't. She smiles and passes out.

Adam carries Phuong to her bedroom. Then, he comes back to the living room. The chime of the clock rings out. It is midnight now. Everyone is tired right now. It is probably the worst birthday of Phuong ever. Ha, Adam says goodbye to Mrs. Nhu, and Michael leaves. Before Adam leaves, he talks to Mrs. Nhu.

"What happened tonight. I think we should not talk about it again."

Mrs. Nhu nods. Then, she returns to the house.

Michael goes to his room and is ready to sleep. Mrs. Nhu tucks him in.

"Grandma, is mommy ok?" He asks.

She smiles. "Of course, she is ok. She was getting emotional tonight."

"Did I make her like that?"

"Never." She kisses Michael's forehead. "Now, go to sleep and forget what happened tonight."

Mrs. Nhu leaves the room. She walks to Phuong's room. Her daughter is still in the dress which Hoa buys her for tonight. She must have been in the spotlight tonight. Turns out, everybody steals that spotlight. Mrs. Nhu helps Phuong to take off her dress and put on her sleepwear even though she is passed out for good. The breath is full of alcohol.

"Sleep tight, darling." Then, Mrs. Nhu comes to her room.

The whole house is in the dark. The night of tragedy had come to an end. The feud, the misunderstood, and the lie have finally stopped. Everyone has what they want at last. But only Phuong is the person who lost the new love of her life, and she has herself a new pain. The flame of hatred inside her has burned everything she built to the ground. It is only ashes right now. What she has to do with her life is vague and gloomy.

PART 3

SIX MONTHS LATER

CHAPTER 14

Phuong

Phuong tries to contact Hoa to talk to him, she even comes to his house, but he is not there. Finally, Phuong gives up. When alone in her room, Phuong opens her phone to look through every photo of her and Hoa together.

They went out for boba, had dinner at some restaurants, went to the beach, or did some weird stuff together. In all those moments, Phuong captured all to make her memory more beautiful and fill out the void in her heart. Parallel with that, she listens to all kinds of sad songs, from Vpop to US music. And befriend with alcohol. Phuong goes through every gift that Hoa gives her before. From jewelry to every handmade gift, from dresses to every cute little animal for decorating. She never realizes how important they are because those are the true love that Hoa has given her. And yet, Phuong only treated him as a "liquid cement" to fill in those voids in her heart and a tool to show Adam that she is still happy with other people. When Hoa discovered everything, it was effortless to understand why he left Phuong.

Phuong has no choice but to accept that she has lost Hoa forever.

One night, she lies on her bed, and again, she looks through the photos of her and Hoa. She cries. But at that moment, she cries because this will be the last time she looks at them. Getting rid of everything that belongs to Hoa is the only way to forget him and move on. Phuong does not do it in the first place because she is still holding the silhouette of Hoa inside her heart, and she always hopes that one day Hoa will come back to her or she will find out where Hoa is to be with him again. And she knows that until then, she would love Hoa for real, and there would be no mistake.

But it is a fantasy of something that will never happen in reality.

She deletes them in order. The last photo is the photo taken of Phuong's birthday before everything happened.

"Goodbye, Hoa." She whispers and clicks "delete."

On a Friday morning, Phuong decides to spend her day going to a temple on the hill, two hours driving from her place. It is the Buddhist temple Phuong, and her mom went to it when she was young. Back then, the road to the temple had been much harder than it was right now. It was a bumpy road, which was full of rocks and dirt. When there was rain, the road turned out to be so muddy that it could create a giant mudslide. So, when it came to that time, no one could go to the temple, and the people in the temple could not go down either.

The temple is on the top of the hill, where trees and unique nature cover it. It is like inside the hands of mother earth. The atmosphere there is so different from downhill. Everyone can breathe well even though they have problems with the respiratory system.

The temple was built back in 1969 by a Chinese Master and then a student of his took over, who is now the Great Master. The architecture was created based on some old temples in China centuries ago. For years, it has only been fixed a few times. But after many wildfires or natural disasters, the temple can still stand without collapsing or being ruined. It is because the Buddha has helped to protect the temple.

The temple is in a place where no one usually comes, and that causes stealing frequently. Nobody knew who spread the rumor that every Buddha statue contained gold and expensive jewelry, and that attracted some gangs in the city or from nowhere came here late at night to steal the Buddha statues. Police started to open the investigation. They questioned everyone in the temple and asked whether they knew anyone had the motive to do such things. The Great Master smiled and said. "We are monks. All of our lives only know how to maintain the peace inside us and spread Buddha's kindness and halo to others. Why do we bother to make a feud with other people?"

The Great Master also told them one thing, which to the police was superstitious. He told them there would be karma for people who blasphemed and disrespected the Buddha's sacred and halo of Him; when the time came, what belonged to the temple would return. So the Great Master decided not to investigate further to look for those thieves. Of course, that was about law, order, and criminal activity, so the police had to do their jobs. For months, there was no new information about the thieves' identities or new clues on the robbery. It seemed like everything had come to an end. But then, as a miracle happened, the Buddha's statues were found coincidentally under the temple's hill. And the thieves were found dead in their houses of some diseases or suicide. Some of them had turned crazy, and they returned the statues. The police department found everything so strange, and in the end, they had to believe in what the Great Master told them, which turned out to be true. From that moment, many police officers decided to come to the temple when they had a chance to meditate, listen to the lecture of Buddha, and pray.

When Phuong was a kid, she hated to come here because it was so dull. Usually, Mrs. Nhu took her here on the weekend or when there were events. They spent time here for days. With a child-like Phuong, all she knew was playing or running around the temple. The monks in the temple looked at Phuong and said she was a shy girl, yet she would do big things in the future. At this place, Phuong was given her Dharma name and became the child of Buddha. Her Dharma name was *Dieu Hue* (*Dieu* meant nice in character, and *Hue* meant intelligence in mind). When Phuong grew up, she realized Buddha's importance and sacredness. She went to some temples in the city on the First or the Fifteenth day of the moon calendar each month to pray, volunteer, help, learn, and find peace. But there was no peace yet inside her soul and mind.

The car stops in the small parking lot of the temple. Phuong gets out of her car and walks inside the temple's Great Hall. The inside is so quiet. The sense of incense has made the atmosphere more sacred and solemn. The Great Hall divides into three compartments. In the middle of the Great Hall is the Buddha statue with fresh flowers and fruits and a bowl of incense with three incense sticks. To the right, there is the statue of Bodhisattva. And to the left, there is the statue of Maitreya. Phuong kneels on both knees, hands crossed. She kowtows three times and says, "Namo Amitabha Buddha." She looks up at the Buddha and starts to pray. Then, she moves to Bodhisattva and Maitreya doing the same.

Suddenly, the bell of the temple chimes out loud. Sun has come up to the top. It is noon right now. The Great Master in the brown Buddhist robe walks in silently. His hands have a string of black pearls. Phuong stands up to wai the Maitreya. She turns and sees the Great Master. She is so happy to see him. The Great Master smiles and greets her.

"Namo Amitabha Buddha," He bows down.

Phuong kneels on both knees and kowtows. The Great Master tells her to stand up.

"Long time to see you, Phuong," The Great Master says. "I have been waiting for you."

Phuong looks surprised. "You are waiting for me? How do you know that I will come?"

The Great Master laughs, but not too loud. "I know many things, my child. Anyhow, are you hungry? I am going to have lunch right now. Do you want to join me?"

"I hope I won't make any trouble for you here." Phuong hesitates.

"When you come here, there is no trouble you bring. Only your peace, mercy, and devotion to the Buddha." He says slowly.

Then, Phuong follows him to the dining room, where some monks and nuns are waiting for the Great Master to join them. Seeing him coming in, they all stand up. He gives the notice for them to sit down and introduces everyone to Phuong, who would join the lunch with everyone here. One Buddhist nun gets a bowl and a pair of chopsticks for Phuong. One novice gets Phuong a chair to sit down. Phuong does not want to blaspheme the Great Master and other Buddhist monks, so she asks to sit at the end of the table. The Great Master agrees, and they start to have lunch. It has been a long time since Phuong did not eat vegetarian. All the food here is so delicious. Phuong feels peaceful and joyful when sitting with the Buddhist nuns and novices, listening to and talking to them. Suddenly, Phuong forgets the things in the city to only focus on this moment.

After lunch, Phuong helped to wash the dishes.

After finishing everything, Phuong looks for the Great Master to talk to, which is one of the reasons Phuong is here today. Phuong asks the monk where the Great Master is, and he says The Great Master is in the Buddhist monastery speaking Buddhist chants. Phuong walks inside.

In the doorway, Phuong can hear the sound of tocsin and the voice of

The Great Master chanting. It sounds so familiar. It is precisely like what Mrs. Nhu did at home every evening.

The Great Master is sitting on the floor, fingers running the black pearl string, and one hand is chanting the tocsin and saying the Buddhist chants. Phuong walks in slowly, kneels, and prays. The chanting stops in a moment, and he kowtows three times. When he turns back, he sees Phuong sitting there. He smiles.

"You should try to say the Buddhist chants. It will help you to maintain the peace in you." He says. "Now, tell me, my dear, what brings you here today?"

Phuong looks at the Master. "There are so many things that happened to my life recently, and it seems like I cannot handle it anymore. My body, soul, and mind have been ruined so badly that I don't know how to cleanse it, Master. I've come to therapy with the hope of finding peace, the balance in my life. But it did not work. Then, I thought there was only one way to find myself back again. I need help from you and the Buddha."

The Great Master nods slightly. "I see. I am glad that you come here to see me today. You know, your mother came here many times before to talk to me about you."

"My mom?" Phuong asks. "Why didn't she tell me anything?"

"Why does she have to tell you? It is her right. She can go anywhere she wants without asking permission from anyone. Including her daughter." He says.

The Master pauses to enjoy his cup of herbal tea next to him. Outside, the wind starts to blow. The leaves were like dancing with the wind. The breeze gets inside the monastery and makes things inside the chiller.

The Master continues.

"I've known about what happened to you recently through what your mom said to me. It made her worry sick about her daughter. She came here to pray for you, but nothing had changed. Do you know why? Even though how many times your mom prays or how much power the Buddha has to change you, it will never work. It is up to you, my dear. You see, you are the master of your life. You control it in the way you always want. Good or bad, you decide. You go to the temple every First and Fifteenth day of the month to pray for yourself. But do you devote yourself to the Buddha? Or are you being enlightened by the halo of the Buddha? Your soul still has so much hate, anger, and dirty thoughts that show clearly outside you. How can the Buddha help you when you are carrying those in you? I've told you to say the Buddhist chant, but I believe you will never do it now."

The Master retakes a sip of tea. "I still remember the day that I gave you the Dharma name. What I saw in you at that moment was a shy girl, but yet, she was kind, she was intelligent, and she had compassion for other people. She would do many great things in the future and lighten up the burden of many people who need it. That's why I gave you the name '*Dieu Hue.*' That gift is blessing you. You've used that gift to save many patients' lives. That is your mission in this life. You were not building the hate or starting the flame of anger. When that thing happened to you, it was a challenge that the Buddha gave you to see what you would do if you were in front of that circumstance. Would you choose to forgive and move on? Or would you prefer to hate and get revenge? It was too evident that you had chosen the second one.

"Hate has a dark power which can destroy things real fast. They say it is easy to hate than to love and forgive. Hate has destroyed your soul and your body. Hate has built up another character inside you, which makes you lie to your son, misbehave in front of everyone else, dive into the lust of booze, and let the new love of your life away in just a second. He came to your life to love you, to help you walk through the hate, to help you to find yourself again, to enlighten. And yet, you threw him away. That's why even though you went through therapy to seek help, it could not help you because you were unwilling to change and open your heart to begin a new life. Don't be the beggar of the past! Think for your reality, son, and mom; think for your ex-husband and best friend. Stop hating them, wish them happiness, and think about your life ahead. Life is impermanent. We don't know when we will die. Hate and anger cannot help you with anything in this life. Only love and mercy can lighten up your life and boost you."

The more Phuong listens to the Great Master, the more she feels everything he says is right.

"What do I have to do right now, Master?" Phuong asks.

The Great Master stands up. He looks at the Buddha statue for a while, then turns to Phuong. "It is not too learn for you to be enlightened. But I have to ask you one thing."

"What is this, Master?"

"Are you willing to do it for real?" The Great Master asks.

"Yes, I am willing to do it for real," Phuong answers sincerely.

What the Great Master told Phuong to do was meditate and learn to say the Great Compassion Mantra. Step by step. She does not need to come here to do it. She can do it at home. But Phuong decides to ask permission from the hospital board for her to take one month off to go to the temple. At first, they don't agree with her request. But after all, she explains to them dramatically that they have to accept. That is one of her talents. She can convince everyone with her mouth. She moves to the temple, leaves everything behind, and only brings her soul and devotion here.

Day by day, she joins the monks and the Great Master to study Buddhism; cleans the temple; meditates in the monastery; says the Buddhist chants. And just like that, Phuong can finally find herself again and move on with life for real.

When she returns, she works and spends time with Michael and Mrs. Nhu. She finds more joy in reading books, talking to patients about how they felt, and taking Michael to a time when she can make him believe in the Buddha more. Seeing her daughter like that, Mrs. Nhu feels happier and more assured. It turns out her prayer has finally listened.

Ha

Now, Ha and Adam are in Seattle, in front of the house of Adam's parents.

After discovering the dirty truth about why Adam and Phuong divorced, they immediately flew to California to see his son. They were so angry, of course. They would never believe their blue-blooded son could do such a terrible thing as that to Phuong, whom they loved as their daughter. They worried about Phuong one, ten to Michael. Adam's parents returned to California to stay with Phuong for a few days. They planned all kinds of things to help Phuong and Michael. But Phuong rejected because she was sure that she was strong enough to raise Michael, and she believed that even though Michael lived with Adam, with his dirty personality, Michael would be happy with Phuong than Adam. That was the moment the battle for Michael's favorite began. They pulled up the play by themselves, no screenplay necessary, and acted until everything was being exposed.

A few years have passed, and Adam's parents have not seen their son because they are ashamed of him and do not want him to come home for holidays or Tet. But when Adam emailed them to announce he would remarry, they immediately called him to tell him to return home with his girlfriend. Adam has no idea what his parents are going to talk about. But whatever they say, he would not change his mind about getting married to Ha.

Six months after the "mask-off" convention on Phuong's birthday, Ha and Adam's relationship has improved. It is somehow strange and unfair for Phuong, the natural person suffering from the pain they caused, who lost her new true love. Ha got divorced from Thomas, no matter how much he begged her to come back to him. Eventually, Thomas is fired from his job in the restaurant due to his bad behavior with everyone there. He always appeared on the job in drunk conditions. He drank a lot after his divorce from Ha. He regretted not loving Ha as she always wanted; he always listened to his mother; he never heard nor understood Ha's feelings and suffering after all these years living in that hell house. Whenever Ha wanted to share her deepest thoughts, Thomas tried to avoid them. Now, what else could Thomas do right now? He could never take Ha back to him.

It is too late.

At first, Thomas refused to sign the divorce paper. It had made the situation worse. He did not accept this divorce because he believed they could work out this marriage again. Honestly, is there anything else being worked out in this failed marriage that one side never understood the other side? Tony, Ha's lawyer, tried to convince the judge, but there was no use. Even Thomas' lawyer did the same. The judge could not rule the decision if Thomas were still hesitating. While the things were in the big mess, there was manna from heaven. Mr. Tan knew that his son was always drunk and that he would not have any self-awareness when alcohol got into him. So Mr. Tan used that "advantage" to do the default dissolution of the marriage to help Ha. He even tried to fake his signature Thomas to complete the divorce case. When Thomas discovered the truth, he turned out to be a crazy man. It was, unsurprisingly. He smashed everything in the house. He got furious with his father. He came to Ha's firm to mess up everything. But there was nothing Thomas could do to reverse it. All bets are off. Ha was worried for Mr. Tan. She wanted Mr. Tan to move out. But he refused. He said that Thomas needed help and would be there for his son. Ha understood that. But she would not leave her father-in-law living alone like that with Thomas. She came by sometimes to help him with cooking or housework.

Since her devious mother-in-law was kicked out of the house after that scandal, Mr. Tan has lived alone with Thomas. He starts to learn everything by himself again, from cooking to housework. But he does not mind at all. He feels relief after he leaves her. He or anyone else in the family cannot believe a person like Mrs. Linh would do such a shameful thing like that. Now, the news about Mrs. Linh remains unknown.

Probably, she is dead.

Life with Ha has been like a fairy tale. Right now, she only wants to be Adam and be happy with him. One evening, while they were in bed after having sex, as usual, Adam asked Ha to go on a trip with him to Vietnam in the summer. Ha was undecided because there were so many things needed to do at the firm. She could not just leave work behind to get on vacation. Adam convinced her hard, and in the end, she accepted.

They spent a month in Vietnam. They traveled from Hanoi to Ha Long bay, then to Hue and Danang, and finally, they stopped at Saigon. Ha agreed with Adam that she would have regretted it if she did not go on this trip. She missed Vietnam. After leaving her homeland to settle in a freed land, Ha never stopped dreaming about returning one day. She was surprised by the fast-changing of Vietnam recently. High buildings, booming economy, delicious cuisines, and the kindness of every Vietnamese everywhere they came.

After 1975, she knew that Vietnam had been so poor and being controlled under government subsidies. It was a tough time. But Ha read somewhere before about archery. When performing it, the archer would pull the string toward them, eyes on the target, and release the arrow. Then, the arrow would fly at high speed to the target board. It meant to move fast forward at high speed. Sometimes, they had to fall behind to prepare for that big jump. Vietnam had been far back for so long; now, it had taken the giant leap, fully equipped for the growth of everything. Ha was so amazed.

While in Saigon, Adam took Ha to a restaurant before they returned to the U.S. the next day. That night, Saigon had had heavy rain since the afternoon. Strangely, when it came to rain in Saigon, everything turned out to be so gloomy. Maybe it was because when it was raining, people could not enjoy the outside activities or being with people they love. In the restaurant, there were only a few guests. Adam and Ha sat at a table near the window with a view of the street. It was still raining cats and dogs. Ha looked out of the window with one hand holding her cheek and the other toying with her fingers. She sighed.

"Why must it be rained on the last day in here?" She moaned. "It is so unfair. We could have been going out in the city instead of staying in the hotel for the whole day."

Adam chuckled. He poured the wine for Ha. "Well, we go out for dinner, don't we?"

"Uh-huh!" Ha kept her eyes on the street. There were cars, motorbikes, and people under the rain who were hustling to come home or find a place to keep themselves dry. Also, people were pushing the food cart to sell. That sense made Ha feel emotional and miss her mother.

"Do you see the lady pushing the food cart over there?" Ha pointed. Adam looked at her, pointing. Adam said yes. Ha continued. "She reminds me of my mom."

Adam turned his look to Ha. "How comes?"

"Well," Ha said. "When we came to the U.S., my mom never had one day for herself. She worked days and nights to raise me. She worked in the restaurants until late at night. She never rested. She even took some clothes home to sew for some spare money for me. So many times, I wanted to help her by getting a part-time job, but she refused it. She said that she could take care of me and that all I had to do was focus on studying. Looking at her trying her best to provide for me, I promised myself that I would do anything to make her proud and that I could take care of her the way she used to do. But when I had that chance, she passed away. It has been suffering to me every day. I never had a chance to pay back what she had done for me."

Ha dropped a few tears. Adam held her hand.

"Hey, look at me," Adam said, and Ha looked into his eyes. "I am sure your mom is proud of you. You are beautiful and successful with your law career, and you have been so strong to go through all the troubles yourself. You always know how to stand up on your feet and move on. That with me is enough to make your mother smile down at you in the other world."

Those words from Adam made Ha smile. She leaned forward to kiss Adam. Ha was never wrong when she chose Adam to be her new lover. She truly felt happy when she was with him. After dinner, they stayed in the restaurant to talk. They remembered all their Vietnam trips, and they even thought they should come back here every year to enjoy themselves. The rain had stopped. It was about nine-thirty. The moon had risen and shone directly at the window where Ha and Adam were sitting. Suddenly, Adam told Ha one more time to give him her hands for no reason. Ha did and laughed.

"What is this?" She asked. And for a moment, her heartbeat fast.

"Babe," Adam said. "for all these years, we have been together from bad times to good times. But after all the stormy days, we can finally be together without any trouble, and nothing can stop us. You are the light of my life; you come to my life as a gift, and you give me the love I never had. I can have it. Ha, I love you so much. I know I am not good enough for you to deserve me, but I want to say that I cannot live without you. What happened in the past had been done. Now, I want to focus on my future, and it would be great if I had you beside me to continue that journey ahead. So," Adam then got out of the chair, took out a red box inside his pant pocket, and kneeled one knee in front of Ha.

Ha looked bewildered. "Darling, what are you doing?"

"Don't say a word right now." Adam opened the box, and there was a diamond ring inside it. He took out the ring and put the box on the table. He held the call toward Ha. "Ha, will you marry me?"

Everyone in the restaurant at that moment paid attention to them. Some were recording. Ha covered her mouth with a joyful expression. She got emotional.

"Are you sure you want to do this?" Ha asked.

Adam nodded slightly.

"I will marry you, Adam. YES, I WILL MARRY YOU." Ha agreed, and Adam put the ring on her finger. Adam stood up, hugged Ha, and they kissed. People around clapped their hands and cheered the moment.

One more time, Ha has to face her fiancé's parents. She is so nervous. She knows that Adam's parents must hate her so much because she is the bitch who destroyed the happiness of Phuong and Adam. She feels like she is sitting on the fire. Ha turns to Adam, just turning off the engine, and holds his right arm. Adam can feel the shaking in Ha's hand and the cold.

"Babe, what's the matter?" Adam asks. "Are you ok?"

"I don't want to get in there," Ha confesses. "I am scared. I have cold feet. I can imagine the face of your parents right now. They will eat me alive, and there is no way they will love me."

Adam does not say anything. He kissed her on the lips. Then, he begins to talk. "Everything will be fine. My parents are not like whom you think. They will love you for sure."

"But..."

"No 'but.' Just come inside with me and remember, be yourself."

Even what Adam said can comfort Ha a little bit, but it doesn't entirely help her reduce her worries. But Ha has the experience of meeting parents, so now, whatever happens, she accepts it no matter what. Ha knows that even if his parents don't take her, Adam and she can still get married and be happy in California. Not living here in Seattle with Adam's parents.

Ha has prepared gifts for Adam's parents. A box of edible bird's nests, which she asked one of her friends to buy for her, for Adam's father. A Coach handbag for Adam's mother. Holding the gift in her hand, she hopes these things can help her to score in their eyes.

Adam is holding the other hand. Tight. Ha takes a deep breath and exhales. Adam knocks on the door. For a few minutes, not so long, the door is opened. An older man, about 70 years old, with gray hair, and a big pair of glasses, appears in front of them.

"Hi, Dad," Adam says.

"Uhm." He says back.

"Hello, Mr. Nguyen," Ha says. "It is nice to meet you."

"Likewise." There is no expression on his face. He does quick research on Ha. From her hair, which she has dyed brown a few weeks before, to her white dress with the belt of Chanel and the high heel. Probably from Steve Madden. Then, he turns to Adam. "I hope your mom will like it. Come on in!"

"That is a good sign." Ha whispers but still keeps the smile on her face. They both walk inside the house.

The house is nothing like Ha had expected before. She thought the house would be full of a Vietnamese vibe, but no, she feels like she is in the place of a typical American family. The decoration is modern, a bit rusty, and still looks luxurious. The beige wall color makes the house more bright. And the sense of lavender has added to the freshness of this house. Ha thinks in her head that whoever did this house's interior design deserves to have raised.

"You go and sit down. I say hello to my mom, and I will be back." Adam says, and he kisses Ha's forehead.

She smiles back. Then, she meets the look of Mr. Nguyen. Now, she is shaking once again. Ha keeps biting her lower lip real hard, her hands holding the gift bags tight Mr. Nguyen can see the tendon on her arms.

Mr. Nguyen gives out the gesture to invite Ha to sit down. Ha bows her head moves to the sofa, and sits down quickly before Mr. Nguyen can sit.

"Shit," Ha spills out that word after she finds out how impolite she is. She stands up again. But "shit" has made her more embarrassed. "I'm...I'm....I'm so sorry for saying that. It was not what I meant."

Mr. Nguyen sighs. "That's ok. I don't mind." He sits down. "My wife and I talked bad words a lot. It is pretty normal." He notices that Ha is still standing and tells her to sit.

Ha sits on the sofa, facing the chair of Mr. Nguyen. There is silence in the room. An uncomfortable one. Ha rests her hands on her crossed legs. Mr. Nguyen placed both hands on the armrest and kept breathing in and out. Ha feels it is weird, so she has to break this silence.

She cleared her throat. "You have a nice house—awe-inspiring interior design. I mean, from the decoration to the furniture. Everything looks great."

Mr. Nguyen looks around the house as if it is the first time he has looked at it. "Thank you! My wife did everything. She used to work for an interior design company."

"Woah, that's amazing. Well organized. I... I admire," She waves her hands around to include everything in this room. "Those."

Mr. Nguyen slightly nods his head. There is silence again.

"So," Mr. Nguyen clears his throat. "I heard Adam tell me that you are a lawyer. What type?"

"Well, uhm, I am a divorce lawyer, a defense lawyer, or a civil litigation lawyer. I do whatever case the firm gives me."

"That's interesting." He says. "Back in Vietnam, I used to be a lawyer. I only practiced for three years until... you know. Fuck communist! Don't get me wrong! I love Vietnam. My wife and I came back for vacation many times. It's just like I don't like the regime. It is so dictated. You know what I mean?"

"I understand that," Ha says.

There is talking coming from somewhere and mixing with the laughing. Adam is shouldering a woman who looks about 60 years old with hazelnut hair, a red button-down shirt, black jeans, and a pair of sneakers. She is wearing makeup, not too much but enough to show she is very detailed in doing it. Overall, she does not look her age at all.

When Ha looks at this woman, the image of Mrs. Linh pops up in her mind one more time.

Seeing the woman, Ha immediately stands up. Adam comes and stands next to her. He puts his arm around her belly. The woman crosses her arms. Her face does not look pleased at all.

"Mom, this is Ha. My fiancé." He turns to Ha. "And this is my mom, Thu."

Ha lows her head to greet Mrs. Thu. "It is nice to meet you. Adam has told me a lot about you."

"Uh-huh. I think the pleasure is mine to meet you finally." Mrs. Thu says. She looks at the bags on the sofa. "What is that?" She points.

Ha looks at the bags and completely forgets about the gifts she prepared for them. She grabs it quickly.

"Uhm, I have a gift for you and Mr. Nguyen." She says. "I hope you will like it."

She hands Mr. Nguyen the red bag. "I have a box of edible bird's nests from Nha Trang. I heard that this one is perfect for your health."

Mr. Nguyen takes the gift. "Thank you."

"You're welcome!" Ha says, then she hands the other bag to Mrs. Thu. "And I have a handbag for you. This is the newest design from Coach. Adam told me that you love luxurious brands. So, I am buying you this because this is my favorite brand."

Contrary to Mr. Nguyen, Mrs. Thu takes the gift without saying anything. She smiles at everyone else. "Let's have lunch, shall we? It is getting cold."

"I'm starving." Mr. Nguyen exclaims, and he comes after his wife.

Ha whispers in Adam's left ear. "I think your parents don't like me."

"Don't be ridiculous! It is just the beginning. Let's have lunch."

They move to the dining room to have lunch with Adam's parents.

They have steak and fries for lunch, served with red wine. The lunch goes well for most of them. They talk about the past, childhood of Adam, politics, world stories, and all kinds of stuff. But they don't say anything or mention one bit about Ha or her accounts. And that is what Ha wants. She keeps praying in her mind that please, please, let the past rest in peace.

After lunch, Adam and his father go to the living room. Ha offers to help wash the dishes. Mrs. Thu does not say anything. When Ha finishes with those dishes, she wipes her hands with the clean white hanging on the cupboard.

Mrs. Thu is sitting at the table and waiting for Ha. She smiles and tells Ha to sit down. Ha sits opposite Mrs. Nhu. There is a tea set on the table. Mrs. Thu asks Ha whether she usually drinks tea or not. Ha says she sometimes drinks when she wants to read a book. It helps her to focus. But coffee is always Ha's favorite one.

Mrs. Thu agrees with Ha. She pours Ha a full of cup of green tea. Ha says thanks and takes a sip.

"This tea is so delicious." Ha gives compliments. "And it smells good."

Mrs. Thu places her teacup back on the small china coaster after she sips.

"I bought it on a trip to providence in North Vietnam, where they had so many fields of green tea. I love that place. One is because of the delicious tea and its beauty. And the other is because it made me feel relaxed there. Can you imagine this? In the early morning, because that place is up on the hill, it usually has fog, and you can see it coming into your room. I took a walk to a town near my hotel. The breeze, a little bit cold, and the scenery there were like cleansing my body and the soul I had in me. I forgot everything that made me feel tired and angry. If I have a chance, and I have, I will go back there one more time."

"Listening to you, I want to go there too," Ha says.

"You should."

Suddenly, Mrs. Thu changes her face into a serious one. She gets her back up straight. "Ha, I want to talk to you about something."

It seems like someone has started the fire inside her. She can feel the burning in her stomach. Maybe tea can help. But wait, tea is still hot. It would add more to the heat inside her belly. She swallows her saliva. It may help.

"Yes?" Ha says with worries.

"You see," Mrs. Thu says. "You know that my husband and I had known about the thing between you and Adam. You stepped into the life of Adam and Phuong, and you ruined everything. We were so shocked and so worried about Phuong and Michael. For all these years, Phuong has been like a daughter to me. She has nothing I hate and all the qualities I always expected if I had a daughter. When I met Phuong when Adam took her home, I knew she would be a good wife and daughter-in-law. So, I accepted her. I thought they would be happy happily ever after until you appeared.

"When I knew about everything, I swore to God that the very first thing I do was find that bitch and kill her immediately. Making her pay for everything that she had done. Yes, I blamed you for what you did—a lot. But then I realized something. It is not 100% your fault. Somehow, the fault belonged to Adam because he had feelings for you and fell in love with you. Just like that, he left his own family to come to you. After we knew, we decided to disown him. Cheating, fucking, betraying. I hate those, and if my husband did the same thing to me, I would have fucking left him. Then, one day, Adam flew here to see us again. He stood outside our door for hours to ask us for forgiveness. But you know, parents will never leave their children no matter what. We welcome him back even though we know what kind of person he is. He told us about everything on Phuong's birthday and how they ended up everything. I felt so pity for Phuong when he told me. But when it comes to the part about you, I can not keep myself together because everything he said about you is all the nicest thing. We had a big fight, you know. Then came the strangest part ever. Some things crossed my mind. The way he said about you, even though we do not like it at all, I could see how much he loves you and wants to have you in his life. That never happened before when he said about Phuong. His eyes have shown me everything. He loves you."

Mrs. Thu laughs. She takes another sip of tea. Damn, she must love drinking this tea. It is about to get cold. She does not mind. "What else could I do at that time? As I said, Adam is our son. Our only son. Whatever the decision he made, we must respect that. Now he has chosen you to be his love; we have no right to obligate that."

Mrs. Thu reaches out her hands to hold Ha's. Ha gets startled and surprised. "Ha, I knew everything about you, about what you'd been through in your life and your last marriage. It is so horrible, so desperate, and so sad. You have been suffering a lot in your life. From being abused by the husband's family, both soul and physical, to the ugly truth that you cannot have a child. To me, it is so cruel to a woman because being a mom is the most important and sacred thing in a woman's life. You'd tried and tried and got nothing—no sympathy from your ex-husband or your mother-in-law. But now, I think it is time for you to settle down with your new beginning. What happened in the past stayed there forever and never looked back. Ha, you are a beautiful woman with kindness and compassion. You think for others before you think for yourself. That is what I can see from you. I have been considering a lot as to whether I should accept you or not based on what you did to Phuong in the past. So, here is the thing I want to say. My husband and I would be so happy to welcome you to our family and be our daughter-in-law. I don't mind if you do not have a child. All I care about is your happiness with Adam. I know one thing for sure you and he would be happy for the rest of your life. I wish nothing more than that."

Every word Mrs. Thu just shared with Ha made her emotional. Sitting in front of her is not a woman who used to frighten her on the first day she met, throws shady words to insult her, or warns her that if Ha makes Adam unhappy, she will cut her throat. It is a woman who loves her and has sympathy for what Ha has been through. Mrs. Thu leaves all the hate and prejudices she had on Ha before behind to welcome Ha to the family. There is nothing to describe my feeling about Ha right now. She can guarantee that she has been into the right family where she can build a happy family.

Ha hugs Mrs. Thu tight.

"Thank you so much, Mrs. Thu," Ha says.

"It's thank you, mom." Mrs. Thu corrects.

"Thank you, mom."

There is the sound of popping Champagne from nowhere. Mrs. Thu and Ha both get startled and laugh at the same time. Adam comes in with the bottle of champagne in his hand, which has been spilled out. Mr. Nguyen walks behind him. He comes to Ha and hugs her.

"Welcome to the family, Ha!" He says.

"Thank you, Dad!"

"Now, let the wedding begin!" Adam shouts in joy.

CHAPTER 16

Phuong

(Three days before the wedding)

On a Tuesday, Phuong takes Michael to the mall to get him something nice for the wedding. Walking through the mall, Phuong turns to Michael to ask what he thinks about his father's remarriage.

Michael shrugs. "I don't know. If that makes him happy, then let him do it." The answer of Michael is plain simple, and short. It can tell that Michael has forgotten everything and opened his heart to changes nowadays, his father will have a new wife, and his mother probably can have her new love too.

The shopping for Michael takes little time. All he needs is a suit and a pair of shoes. Phuong decides to choose the newest design of Calvin Klein for children. It is a white suit, tailored perfectly as if it were designed for Michael. When he tries it on, he looks like a Hollywood movie star. Michael looks at himself in the mirror. Phuong stands behind him.

"You will steal the show, babe," Phuong says.

"Do you think it is too tight for me?" Michael asks.

"No, I think it fits you well."

When Adam and Ha came to Phuong's house to announce the news, everyone was so excited and congratulated them. Of course, they knew this day would come. Ha had asked Phuong to become her bridesmaid, and she accepted. She said nothing would be more privileged and honorable than doing for her best friend.

In the last weddings with Adam or with Thomas, they became bridesmaids of each other. It was a good time until everything shattered. Maybe there was a curse. Phuong became the bridesmaid at Ha's wedding with Thomas. Ha divorced. Ha became the bridesmaid at Phuong's wedding with Adam. Phuong divorced. But they did not care about that superstitious thing.

They discussed the wedding plan together: where the wedding would be held, what to wear, what to eat, how many guests would be there, etcetera… Sitting opposite Mrs. Nhu and Phuong, the couple held hands and smiled. They were so happy. Phuong looked at them as if someone had flipped the pages back to the previous chapters in her mind.

Phuong's wedding with Adam many years ago was somehow the most beautiful time in her life. Phuong was in a blue dress, crossing Mrs. Nhu's arm, and walking down the aisles. Everyone in the chapel stood up and looked at Phuong. Some were whispering to give Phuong the best compliments. Standing in front of Adam with the Father reading, Phuong knew that from this moment, she finally could belong to Adam, and she wanted nothing more than to be happy with him for the rest of her life. At the ball, "Can't take my eyes off you," which was both Adam and Ha's favorite song, was being played. Adam took the lead like a natural professional dancer (he had been practicing for months). Phuong followed his lead. A little clumsy at first, but just looking at his eyes, Phuong got the energy, and she danced through the song.

Thinking back to that moment, tears came from nowhere. Mrs. Nhu looked at Phuong and whispered.

"Are you ok, dear?"

Phuong wiped the tears quickly and smiled. "I am fine. I'm…just happy for them."

Mrs. Nhu nodded her head. She would not give any further talk or advice because she trusted Phuong had changed, and she was truly happy for Adam and Ha.

After the shopping, Phuong takes Michael to a small restaurant in the mall, where they sell ramen and Japanese food. Michael loves it because he watches a lot of anime and uses Adam's Netflix account. He is obsessed with Japanese culture.

Phuong remembers one time she walked through Michael's room and listened to some weird noises. She pushed the door, not too broad, just enough for her to peek in. And there was Michael speaking something in his high voice; he was in a colorful costume and did some actions which Phuong could not understand. But one thing was for sure, what he said was not in English. Phuong was afraid that someone had possessed him. Later, when Phuong found out that what Michael did was based on some cute characters in some anime he watched. That is called cosplay. She is glad that nothing wrong with him.

They order two bowls of ramen and a dish of sushi rolls. Phuong must figure out what to eat because she has never tried it before. Michael helps her to order. Phuong loves spicy, so she has a bowl of Spicy Miso ramen. And Michael has Chicken ramen.

"Are you excited about your father's wedding?" Phuong asks while Michael is sipping his noddle.

He swallows. "Yes, of course. It is a big day for him." And then he drinks some water.

"Uhm." She continues with her noddle. "You know, I feel happy for him too. He can find a new love for himself."

"You do? After what he did to you?"

"Babe, it is the past. I'd forgiven him. And you've forgiven him too. Let it rest in peace. He is my ex-husband, but it doesn't mean he is a stranger. He is family to us. Without him, I would not have had you in this life. Agree that I used to hate him and Ha so much, but after time, I found out that hating him and she did not bring me anything, only tiredness and trauma in my head. And then, when I finally can have a new love in my life, I turned it to dust."

Phuong realizes she is too mushy and too dramatic. She changes the subject. "Let's finish it and go home to prepare dinner with daddy."

"You miss him, don't you?" Michael still wants to talk about this.

"What?" Phuong asks. She chuckles. "Why do you ask me like that?"

"I don't know. It's just... I-I can see it in you."

Phuong rubs Michael's head. "There are things that you only want to keep for yourself. No matter what happens."

They leave the restaurant after finishing lunch. As they are walking, Phuong suddenly stops in the middle of the road and looks to the left. A unit is closed, and outside hanging, a sign on the door. "For Lease." Phuong looked at that place for a moment.

Michael saw his mother had not come with him, he came to her and shook her hand.

"Mom, Mom, MOM!" He yelled for the third time.

Phuong startles. She looks at Michael.

"What are you doing, mom?"

"Oh, there was nothing. It's just..." Phuong cannot continue as if there is something stuck in her throat. "Let's go!"

Then, they leave the mall to go home.

That place used to be an ice cream place where Hoa took Phuong and Michael for the first time. And soon, it became her favorite ice cream place, and Hoa and her dated after that every dinner. Because of the blooming of many other drinking places in this mall, the business started to go down, and shortly, they shut down. At that moment, as if someone had put sugar inside her mouth, she felt the sweetness of vanilla, her favorite flavor, at the tip of her tongue. She remembers that Hoa used to feed her ice cream. His smile was so beautiful and so charming. Thankfully, Michael has taken her out of that "la-la land." Phuong returned to reality.

On the way home, she asks Michael whether he wants to have ice cream or not. Michael agrees, and they go to the same ice cream place to have delicious ice cream.

CHAPTER 17

Ha

(Two days before the wedding)

Like fate has settled, all three of them could never be separated. Life always brought them back together, no matter what.

Ha comes to Phuong's house one night to talk to Mrs. Nhu about her worries before the wedding. Ha chooses the night Phuong has her night shift at the hospital so that she can be more comfortable because she is going to marry her best friend's ex-husband.

"I felt so terrible right now, mom," Ha says. "Is it even fair for Phuong at all? I mean, after all, I had stolen her husband."

Mrs. Nhu smiles. "Why, until now, do you still have that thought?"

"I don't know. I feel like that."

"Babe, you love Adam. And he loves you. That's it. You guys will be happy together because, after everything, your love for each other has not changed a bit. That's something that not everyone can do. Phuong and Adam used to love each other, and they failed. I always blamed Adam for his fault for letting that happen. But I always believe that when a relationship ends, both must have responsibilities for that. Much or less. One fault is that Adam betrayed Phuong. One fault because Phuong, in some parts, had ignored her happiness to focus on something else she considered to be more important. You see, now they had learned some lessons, and they had realized it. But it was too late. Adam had a new beginning with you, and I am sure he won't make the same mistake again this time. And Phuong, well, after Hoa went away, she finally realized she could have loved him and felt his love. Now, I hope Phuong is happy in her life."

"I hope so, too," Ha says.

Suddenly, the thunder roars. Both Ha and Mrs. Nhu startles. The chime of the clock in the living rings. It is 9 p.m. Outside, it begins to rain. According to the weather forecast, tonight will have heavy rain, the heaviest rain in the last five years. When it comes to the rain, things feel like being reborn again. It can recover everything that has been damaged by the heat of the sun.

When Ha was young, Mrs. Trang told her, "whenever you felt angry or anxious, just immerse yourself inside the bathtub with warm water and let the water wash away everything that caused you tired." And it worked. During their time in that hell house, Ha never spent less than 15 minutes in the bathroom. She soaked inside the bathtub with red rose petals and bath oil, listened to classical music from Bach or Beethoven, and ignored the outside world. With all the pressures in life plus the torture from Mrs. Linh, Ha forced herself to live in her world. There was no wonder the family's water bill was always raised.

Ha stands up and comes to the window near the sink. She looks outside. The water pours down from the roof and flows away. It is like all the depression being washed away and down to the sewage.

"Rain has a power, doesn't it, mom?" Ha asks while her eyes are still outside.

"I cannot agree more." Mrs. Nhu says.

Ha sighs and returns to her seat. "Mom is there something I want to ask you."

"Go ahead, dear."

"Would you be the person who walks me down to the aisle on my wedding day?"

Mrs. Nhu used to walk Phuong down the aisle at Phuong's wedding, and to her, it was the most honorable moment that she could do for her daughter. Holding Phuong's hand and walking, she had to keep her tears inside because she did not want Phuong to see her crying, and Phuong might cry too in front of so many guests. Also, she did not want her makeup to wash away. Before Mrs. Nhu gave Phuong's hand to Adam, she looked at Phuong and said nothing. She just gave her a slight kiss on her left cheek. She returned to her seat to watch the ceremony.

When the Father announced that Phuong and Adam were finally husband and wife, Mrs. Nhu understood that her only daughter had finally walked out of her life and be with her husband. All the memories with her daughter started returning to her mind like a movie. From the moment Phuong was born to the day she first called her mom. From the day she and Phuong came to the U.S. to the day she became the hospital dean. It was like just yesterday. At that time, she could not hold the tear anymore. She cried. Mrs. Trang sat next to her and noticed her friend crying. She smoothed her and held her in her arms. Mrs. Trang understood Mrs. Nhu's feelings because she had been through that situation when watching her daughter, Ha, belong to Thomas' family.

Mothers' love for their kids will always stay forever, no matter what. They carry their kids inside for nine months and ten days, and by the milk line, they raise their children. They give them everything they want; they sacrifice anything, even their happiness, to provide for their children. Not only the mother but also every father would do the same. There is a saying that when a child loses their parents, that child has lost wings, but when they lose a child, they lose the whole world.

Mrs. Nhu smiles and hugs Ha. "I would love to do so. It will be my honor. But..." Mrs. Nhu pauses and releases her. She holds Ha's hands. "I have to say no."

Ha's eyes open widely. "What? Why?"

"I will leave that honor to somebody else. Somebody that loves you like a real daughter. It is not because I don't want to do it. I would love to. But that person would be a perfect choice for you."

"Who are you talking about?" Ha asks.

Ha takes a deep breath and breathes out. She knocks on the door. It takes a few minutes for someone to open the door. In front of Ha, it is Mr. Tan. He is wearing glasses, his hair has turned all grey, and he smiles at Ha. Before Ha can do anything, he hugs her first. Ha is still surprised, but suddenly, she feels the warmth from Mr. Tan. She was clutching her father after many years of going away. It is cozy, strangely, and Ha misses it. Ha hugs him back.

"I miss you so much, Ha." Mr. Tan says.

"I miss you too. Dad." Replies Ha.

They come inside. She never thinks of returning to this hell house from the day she walked out of this house without bringing anything with her. Right now, it is precisely like a hell house. Everything around runs down back. There are boxes on the floor. Some stuff is lying on the floor. She can smell the mold too. In the day, Mrs. Linh spent so much money repainting the house every year. She would never let her home run down poorly like this.

"What happens to this place?" Ha asks. "It looked terrible, dad."

"I will not make any argument on that." Mr. Tan says.

"Are you leaving?"

"Yeah, I will sell this house and move into a smaller house in San Diego."

"Why are you moving?"

"Well, I want to change." Mr. Tan looks around the house. "There are so many bad memories in this house. Don't you agree?"

Ha nods.

Mr. Tan continues. "Besides, I want to sell the house to have money for Thomas to begin again. He wants to open his restaurant since nobody wants to hire him anymore because of his past. I know that he deserves it after what he has done to you in the past. Karma, as they always say. But after all, he is my son, and I would not bear to look at him like that. He gets drunk every night and can't even control himself. I want him to be happy, of course. I suggested my plan to him, and he seemed very excited. He is on the way back to normal. He learned more about new dishes; he told me many ideas about his restaurant. Believe it or not, I think my cholesterol is increasing because I try his food daily. But it is good to see Thomas be on his feet again."

"Yes, it is great," Ha says. "I am glad that he can find something to hold on to. Cooking is always his passion. It will never change no matter what."

"I agree with you." Mr. Tan says. He suddenly realized something. "Oh, where is my manner? Do you want something to drink?"

"Oh, no. Don't mind me, dad." Ha says. "Where is Thomas?"

"He is going out to buy some stuff to cook and looking for the location for his restaurant. He won't be back until afternoon." Mr. Tan wipes his hands with a white cloth in his pocket. "Packing up is so tiring. I never know so much stuff in this house like that."

"Do you need help?"

"No. I've almost finished. Tomorrow, the truck will come and carry everything to my house in San Diego. The rest will go to donations. By the way," Mr. Tan turns around to look for something.

"Where is it?" He murmurs. "I remember I've put it around here."

He runs through every box with a label on it. But he cannot find the thing he wants anywhere.

Seeing Mr. Tan struggling to find something, Ha asks what he is looking for. Mr. Tan says it is the box of Ha's stuff.

After she left and never returned, Mr. Tan carefully packed everything that belonged to Ha in one box and left it in the garage. Ha appreciates that, but she declines, says she no longer needs it and tells Mr. Tan to give it to the donation.

With Ha, when she says she never wants anything to do with this family, she truly means it, even her own clothes or stuff. No, thank you. Those only bring bad memories back to her. She does not want it at all.

Mr. Tan stretches out and groans. "It is so tiring. Oh, why are you here today?"

Ha tells Mr. Tan to sit down. "I am going to get married tomorrow. With Adam."

"Really?" Mr. Tan gets shocked. He was shocked because he would not think it was so fast. It has been six months since Thomas and Ha got divorced. "Woah, congratulation to you and him. You must be thrilled."

"Yes, I am happy." She says. "And I want you to be there."

Mr. Tan laughs and shakes his head. "I don't think it is a good idea. I am nothing to you after your divorce from Thomas. My appearance there will only make you uncomfortable, and I think nobody wants me to be there, at least after what they knew our family had done to you."

Ha expected Mr. Tan would say something like that. She can understand the complexity that Mr. Tan has inside him.

After many years of living in a house, he is cuckolded by his wife, who sleeps with young men and lies to him under the cover of a faithful wife. She is nothing but a faker and a hypocrite. And his son is an abuser of his wife. And yet, Mr. Tan could not do anything to stop or prevent it from happening. He feels so sybaritic. But Ha, does not care about those things. Since she stepped into this house, Mr. Tan has been there for Ha. He is the only person who stays on Ha's side whenever Mrs. Linh throws terrible words at her. He gave her advice in life whenever Ha had troubles in her life.

And more than that, Mr. Tan never treats Ha as a daughter-in-law. She is a daughter to him. A biological daughter to him. Ha was growing up without knowing her father. She always desired to have a father in her life, spend time with him, let him take her to school, hangs out with him, and be loved like other children. Mr. Tan is more than a father in her life.

Ha stands up, comes to Mr. Tan, and kneels. She places her hands on Mr. Tan's lap.

"Dad, I am not asking you to be the guest at my wedding tomorrow. It will be the worst thing I do to you. You deserve more than that. You are like a real father to me, and your position in my heart will never be shifted. What I am asking you today is that I want you to be my father walking me down the aisle on my wedding day. It will be the best thing that ever happens in my life. Please, Dad!"

Mr. Tan looks into Ha's eyes. He can see the sincerity in those. If that is what Ha wants him to do and could make him feel less guilty in his soul, then he would have no other choice.

"Are you sure about it?" He asks. "I don't want to be a burden there."

Ha nodded slightly. "It will make me the happiest girl in the world."

"Then, let's do it!" He says.

FINAL

The Wedding Day

The wedding is about to begin. Everyone arrived and sat in the chapel. Adam is in a white suit. He is a little nervous, but he tries to calm himself to stop shaking. He feels like he is about to pee himself. The best man behind him, Mark, his best friend, sees his butts banging each other; he steps up and whispers to his left ear.

"Stop doing that. It will be ok."

Adam breathes in and breathes out. "I can't. I am too nervous."

"I know, but it is happening, ok?. You have to deal with it. We have been practicing this before. This is your second wedding, and you've your experience already."

"It is different."

"How is it different?"

"It is fucking real."

Father hears that. He clears his throat. "We are in the church. Please watch your language!"

The groom turns to Father. "I am sorry. I am nervous."

In the makeup room, the bride is all alone. The makeup is done, and the dress is beautiful. Ha keeps walking to practice her vows. Gosh, she needs a cigarette right now. She looks at the clock, twenty more minutes until the ceremony.

Cigarette, Cigarette. Cigarette. Yes, Ha has begun smoking again recently. Probably, Adam has a bad influence on her.

She throws the notecard with vows in it into the trash. She goes through her handbag, but no cigarette. Maybe her mother knows about this and took it away. Ha gets out of the room. There is no one outside. She walks down the hall to find somebody with a cigarette. And as she wishes, a janitor is mopping the floor. She comes to him.

"Hi, do you have a cigarette?" She asks him quickly.

The janitor looks at her curiously. "What?"

"Do you have a cigarette?" She raises her voice to him.

"Yeah, so?"

"SO?" Now, she is super angry. "What the fuck is wrong with your brain? When someone asks you that, you must know they want it. Jesus Christ!"

The janitor takes out of his pocket a pack of cigarettes. He shakily gives it to her. She grabs the pack and gets a cigarette.

"Lighter, please!" The janitor lights up the cigarette for her. The bride smokes, and she feels much better. So satisfying

"You don't know how much I need this shit. Thank you for making my day."

Then, she throws the pack of cigarettes at him, and he catches it. The bride leaves. He looks at her and shakes his head. "What a psycho!"

"I've heard that."

Ha returns to the makeup room. She closes the door ten more minutes until the ceremony. She lies on the couch, puts her left hand on her forehead, and enjoys the rest of the cigarette. She closes her eyes and starts thinking about her life after she says, "I do." It will be a wonderful life. Indeed, there will be no more suffering, no more painful moments, and no more crying about her miserable life. That is what Ha knows for sure.

Someone knocks on the door.

"Come in," Ha says.

That person opens and walks in. It is Mr. Tan. He is in a blue navy suit. He walks to the couch where Ha is lying. He starts to get angry when he sees a scene he does not want to see.

"Oh my god, are you fucking kidding me?" He takes the cigarette from her mouth. "What are you doing?"

She sits up. "I am nervous."

Mr. Tan sighs. He throws the cigarette into the tin trash can, returns to the couch, and sits next to her. He holds her hands.

His hands are so warm and soft. It is hard to believe they belong to an older man. Ha always likes to touch his hands. And she envies it too.

"Listen, dear," His eyes meet her eyes. "I know it is tough for you. I wanted to leave the church and flee away when I got married. I was so nervous that I almost peed myself. Well, I peed myself, not a lot, but no one noticed. Thank God for that!"

They both laughs. He continues. "You've made the right decision, dear. The man outside was born to be with you. Your marriage with Thomas is a failure, but this time with Adam, I believe, will work. Adam may not be perfect like other men, but I can see the love he gives you, the future he can assure you, and the truthfulness he has for you. That man is very hard to find nowadays. Maybe you are worried about your decision right now, but you will be happy when you are with him in one house. Ok?"

"Really?" Ha asks.

"I swear."

Ha gives Mr. Tan a big hug and kisses his left cheek. "Thank you so much. I love you."

"I love you too!" Mr. Tan says. He released her. "It's time now."

The time has come. They are standing outside the chapel, waiting for the door to open. They look at each other and smile.

"Are you ready?" Mr. Tan asks.

"Yes, let's do this!" Ha says.

He offers his right hand, and the bride holds his hand. The door opens. The wedding music is on. Everyone stands up and turns to look at the bride and Mr. Tan, who is walking down the aisle. Then, Mr. Tan lets her go as the bride stands before the groom.

Phuong, who is in a pink silk dress, stands behind Ha. She taps on Ha's shoulder. Ha turns back.

"You are so beautiful," Phuong says. "I am so happy for you."

Ha strolls to Phuong and hugs her. "Thank you so much."

Then, Ha returns to Adam, and they look at each other. Now, he is no longer nervous.

He mouths. "I love you."

She mouths back. "I love you too!"

The ceremony begins. Father goes through everything. Adam and Adam say the vows to each other. And the critical part is here.

Father looks at Adam. "Adam, do you take Ha to be your lawfully wedded wife?"

"I do," Adam says.

Then, Father looks at Ha. "Ha, do you take Adam to be your lawfully wedded husband?

"I do," Ha says.

Father says. "I announce you, husband and wife." He turns to the groom. "You may kiss the bride."

Adam opens the veil of the bride. He smiles and kisses Ha. The music goes on. The whole chapel bursts out in happiness. They clap and cheer for the newlywed. Then, hands in hands, Adam and Ha walk out of the chapel to the restaurant. Everyone looks at them and gives them their best wishes.

After the ceremony, everyone gathers in the restaurant. Mr. Nguyen uses the silver spoon to cling to the champagne glass. Everyone stops talking and looks at him. He clears his throat.

"Thank you so much for coming here today to attend my son's second marriage. I believe he is better than me right now. He has two wives." Everyone laughs. "I'm just kidding. This is the second time I have given a toast to Adam and his bride. For the first time, it was him and Phuong. I used to believe he and Phuong would be happy together for the rest of their lives. But life was not what we all had expected. It will take another turn if we don't know how to control it. Yes, my wife and I were pissed at Adam after we knew what had happened. We decided to disown him because we were ashamed to have a son like him. But parents will never leave their children no matter what, right? After all, it is his life and his decision, and we must respect that." He turns to Adam and Ha. "You guys are finally together, and you are husband and wife. I believe both have learned something from the past. Throughout time, I can see your love for each other is real. I hope you will keep that love. I wish nothing but the best to you. Be happy and swear to God, I don't want to attend another marriage from you. Ok?" People laugh. He turns to Ha. "And to you, Ha, welcome to our family."

Ha says. "thank you."

Mr. Nguyen raises his glass. "To Adam and Ha."

Everyone says and raises it all together. "TO ADAM AND HA."

People go on and enjoy the party dinner. They dance, they drink, they talk, and they sing. Some of them have "funny" voices. Phuong sits quietly at a place and watches Adam and Ha having fun. Inside her, she feels happy too. Even though life is not what Phuong expected, Phuong always believes that life has a plan for them.

So life has another plan for her head, which she has not known yet.

From afar, Michael runs to Phuong hurriedly. He grabs her hands and pulls her out of the chair. Phuong does not know what her son is doing. She asks him, but he tells her to stop asking and follow him. Finally, they stop outside of a room with a white door.

"What is this?" Phuong asks. "Why do you take me here?"

Michael smiles at her. A smile of excitement. "I have a surprise for you, mom. Just come in, and you will see."

Then, he runs away and leaves Phuong bewildered. She does not do what Michael has planned. She opens the door and walks in.

Nobody is in here. Phuong sighs tiredly because, probably, Michael puts a prank on her. Phuong walks around. There is nothing much. It is a room for couples to take wedding photos. A piano is next to the window with a white curtain. The fake fireplace is made of plastic, and the fire is just some red glow rocks. A green screen and some props for a photo shoot are in the corner. The lights are all on as if there will be a couple having a photoshoot. But today, they close for the wedding of Adam and Ha. In the middle of the room, there is a black wooden table in the middle of the room, which gets attention of Phuong the most. She comes near the table and looks at the bouquet of red roses. She touches the petal. It is a natural flower. At least there is something real in this room. In today's world, everything is so strange. When someone looks at something that amazes them, they will say it is beautiful, as if it is artificial, even though it is accurate. And when they look at something unnatural, they would say it looks natural.

Phuong looks closer at the bouquet and notices an index card placed among the flowers. She picks it up to see. It says "For the most beautiful girl in the room."

She smiles as if this is for her only. She puts it back because she knows it is not her business. Perhaps, this one is for the girl who is going to have a photoshoot with her fiancé tomorrow.

"There is only one beautiful girl in the room now." A voice came from behind Phuong.

She does not get startled, but she hears the voice so familiar. She smiles in tears. Then, Phuong turns back. She knows this time for sure that she will not let this person go away one more time.

The End